MW00439384

# THE SCORNED WIFE

## THEO BAXTER

INKUBATOR
BOOKS

Published by Inkubator Books
www.inkubatorbooks.com

Copyright © 2024 by Theo Baxter

Theo Baxter has asserted his right to be identified as the author of this work.

ISBN (eBook): 978-1-83756-329-6
ISBN (Paperback): 978-1-83756-330-2
ISBN (Hardback): 978-1-83756-331-9

THE SCORNED WIFE is a work of fiction. People, places, events, and situations are the product of the author's imagination. Any resemblance to actual persons, living or dead is entirely coincidental.

No part of this book may be reproduced, stored in any retrieval system, or transmitted by any means without the prior written permission of the publisher.

# 1

Amelia Gray had finally gotten to a point where she could stop crying.

It had taken her six months.

*But that doesn't change the fact that there isn't much left to do.*

She was sitting on a leather couch in her Manhattan apartment. On the coffee table sat an untouched glass of wine next to an untouched bottle, all next to an untouched plate of tomato sandwiches.

What bothered her was that she'd had it all prepared since noon.

She wasn't sure if she'd wanted to get plastered since high noon, or if she'd just pretended to and let her stuff sit there, collecting air, for hours. She wasn't entirely sure which was worse. Both seemed pretty sad.

Across from her, the TV was playing, also for hours. She wasn't sure what. She had long ago stopped paying attention. But at least it filled her home with noise.

Might as well actually get up and try to do something

productive. And so, with a little bit of a heave, she pushed off the couch and moved toward the studio just across from the living room.

In truth, the entire area was a studio apartment. From one end—at the kitchenette—she could look across the whole apartment and see her bedroom at the opposite end, with her living room and her de facto "studio" in between. But she still appreciated being able to think of these aesthetically different areas as "rooms." They allowed her to have a different feel depending on where she was. In her mind, she could trick herself into thinking that she was in an entirely cordoned-off area.

Sam never thought of it that way. If he knew Amelia was at the opposite end of the apartment, he would just yell across to her. Whenever she wanted to talk to him, she would cross the apartment to wherever he was and talk to him as if she had just entered his room. It always made him snicker.

*In retrospect,* she thought, *maybe he was laughing at me. Pathetic little dim bulb.*

*Well, nothing for it now. Time to get back to work. Whatever that means.*

She walked over to her easel and a collection of paintbrushes facing the outdoor window in her studio. Then she grabbed a small canvas and placed it on the easel, tightening the holders and setting it in place. She took some charcoal and started sketching a simple vase that was on a stand next to one of the windows. Getting some of the buildings in the background behind it. There was sunlight bursting through the afternoon clouds, making some nice rays. She tried to capture that as well.

For the most part, it just looked like she was drawing lines. Nothing really there. Nothing inspiring, anyway.

She got up from her stool, put the charcoal away, and headed back toward the kitchenette. She didn't even bother hanging a sheet or anything over the canvas to protect it from dust. There was no paint there to damage. Besides, the image was forgettable. If she threw it out the window, she wouldn't feel any loss on her part. Hell, the canvas was one of the few things that Amelia had purchased without needing money from her father to pay for, so at least her mother couldn't complain about it.

Though Amelia was sure her mother would find a way.

Her parents were paying for the apartment. Even when Sam had been living here. Amelia was proud of her work, and she had something of a small following and loyal clientele. But she was barely making enough to even worry about paying taxes on it. Sam was a civil engineer and certainly earned a fair amount, but also lost an awful lot of it on bad investments. They'd made enough to get by, but Sam had always found a way to screw it up and keep them from growing independently wealthy or even comfortable. So, her parents' money it was.

On the way to the kitchenette, Amelia passed by a book-shelf made of boards and cinderblocks. Very "college life-style," if not for the fact that the boards were well polished and protected by lacquer, and the cinderblocks were painted all different shades of gold, silver, and mahogany. Then there was the artist's easel, the random knick-knacks around the apartment that looked like they had been pulled out of a garbage dump but were actually expensively designed to look that way and had been purchased from a luxury store.

The more Amelia thought about it, the more she realized

that her parents were paying quite a lot of money to create the illusion of their daughter living like a vagabond. In one of the most expensive places in one of the most expensive cities in the world.

When Sam had lived here, he didn't mind the dorky posters or the mattress on the floor—on top of an expensive kotatsu heater, of course—truly, he'd never complained about anything. Amelia assumed that everything in their marriage was fine. It wasn't until now, with the advantage of retrospect, that she realized he'd rarely mentioned anything at all. It was almost like he had hardly ever even been there.

At the kitchenette, she opened the fridge and wondered what she was going to make for a snack. The refrigerator was almost bare. A few vegetable dips and bottles of kombucha here and there. A stick of butter defrosting. Maybe she could make a sandwich or something ...

Then she suddenly remembered that she had already made tomato sandwiches over four hours ago.

She leaned over and rested her head on the refrigerator door. *I am really starting to lose it,* she thought.

Closing the door, she wandered back over to the living room. She was about to sit down when there was a knock on the door. The building was rather secure—had its own pin code entryway, doorman, and everything, no expense spared —so there were very few ways that a random person could knock on her door without her approval.

Then she remembered. She knew exactly who it was. She went over to the door and threw it open.

"Oh," Mark said, obviously startled. "Hey there, Amelia. Groceries!" He held out a bag.

"Excellent," replied Amelia, grabbing the bag. "Thank you. I mean that. It's a big help."

"Well, absolutely. I'm always here for you, whatever you need."

Amelia gave a smile and a nod and was about to close the door when Mark reached out with his hand, stopping her, evidently about to say something. Amelia held the door for a moment, wondering what was up. But Mark just stood there, then nodded and backed away, giving a polite little wave.

Amelia closed the door and headed back in.

For the past few months, Amelia had found it hard to go out and pick up her own groceries. It wasn't like she didn't have the time—realistically, she had all the time in the world. She just found that she no longer had the energy to give a damn. It seemed like such a waste. She never wanted to leave the apartment, she never wanted to walk down the steps or down the sidewalk, and when she was at the grocery store, everything always seemed so ... colorful. Filled with energy and spirit.

Sometimes, it felt overwhelming.

So when her next-door neighbor Mark offered to help out by picking up some groceries for her, she appreciated the gesture. Certainly, it saved her a lot of time.

Gave her all the time in the world, she thought, for all of the nothing she'd been doing recently.

Finally finding a reason to go into the kitchenette, she filled up her fridge. She was probably going to make something simple tomorrow. Like soup.

She turned off the TV, then sat down on the couch. In the quiet of her apartment, she could finally be alone with her thoughts, and that was when she remembered why she let the TV play all day long—to avoid those thoughts. To not have to remember.

About a year earlier, she had begun finding evidence that

Sam was cheating on her. At first, Amelia was horrified and in denial. Then she got very upset. Until she thought it through and decided that maybe it was better this way.

After all, she had grown up in a household where her mother gossiped about women who got divorced, and her sister teased and belittled them. Amelia didn't do any of that, but, if she was being honest, she knew their opinions had had a subconscious effect on her. She grew up believing that divorce was something that happened to other women. Poor, unfortunate, suffering women.

Therefore, what would be the point of confronting Sam about his having a mistress? Was she really losing out on him as a lover? Sex between them had slowed down considerably by that point, so it wasn't like anything had really changed. Was she having her intelligence insulted? She knew her husband was cheating on her, but he didn't know that she knew. So she had the upper hand there. Was there a change in their home life? Honestly, not really. Everything was about the same. If anything, Sam seemed to be filled with even more energy. She didn't want to admit it, but it seemed reasonably easy to defend the idea of her husband sleeping with some bimbo if it meant a happy home life. For the life of her, she had trouble finding a downside.

Until six months ago when Sam didn't even have the courage to face her as he spoke to her over the phone about how he was leaving her. About how he was going to file a legal separation.

And just like that, Sam had decided that their marriage was over.

Amelia didn't even feel bad about losing the marriage, so much so as she felt bad that she was becoming one of those shameful divorced women. She couldn't stop crying and screaming at Sam over the phone, asking why he would do this to her.

But those demands meant she had to listen to his callous response when he said he'd found a younger girlfriend, whom he enjoyed having sex with. He didn't even try to hide it or pretend that there was some sort of ulterior, higher, psychological motive to it. He didn't talk about falling out of love, or needing to find himself, or whatever other nonsense a coward could devise.

She was expired. And wasted. And now, she had the black mark of divorce upon her. She was just an old artist lying around in a Manhattan apartment that she couldn't afford, surrounded by a life that used to be theirs, and now, she didn't have the energy to do anything about it being just hers.

No, she was one of those women.

Raising her glass, she gave a toast to nobody in particular: "Here's to a lousy marriage."

It wasn't the right type of toast, but she wasn't quite sure what sort of toast to make. There really wasn't anything to toast. Her divorce wasn't finalized yet. She just wanted to be able to acknowledge that she was doing something about it, even if it was simply having more wine.

If anything, the toast was merely a celebration of her ability to finally acknowledge where she was in life.

She gulped down the glass of wine. It was bland and aerated. Almost tasted like flat bubbles mixed in with warm grape juice. It had once had life, but over time, it had become fruitless. Easy to disparage and toss aside.

*Even the wine is mocking me,* she thought.

## 2

———

"Oh," said Wendy, nursing a macchiato. "So you actually got back to painting something?"

Amelia was at a café with her best friend, Wendy Stahlman. Wendy, at thirty-three, was only a year younger than Amelia, and they'd both majored in fine arts at New York University. They had a similar sense of humor, and they always comforted each other through the hard times. Wendy was, by far, the most trustworthy friend she'd ever had. And certainly, the one with the kindest heart.

"Hardly," replied Amelia, rolling her eyes. "I just did a little sketch work with charcoal. A vase in a window. I was hoping to do something, well, a little more interesting than that."

"Yeah, I guess I can see that. But as I recall, you haven't drawn anything in ages let alone painted anything. So it's a good place to start."

Amelia smiled and nodded, sipping on her own latte.

"And you're still dealing with your mom?"

Amelia sighed. "Yeah, I guess. I mean, I have to. Income

isn't very steady right now. I'm thinking that, maybe, I'll have to get a side job that I might be able to incorporate my art into."

"My gallery has one of those community art teaching clubs. Maybe I can see if they need an instructor."

Wendy worked the front desk at a major art gallery. Amelia knew that, although Wendy was fond of the art world, she didn't want to risk it all to become an artist herself. To her, it was a sweet and youthful dream, but she didn't mind the idea of simply daydreaming while living out a comfy little life.

"You could come in once a week and teach moms and retired ladies how to paint a flower," Wendy said. "At the very least, you would still be able to work on your own stuff while you're there. And bonus! Those people will probably think you're the best painter in the world."

"Oh! You would pay me to be a show-off? Sounds sweet."

"Well, the gallery would pay you. I would just be able to bug you."

"You would definitely have to pay me for that," Amelia said with a laugh.

"And what about that guy who lives next door and used to get your groceries?"

"Mark. And he still gets me my groceries."

Wendy narrowed her eyes. "Oh, does he now?" she replied, with a slight twinge in her voice.

"Yes, Wendy," Amelia replied. "I believe he's single. And he loves animals; his day job is taking care of dogs. I can introduce you, if you like."

"I'm sure I'll get to meet him on my own," Wendy replied, smiling behind her macchiato.

Amelia knew exactly what Wendy was thinking. She had

a very flexible comfort level about guys. Namely, she enjoyed going after cute guys, and she wasn't afraid if anybody knew about it. If anything, she reveled in it.

The more Amelia thought about it, the more she realized that Wendy had been that way for as long as she'd known her. Even back in their school days, whenever they took the courses that involved drawing nude male models, Wendy would rate them and feel very comfortable sharing her rating system with Amelia afterwards. Back then, she was bold enough to slip her phone number into whatever personal effects the model had tucked away. One time, Amelia remembered Wendy slipping her phone number into the backpack of a female model.

Which was a pretty bold move, considering that it usually worked. With most of the guys. Even with the girl.

Suffice it to say, Wendy was more interested in having fun with men than having a permanent relationship. She made it plain that she was never out to hurt anybody, but also never hid the fact that she was looking for more of an adventure than a true relationship.

"Well," added Wendy, "if you want, I'll check in with the clubs and education department and see if they're looking for any new instructors. And I'll tell them I have a friend who would be perfect. But they rarely need anybody new. Could be a while."

"I know," replied Amelia, sinking her chin into her hands. "It just means I'll have to ask for Mom's help more often. Not the easiest thing in the world to do, but, then again, I enjoy eating."

"I'm surprised she hasn't pressured you into real estate or selling cars by now."

"That would require effort. I think she's too tired of me to invest so heavily in my life."

"Maybe she'll get so tired she won't invite you to your own birthday parties anymore."

"Regrettably, the next one's coming up soon, and there's no chance that I can avoid visiting my family."

"Including your sister."

"Yeah, including Cara. Mom insists I'm supposed to be more supportive of her, now more than ever."

"And your mom knows what your sister did to you?"

"Spent her life constantly sleeping with all my boyfriends? Yeah, she knows. I mean, maybe she doesn't know about every boyfriend of mine she slept with, but, yeah, most of them."

"Amelia, I'm trying to be polite here, but it's getting harder and harder to describe your mother as anything other than narcissistic."

"I get it. She's a total bitch. I'm just saying they both are. I guess they always seemed to gel together a little more than she ever gelled with me."

"I've always wanted to badmouth your family in front of you, and now I'm starting to think that maybe I have your permission to do so."

"I am certain there's a line you're not allowed to cross, but somehow my family manages to keep pushing it a little further away."

"Well then, your sister is a narcissistic slut, your mom is an affluent sociopath, and your dad, well, I hardly know him, but I still don't understand why he would sit back and allow any of this."

Amelia, regrettably, agreed with her.

"And now we can officially add Sam to the mix," Wendy

went on, hitting her stride. "He's a rake, and a childish one at that. He can hardly maintain himself and doesn't know the first thing about keeping his future in perspective. Which is why he threw away a perfectly good wife for some slutty young thing. And trust me, he's not getting anything he thinks he is. Other than laid. And that won't last."

"Oh, wow; that is a perspective," replied Amelia. There was a time when even the suggestion of any of this would've sent her bawling into tears. Now she thought she'd finally gotten to a place where she could just treat it like conversation. It really felt nice, being the stable one. She felt like she had grown far more secure than she ever felt she deserved.

Amelia thought about what Wendy had said and lingered on something for a moment. "Wait. You said he's a rake. What's a 'rake'?"

"A rake is basically a male slut. Except I don't like that term because it implies that a female slut is the standard, and then there's variations of it. A 'rake' was a common term back in the seventeen and eighteen hundreds. I like it. I kind of want to bring it back."

"How do you know all this?"

"I learn stuff when I read. I pick up little things here and there along the way."

"You pick up vintage terms for slutty guys 'along the way'?"

"And not just vintage terms either," Wendy replied with a wink. "If you want to spend some time with a guy, I could make some suggestions. There's kind of a club, of sorts—"

"No, stop," Amelia said, holding up her hand. "I don't need more drama in my life right now. I'm scarcely getting up off the couch as it is."

"Yeah, fair. Family, divorce. Oh, and on that subject, is it working out? The proceedings, I mean."

Amelia smiled. "Yeah, it is, actually. The lawyer you recommended is great. He works fast, and he really lays it down on the table. God, I couldn't even imagine trying to find a lawyer when I was in that devastated state. I would've been in trouble."

"Well, I don't think I could've lived with myself if I was able to help and didn't. So that's both of us who are grateful."

Amelia nodded. After Sam had announced he was going to divorce her, she was absolutely torn apart. Frankly, those first days were a blur; she had trouble recollecting exactly how things went down, how the passage of time moved. Wendy had swooped in, took care of her, took care of everything. Found a lawyer who promised to keep Amelia's interests at heart and fight like hell to make sure she wasn't taken advantage of in the divorce court.

Wendy knew when to badmouth her family and when to badmouth her ex-husband. She knew when to offer coffee and when to stop offering men. And, especially, she knew when to make her laugh.

Amelia couldn't imagine ever being able to find a better friend than Wendy.

## 3

Amelia discovered one interesting advantage to being single and living on her own: she could pretty much do whatever she wanted in her apartment.

If she wanted to open the windows during a storm and listen to the rain falling over the city, she could. And if she wanted to head out into the world before the sun rose, there wasn't anything stopping her from doing that either.

Amelia set her alarm for 3 a.m. and only vaguely remembered doing so when it actually woke her the next morning. She got out of bed around three thirty, after hitting snooze a few times.

A quick shower and a prepackaged breakfast later, and she was in the car. She was a little delayed due to the fact that she hadn't planned on how to fit her easel into the backseat and had to angle it a weird way that she wasn't expecting. That, and she hadn't planned on how to transport any of her materials either, realizing at the last moment that they could spill in the car if she placed them wrong.

Improvisation, plus a desire to sleep. There was a very realistic possibility, she told herself, that she wouldn't make it to the sunrise.

Fortunately, as she pulled into the paid parking area of the Raritan Bay Waterfront Park, she began to see a glimmer of light inching over the horizon out into the sea. Again, more improvisation. She wasn't entirely sure where she was going to find her perfect painting location. She just knew that she had a few criteria to hit, and Raritan Bay seemed like a reasonable enough spot to find what she was going for. She needed a clearly visible sunrise. But she also needed to see it peeking out over a certain amount of waterfront and coastline. A little of the city skyline on the horizon would be acceptable, but she wanted something slightly flatter, more natural.

Given that she had to look slightly northeast from the bay in order to see Long Island, she wondered if the angle of the sunrise would come out a little awkwardly. Hopefully not.

Thankfully, the easel had not been damaged when she'd unceremoniously shoved it into the car, nor when it had slid and whacked her across the head as she was driving down the freeway. Her paints and varnishes had not spilled on the floor in front of the passenger seat. Everything was going smoothly.

*Much like everything else*, she thought.

Walking through the park, hoping that she wouldn't run into any police officers—she was legally too early to be there—she eventually arrived at the waterfront gazebos, which not only had a nice steady, flat surface for a floor, but also looked out at a clear view of the coastline. Perfect, really. Also, no police officers, as it turned out. The only other folks out at this hour were a dog walker, a homeless man sleeping on a bench some distance away, and a seemingly happily married couple taking an early morning jog.

*Happily married couple*, Amelia thought. It all seemed like a distant memory at this point.

Not too long after her coffee shop chat with Wendy a few days ago, the details of her divorce from Sam had been finalized. Her lawyer certainly did a great job and protected her interests, but frankly he didn't seem all that necessary. Sam didn't fight her for anything. It almost seemed as if he didn't have any financial interests at all.

Sam didn't have any claim to the apartment because Amelia's father had paid for it during the majority of the marriage. Whatever little money Sam had contributed at the start of their residence was only a fraction of the full amount. The same could be said for any of the furniture, personals, or the car. He got to keep his computer and his suits, which was perfectly fine with Amelia, even though she knew he probably didn't pay for all of them himself either.

Curiously enough, he didn't ask for any alimony, and Amelia wondered why. After all, he was doing fine as a civil engineer, even if he probably did have to live somewhere considerably farther outside of New York now, but he still didn't have the kind of money that Amelia's parents did. Did he not ask for it because he knew he would have to justify it, seeing as how he was the one who'd instigated the divorce, and his only reason for that was his own infidelity? Maybe it was toxic masculinity; maybe it was that old idea of a man not having to live off his ex-wife's alimony.

Whatever it was, it certainly helped her financially. She got to keep everything, didn't have to pay anything other than her own legal fees, and they didn't have any children to worry about harming.

Having finished setting up her easel, Amelia stared out at the sun as it began to rise over the horizon. It created a radiant burst of orange, which mixed in very chaotically, yet very passionately, with the dark purple of the night slowly fading away. She started painting away, struggling to figure out how to mix her different paints to capture the shade before it was gone forever.

Thanks to a lifetime of experience, she knew how to blend quickly and apply efficiently. She captured the sunrise moment in the skyline beautifully. Somewhere behind her, she could sense that somebody was staring at her work. Admiring it, by the look of it. Thankfully, this person didn't bother her, and she didn't turn around to thank him or ask him to leave. It was just a nice little moment. One of the benefits of being an artist: the admiration of the general public, and the acknowledgment that your work is beautiful.

As the sun rose, the miraculous collection of oranges and stunning rays of light eventually shifted into just another sunny morning.

She studied her finished work. It was very pretty. Good colors, good brushwork, good technique. She could probably sell it for a couple of bucks at one of those kiosks at the mall.

Otherwise, it was just an average painting of a sunrise over a New York skyline. It was a touristy thing. It had no real relevance other than its aesthetic beauty.

Still, painting a nice nature scene, no matter how commercial and mass produced it seemed, was probably a step in the right direction. It got her painting muscles back into action, and it was good to get out of the house. Make a decision in her own life about where she was going to go, what she was going to do. Feel like she really mattered, like she really accomplished something, and really started to get something done.

It was a nice morning.

Dull, but nice.

Sufficiently disappointed in her work, she packaged her still wet painting into a specially designed carrying case, collected her paints, varnishes, brushes, and easel, then threw them back into the car. It was now well past eight in the morning, and she figured she might as well get breakfast somewhere. Another benefit of doing whatever she wanted; if she woke up at three in the morning to start her day before the sun even rose, she basically had the rest of the day to herself.

After dealing with rush-hour traffic, she arrived at Confectionery Bakery, where she picked up a fresh loaf of bread—still warm, still emanating the scent of new dough— and some high-quality cheese Danishes. It was going to make for a fantastic morning.

Another quick drive, and she was back at her apartment building. She fully expected the vast majority of occupants to be at work, so she was surprised when she stepped off the elevator and found Mark peeking out of his doorway.

He gave her a smile and an enthusiastic wave. "Hey, Amelia!" he called out. "Do you have a moment?"

Amelia obviously had her hands full with her easel, painting supplies, and breakfast. Apparently, for some people, Amelia thought, this state was the universal sign for "eager to socialize."

"What is it?" she said, desperately trying to seem polite as she approached him.

"Well, I've been thinking," said Mark. "I mean, I don't

mean to pry, but I'm aware you've been going through some pretty rough times recently."

Amelia remembered mentioning to him that she was getting divorced. She didn't quite understand why. Probably just to have somebody, anybody, to talk to. "Mm-hmm," she said through tight lips.

"A lot of people consider animal companionship to be very therapeutic. I'm not suggesting you should go out and adopt a pet, because that's quite a commitment, and I don't know if you'd have time for it."

"Sure." Amelia nodded, hoping he'd hurry it along.

"I have access to adorable dogs all the time, given what I do for a living. So if you're in the mood for hanging out with a playful pup, you can always ask me, and I could set you up with a sweet canine friend for an hour or an afternoon or whatever."

Amelia's arms were starting to strain against all the stuff she was holding. "That's really nice," she said, moving past Mark toward her own door, "but I'd have to give it some thought. I'm already busy, and I'm not sure I'm looking to be buried under a dozen dogs or anything like that."

"No, no, it doesn't have to be that many. I could just loan you one, they're very friendly, and they just warm your heart instantly."

"Aren't these your clients' dogs?" Amelia said, aware of the challenging note in her voice. "Aren't you just watching them?"

"Oh, no, far from it. You don't get to be successful in this line of work unless you provide something more than simply walking and leashing. My clients are paying for their little guys to have a friend who cares about them for a couple of hours. I talk to them, give them scratches, learn about their personalities. You know, really give them an afternoon to hang out with a friend. Learn which ones are real jerks, and which ones are misunderstood jerks."

Amelia smiled. "You're funny," she said. "Look, maybe, but not right now. I'll keep the offer in mind. So, thank you."

"No problem," he called out. "And if you ever change your mind, you know where to find me."

Amelia closed the door behind her, walked into her place, and unceremoniously plonked the bread and Danishes down on the counter before gingerly placing the easel, paints, and her most recent work in their proper locations. She knew where her priorities lay. Even if it was a simple sunrise painting of no real consequence, it was still a work of art. It still had a little piece of her inside it.

She had to respect it. Believe in it.

Going back to collect the bread, she took it over to the kitchenette, where she threw one of her cheese Danishes into the microwave to give it some warmth, while cutting up the loaf, savoring every aroma that floated out with every slice. She plied a little cream cheese to it, unapologetically knowing that this bonus brunch was effectively going to be her eating all sorts of very sweet, very creamy cheeses. Again, one of the bonuses of living her own life at this point. Nobody could tell her what to do.

As she sat down on her couch, ready to eat a chunk of fresh bread and cheese Danish, believing she had the freedom to do anything she wanted to do, the one person who could prove her wrong decided to call.

Her phone vibrated in her jeans pocket, and while munching on a bite of her sandwich, she pulled it out to take a look.

It was her mother.

It was just after nine thirty in the morning. This was far too early to be bothered with her nonsense.

On top of that, Amelia wondered why her mother was even trying to pretend to not know that her daughter was free at nine thirty in the morning. To rub it in her face that she was unemployed, she supposed.

All the same, she certainly didn't want to deal with replying to a passive-aggressive voicemail message, so she picked up.

"Hello," she said quickly.

"Oh good, you're awake," her mother slurred.

Amelia could hear clinking in the background, and the heavy exhales coming from her mother's nostrils, as well as her lips smacking.

She knew what her mother sounded like when she was drunk. She just wasn't expecting it quite so early in the morning.

"Hey, Mom," said Amelia. "How are you today?"

"Oh, like you give a damn," replied her mother. "It's not time for me to pay your rent, so I guess it's not time to pick up a phone and call me up, now, is it?"

"I've been busy."

"With what? You don't have a job, and nobody's buying your paintings."

"I've noticed. I've been busy painting."

"Yes, well, I've been busy doing things that don't earn me an income too, but at least they're fun."

"Why are you calling?"

"What? What are you ... Oh, right, yes, the reason I'm calling. Sorry, I've been up all night. I must sleep soon. No, no. The reason I'm calling is because I was hoping you could pick up a forest cake for your birthday party."

"I don't like forest cake."

"I didn't say it was for you, did I? We're going to present it to your sister's new boyfriend."

*Oh, right*, Amelia thought. *That whole thing.* "Mom, didn't you tell Cara that it's my birthday, and she doesn't have to bring anybody with her? I don't want to deal with her."

"We're trying to be supportive here, Amelia. It's not all about you."

"It's not all about me on *my birthday*?"

"Well, it's not like you don't have those every year. But this year, Cara just happens to have a new boyfriend. And you know how much trouble she has holding onto one of those for very long."

*Yes*, Amelia thought. She certainly knew why.

"I thought we could make this into a bit of an encouragement situation. Really show her that we're rooting for her this time."

"I don't know why I'm bringing a cake I don't even like to somebody I don't want at my birthday party that I don't even want to attend."

"Oh, I'm sorry, Amelia, were you planning on spending your birthday in my apartment?"

"In ... what?"

"I was under the impression that you knew you were living in my apartment in lower Manhattan that I was paying for with my money. But apparently you need a reminder about who's actually paying for the place, now, don't you?"

Amelia, of course, was very aware that her mother— through her father, at least—was paying for her apartment. She just wasn't expecting her mother to shove it right in her face like this. This was low, even for her.

"I suppose if you don't want to be practical about who in

your family is thinking about you," her mom continued, "then I can tell your sister exactly what kind of person you really are. At least she's coming to your birthday party. You'd think you'd be a little grateful. But I don't seem to recall you ever coming to her birthday parties."

Amelia knew full well that her mother knew Cara never invited her to her birthday parties. But, then again, they all knew that it was because Amelia would never come anyway.

"Look, I'm coming," Amelia said, exacerbated. "Of course I'm coming. I just don't understand why I have to go buy a cake with my money."

"Oh please," her mother managed to slur. "When has it ever really been your money?"

Amelia waited her turn to respond, but all she could hear was her mother make some other comment, too weak and too quiet to have any effect, before she hung up on her.

Yes, sir, Amelia now knew, she was definitely going to her birthday party. Which she would've rather spent alone, or at least with Wendy. Somebody who would've actually made her feel welcome.

Somebody who actually felt like family.

## 4

Amelia drove from Manhattan up to New Haven, Connecticut, where her parents still lived. Amelia's birthplace was in New Haven, but her dad had been born somewhere else in Connecticut, while her mother was from Massachusetts. She vaguely remembered hearing that her grandparents were from Vermont. Basically, a lot of old money in the family.

The type of old money that caused a family to learn to respect it, no matter how disrespectful it might become. They never questioned the idea of money.

Which was probably part of the reason why her parents had trouble with the fact that their oldest daughter ended up going to art school. Amelia had been good at math and science back in school and probably could've gone into some sort of applicable academic field. It was just that none of it really excited her.

And that, in part, she knew, was because it never excited either of her parents either. Her father was a business owner and stockbroker. Her mother was a socialite.

Cara was a different matter entirely. But not that different, the more Amelia thought about it.

Women's liberation never seemed to have gotten into the minds of her family members. Her grandfather, dad, and uncle were invested in stocks, and their wives were invested through them. The women made sure that the house was lovely and that they were in those lovely houses to greet their husbands when they came home from work.

At least, that was how the women in her family always seemed. They certainly dressed the part, always looking more than presentable. She knew her father was very wealthy, and her mother wasn't particularly inclined to start scrubbing the toilet, and she recalled there were always cleaning staff coming in. So the woman's job was to pick up the phone and call various services. And then find something else to do. Sometimes liquor was involved.

She adjusted the driver's side visor to block out the sun before it almost blinded her as she drove up the highway. She had just passed a sign saying that Milford was only a few miles away, and that she needed to slow her speed. After Milford, New Haven wasn't that much far ahead. And neither was her birthday party. And, of course, her family.

Amelia was assertive and inclined to live her life the way she wanted to. Her family was never going to be agreeable to this notion. She was hard-pressed to imagine a circumstance in which she upset the family morality to such an extent that they cut her off entirely, but neither would they stop telling her what a horrid disappointment she was, how embarrassing she was, how she was the daughter who couldn't be more like her sister.

Because, of course, Cara was preferable. She was younger, and she put in every effort to be a little more doll-like, a little more girlish, a little more adorable. She was obedient, gracious toward everything her parents said—in the few times they ever said anything to their girls—and more willing to be everything that a girl was supposed to be. Not like Amelia.

And so, her parents liked Cara and always forgave her. Whenever Cara caused damage, she would blame it on Amelia, and everyone would accept her words as truth. If they ever broke out into actual fights, over toys or TV or whatever, it was always Amelia who was supposed to be more responsible. Cara was more precious, and boy, did Cara know it. And boy, did she use it.

And the more she grew up, the more she realized she could never stop using it.

Cara was the hottest thing in school. And she kept that popularity up by berating and destroying her older sister, the weird art nerd. Every girl wanted to be associated with Cara. They would do anything to stay on her good side. Even do everything in their power to humiliate and hurt Amelia.

She had to spend all her school years struggling to find anybody to talk to, or simply socialize with. Cara always treated her like a stepping-stone, an opportunity to be even bigger than she was before.

Especially with boys.

When Amelia's first boyfriend eventually broke up with her, he never gave her a reason why. Amelia didn't understand until she came home one day and saw that he was in the house, with her sister doing some rather "adult" things to him. She hadn't even been sure Cara knew anything about sex yet, but here she was, taking advantage of the situation. Taking more of Amelia's toys.

And it had only gone downhill from there.

It seemed that Cara had always used her body to lure every guy away from Amelia with the promise of sex. Which, even at a young age, Cara had known how to do very well. It had confused Amelia how Cara could be so adult about these things.

Whenever Cara stole any of her boyfriends, Amelia would ask her mother why she didn't reprimand Cara. Instead, her mother would chastise Amelia for being incapable of keeping the boyfriend in the first place. Obviously, Amelia should start taking advice from Cara; maybe then she'd see what she was doing right. If Amelia brought up the fact that her sister was always deliberately going after her boyfriends, and not just random boys, her mother would blow it off as a phase.

Once, when Cara stole one of Amelia's boyfriends, she didn't actually keep him for very long. Funnily enough, after Amelia got over the whole experience, so did Cara.

Almost as if the boy hadn't meant anything to Cara beyond simply taking things that meant something to Amelia.

Amelia had a clear memory of tearfully bringing this to the attention of her father, hoping he would do something.

He didn't.

That should never have been a surprise, she knew.

And so, her sister hated her: her sister deliberately, vindictively behaved in ways designed to hurt her. Her mother hated her, though she was more absent and nauseatingly sarcastic than actively vindictive. And her father didn't care about anything that didn't directly affect him.

Amelia was alone.

Whatever ambitions the family had for her to be a loving, respectable housewife never seemed even remotely

possible, considering that her sister kept ruining every relationship she ever had. Even her parents, the two people who
would likely have been the most invested in her finding, and
keeping, a man, didn't consider it particularly plausible or
realistic. It was always Cara who seemed as if she could be
the perfect housewife, even if she did leave a trail of men
behind her, none of whom she was willing to hold onto.

Amelia knew that she was a family issue to be dealt with,
which ironically enough made it easy for her to go off to art
school, since she knew her parents wouldn't mind being rid
of her, but such a course of action didn't make her feel any
more wanted.

Case in point, she arrived in the driveway of her family's
mansion in Connecticut for her birthday party that, frankly,
she knew wasn't actually for her. She couldn't do anything
about that. Just stomach it and move on.

She parked in the driveway and noticed some cars that
she didn't recognize. Presumably, her parents had bought
some new ones, but she also had to consider the possibility
that maybe Cara's current boyfriend had one of his own here
as well.

She stepped out of her car and looked over at the driver
getting out of the car opposite her.

It was Sam. Her ex-husband.

Was she was losing her mind?

Amelia watched, aghast, as her little sister hopped out of
the passenger side and ran around the car so she could grab
onto Sam's arm.

She made sure to glare at Amelia the entire time.

# 5

During dinner, Cara and Sam were seated across from Amelia. They sat close together, very deliberately trying to be as intimate as possible. Right in Amelia's face.

Amelia had to endure almost forty-five minutes of Sam and Cara smiling at each other, touching each other. Whenever Amelia would turn to look away, or breathe deeply to help tolerate the whole experience, she noticed Cara would up the ante: she would start pawing at Sam, gripping his thigh close to his crotch. At one point, when leaning in for a kiss, from an angle that her parents wouldn't have noticed— if they were even paying attention—Cara pushed out her tongue and licked it all the way up Sam's neck. Holding Amelia's gaze the entire time. Making sure she knew the show was for her.

It was excruciating, but nothing that surprised Amelia. She fully expected this from her horrid, sadistic little sister.

What she hadn't been expecting—and what really broke her heart—was how Sam reacted. He didn't seem shocked by how Cara was slobbering on him, both figuratively and literally, in front of her parents. He closed his eyes and took her attentions with obvious pleasure.

It dawned on Amelia that Sam had been in on this the entire time. Because Cara was the woman he had been cheating on her with.

It was simultaneously a shock, simply because this time Cara had gone out of her way to steal Amelia's husband, and not really that shocking at all. At least not since her sister was involved.

But the more Amelia thought about it, the more she realized how depraved Cara really was. After all, at the time, Sam's request for the divorce was so distressing that Amelia was too stunned to analyze it properly. Now, in retrospect, she realized there was a lot to analyze. Sam readily admitted that he wanted to have sex with a younger woman. Who did that? Who was so forward about their infidelity? Who had no shame in hiding such a thing, without even a hint of trepidation about being the bad guy in the situation?

It all made sense now. That wasn't really Sam talking. It was Cara. She had been coaching Sam on what to tell Amelia over the phone.

Cara had orchestrated her plan months ago. From the infidelity to the revelation, to this new, even bolder revelation that was playing out right now.

And Sam was an active participant in Cara's plan. Why did Sam hate her this much?

Amelia's mother finally got up out of her seat and headed into the kitchen to find something, in her words, "stronger than this weak shit," meaning the wine.

The perfect opportunity, Amelia thought, to confront

her. "Mom, what the hell are you doing?" she shouted, realizing that she had been waiting a very long time to yell that.

For the first time this evening, Amelia could see in her mother's eye a look of gross disappointment, of anger at being yelled at.

"What's gotten into you?" replied her mother. "Stop that yelling."

"That is Sam! That's my ex-husband!"

"I said stop yelling in my house."

"What do you expect me to do? How do you expect me to react? That's Sam. You don't have a problem with this?"

"Wait," her mother said, focusing more fully on Amelia. "How do you know Sam? Have you met him before?"

"He's my ex-husband."

"Wait, are you telling me ... *that's* Sam? The same man?"

"Mom, you know my ex-husband."

"Well, hardly. It wasn't as though we were invited to your wedding." Her mother shrugged. "I mean, you rarely ever brought him over, so it's hard to place him. Though, I guess, yes, he does look the same."

Amelia was exasperated beyond measure but knew better than to accuse her mother of lying. It was true, she and Sam had gotten married at the courthouse, and she had rarely brought Sam over. Mostly because she rarely went to visit her parents herself. In the few instances that Sam ever visited Amelia's parents prior to their wedding, they'd made it clear that they were not impressed by the man, which was why they'd gone to the courthouse in the first place. Considering the amount of money flowing through their family, a civil engineer was more of a factoid than a term of praise. In that moment, Amelia had every confidence that her mother genuinely couldn't remember her own daughter's ex-husband. Nor did she even care.

"Mom, for God's sake," replied Amelia, in pure aggravation, "Cara just brought her new boyfriend to the dinner table, and she very deliberately brought the man whom I was married to for a decade. Can you at least understand why that might *bother* me?"

"I'm not an idiot," replied her mother, finally finding a glass to go with her vodka bottle. "Anybody would be hurt and disappointed. But you really do have to look at the bigger picture. Marriages don't fall apart at the snap of a finger after ten years. So, at a certain point, wouldn't you have to say that your marriage was always slowly failing?"

"Mom, it did suddenly die," Amelia protested. "Sam told me it was because he was leaving me for another woman. And that woman turned out to be my little sister. She did this deliberately."

"Maybe it'll work out better for them," her mother said, tipping a hefty measure into her glass.

"Cara doesn't care about Sam. She's just using him, enjoying this in her own sick way."

"You know, Amelia, some people would call it proactive."

Amelia's eyes went wide. "Excuse me?" she said quietly.

"Well," said her mother, gulping down her vodka and pouring herself another, "think about it. What can you do for a living? Do you have your name in any books or on any walls? Are your artworks hung in any galleries? Honestly, if you weren't my daughter, do you think I would have even heard of you?"

Amelia gaped at her mother.

"No. No, darling, I pay for your hobby," her mother breezed, lifting her glass as if to prove her point. "I pay for your home. All you had to do was find somebody else to support you, and you couldn't even do that. Just shacked up with some twat for ten years. And you couldn't even keep him satisfied enough to hold onto him." She knocked back another slug of vodka, adding fuel to her spiteful fire. "Do you think I enjoy being married to your father day in, day out? But at least I'm good at it. Could be worse. I could waste my time and everybody else's money too. You can say what you want about Cara, but at least she has the know-how to keep a certain perspective in life. If it's not this one, she'll find someone else. She'll make something of herself. And she'll know how to keep her man. She'll know how to do it right."

"Do what 'right,' Mom?"

Her mother raised her eyebrows, as if that were answer enough. "I'm just so tired of you not listening to me," she snapped.

Amelia stood silently as her mother wobbled past her into the dining room. The sad truth was, Amelia knew exactly what her mom was talking about.

Effectively, without spelling it out, her mother was admitting to prostituting herself in order to have a comfortable home life. And somehow surviving the experience by always finding another bottle to drown herself inside. Whether she was happy or sad about it didn't really matter at this point. It was what she expected of herself, and it was what she associated with success in her life. Cara was willing to do the same, so she saw that daughter as successful.

Amelia, not so much. Maybe her mother didn't really like her, but, frankly, Amelia knew her mother better than that: the truth was, she didn't like women at all.

So it made ironic sense that she ended up with her

father, Amelia thought. Her father had wanted sons. But he never got any.

Amelia stormed out the opposite door of the kitchen, into the main hallway, where she caught a glimpse of her father in his study. Apparently, during her little tirade with her mother, Dad had gone off to get his own drink from his liquor cabinet. Regardless of how much he drank, though, he somehow managed to remain comparatively far more stoic; there was no swaying, no looking like he was about to collapse.

If anything, he seemed almost lifeless.

Daring to go into the study, Amelia came up behind her father. He scarcely registered that somebody was coming into his room; looking behind him, he saw that it was his older daughter, then went back to staring and drinking.

He was staring at an old family photo. Younger parents, teenage daughters. Everybody had been very warm and loving to each other back then.

"Dad," Amelia said, almost pleading, "you know that's Sam, right?"

Her father was silent for quite some time before answering, "Yes."

"And ... and you're fine with that?"

Her father swirled Scotch in his glass. "He won't last. Just like all the others."

Amelia shook her head, despairing. "You know why she's doing this, don't you?"

Another long silence. "I would appreciate it if you returned to the dinner table," he finally said. He placed his glass down and walked away.

Amelia stared at the family photo a little while longer.

Then, turning on her heel, she did just as her father had requested.

Planting herself down in the chair opposite Sam and Cara, she looked around at the food. All of it very rich and well done and, to be perfectly honest, far more than five people could consume. It was a crass amount of food. All of it was for show, she thought.

The furniture was equally luxuriant, mahogany with leather covering. It was also just for show. Nobody actually ate in this room except on special occasions.

Her mother's celebratory mood was for show. Her father's willingness to even be here was for show.

Their family show of togetherness was for show.

And anything Cara did with her man was, in truth, just for show. Any emotion Sam claimed to have in his heart was for show as well.

As Amelia looked at everything in front of her, she asked herself, why was she even involved? What was she getting out of this anymore?

"Aw," Cara said, speaking up suddenly, noticing how calmly Amelia was sitting, looking at the world around her. "Did somebody finish having a good cry?"

There just wasn't any reason to play along anymore, Amelia realized. She rose out of her chair, flinging her food at Sam and Cara. "What the fuck is wrong with you, you crazy whore? And you"—she shifted her gaze to Sam— "you're stupid enough to get caught up in it. You mean nothing to her. You threw everything we had away for *nothing.*"

For the first time, it almost seemed as if Cara's veneer had dropped. She was obviously expecting tears and pathetic whimpering from Amelia. Instead, Amelia had begun to fight back. For the first time that Amelia could remember, Cara looked like she had no idea what to do.

*Good*, Amelia thought. She was so sick of everything.

She stormed off, just fast enough before her mother could stagger to her feet and start demanding why Amelia had thrown food all over the expensive carpet, which would now need to be cleaned. She also yelled something about how the dishes were genuine antiques and irreplaceable, but Amelia barely caught any of it. She was already storming off toward her car.

By the time she got behind the wheel and revved her engine, her mother had charged out the front door, struggling to put on her shoes, shrieking as she stumbled down the driveway. She really looked quite a sight, hysterical in her manic, drunken rage.

"You ruined the birthday party!" she yelled. "This was your birthday party! This was all for you!"

It was funny to Amelia that in all of this, she'd almost forgotten that it was her birthday party. The word birthday had never come up once during the evening.

No, the party was nothing more than a show. Just like Cara's relationships. Just like that whole house, the whole family.

Just like Sam and his integrity as a husband and as a man.

Just like her father.

# 6

On the drive back to Manhattan, Amelia's phone vibrated. She knew that the only person who would be calling her at this moment was her mother: to demand that she get back to her own birthday party and stop ruining it. She let the phone go to voicemail every time, until her mother had, evidently, flooded her voicemail feature until it was full. For a while it didn't ring, but then it started vibrating as her mother messaged her.

By the time she got home, the phone was still vibrating. Amelia only caught a glimpse of the screen, indicating dozens of texts from her mother, all short and aggressive, before she shut off her cell phone.

She was done. There was nothing left.

She immediately sought out the bottle of wine that she had purchased not too long ago, and wished it was something that could take her pain away.

She poured a glass and swallowed. It was filled with bubbles, bitter fruit, and entertainment. It tricked her throat and her chest and her stomach into thinking that everything was all right. But her mind knew that it wasn't, so she poured herself another glass before finishing that one off as well.

But the glass wasn't large enough to contain all the wine she needed. She dropped it off in the kitchenette and began drinking directly from the bottle. It flowed.

She was wondering what might happen if it flowed so intensely that it went down the wrong way, causing her to choke herself on so much wine. Would her gag reflex kick in and save her?

Or would it feel comfortable?

Her head still throbbed from the reality of the situation. She drank more wine to alleviate her headache, only for the alcohol and the wine to dry her throat, dehydrate her, and bring the headache back with full force. It was a never-ending cycle of pain. She was getting far more intoxicated than she should. Even though she knew the drink was only magnifying her pain, it didn't change the fact that she felt like pain was all there was left for her anyway.

In retrospect, Cara had always been flirtatious with Sam. At the time, Amelia never thought anything of it because this wasn't a boyfriend, it was her husband. There was commitment involved, a trust. She wouldn't have been surprised if Cara had tried to go after her husband, but she had fully expected nothing would come of it, that she would just be embarrassing herself by continuing an old stereotype they'd performed when they were high-school kids.

But now Amelia drunkenly collapsed onto her couch, feeling the cold of the cushions press up against her swollen cheeks. Sam had cheated on her with Cara, her little sister. They had obviously been doing it for several months before the divorce was even mentioned, so Sam probably realized he could keep doing just that. Remain married and practice infidelity. In truth, there was no need to get divorced. He was already doing what he wanted with his side bitch.

Therefore, not only had he agreed to hurt his wife by cheating on her, but when, later, his mistress suggested fully terminating his relationship with his wife, he'd gone along with that too.

So Sam had gone out of his way to hurt Amelia. Did he really hate her that much? Or, more likely and more to the point, did he like what Cara had to offer so intensely that he just didn't care what the cost was?

Amelia turned over on the couch and stared out through her windows at the night sky. The room swayed, and the window glass began to melt and twirl into strange colors. The fluttering bits of lint that danced around in her eyes seemed to be the only lifelike movement she would ever enjoy again.

If she kept drinking until she suffered alcohol poisoning, would she belch up everything in her stomach all over her floor? Or would her body just give up, and her vomit never quite escape her throat, choking her out, killing her?

She wondered if she should give it a try. After all, she was obviously of no use to anybody anymore. If she died on this couch, Amelia thought, nobody would notice. Nobody would find her body for weeks, maybe even months. And, certainly, nobody would care.

Amelia felt that there really was nobody in her life who would be willing to talk to her, to love her, or to help her. Nobody would ever come over for coffee or a chitchat ...

There was always Wendy.

Amelia didn't want anybody to see her like this. But she didn't want to be alone either.

She grabbed her cell phone and turned it back on—the

moment she did, another ninety-seven messages showed up ahead of all the other ones she'd not opened—and contacted her best friend.

Amelia vaguely remembered Wendy saying, "Hey girl," when she picked up the phone. Amelia felt her eyes growing redder underneath the swirling of the world before her as the tears kept everything from standing still in her view. She asked her best friend to come over.

Wendy immediately said that she would, then hung up, and that was that. There wasn't any need to beg; there wasn't any need to convince her or offer her anything. Wendy simply knew she had to help.

Her head spun with pain, with the memory of that horrible birthday party that she knew she was never going to get past, and she almost fell unconscious while waiting for Wendy. But when the buzzer sounded, she found the energy to lift from the couch and sway toward the door. She knew that her friend wouldn't be able to get in unless she buzzed her in, so she watched the world spin wildly as she staggered to the camera display, where she vaguely bashed her hand up against the keypad until she hit the correct button.

There was a banging, followed by Wendy's voice asking her if she could come in, some more hobbling, and even a falling to the floor once, but pretty soon, Amelia was at her front entranceway, unlocking the door and letting Wendy in.

Although Amelia didn't remember all the details of what came next, she knew that something good must've happened in her miserable life, since she eventually found herself falling asleep, and then waking up, very hurt, very hungover, and still in pain from everything she'd endured the night before.

Except, this time, she'd endured it with her head in her best friend's lap.

Another thirty minutes, along with some very heavy-duty painkillers, and her headache was gone. But that didn't stop the pain in her heart.

At first, Amelia didn't want to bother her best friend anymore, considering that she'd spent the night in her apartment. Still, Wendy revealed that, even though she was sitting upright, she had eventually got to sleep for at least a couple of hours. And the reason why she was here at all was because she needed her friend to be okay, so she was well prepared to deal with anything Amelia could throw at her.

Amelia felt the tears well up again. A mix of despair and elation this time, since she couldn't imagine a better friend. She told her everything.

Wendy, the most devoted friend and kind-of therapist in Amelia's life right now, patiently listened to every word. Until, finally, Amelia felt like she had nothing left to say, and Wendy slowly faded into the conversation.

"Well," she said, swirling the coffee in her cup, "I think it's pretty straightforward. Your family are a bunch of sociopaths."

Amelia started laughing. She couldn't imagine having any reason to laugh, but she loved the fact that Wendy wasn't all that far off.

"Yeah, I know what that sounds like," Wendy added, "but I really mean it. Your mom sees your ex-husband hopping from sister to sister, and apparently that doesn't faze her. Your sister literally makes plans, months ahead, based around the idea of very specifically being a jerk to you. I don't know what else to say except that it's not how normal people act. That's how poorly written clichés in bad femme fatale novels act."

"Yeah, no kidding."

"And your dad just sat there? Didn't comment on it, didn't question it?"

"No." Amelia shook her head. "In fact, he couldn't make eye contact."

"Okay, so that aside, your mom and your sister have a dedication to an obsession, and they won't let it go. Unfortunately, in both cases, these obsessions completely involve you and your willingness to suffer through them."

"And people say that young people don't spend enough time with their families anymore."

"The way you describe them, spending more time with that family in the *Texas Chainsaw Massacre* would probably count as a vacation."

"Heh, yeah ... so, I really would like to know what else you're thinking."

Wendy put her coffee cup down and rested her chin in her hands. "Well," she said slowly, "it's a shit situation. Your sister isn't going to listen, your mother is going to insist that you're not listening, and Sam's a hopeless case, but he's there anyway. You can't really escape those people unless you go no contact, which we both know you won't do. They want you involved, and they want to rub the situation in your face. I'm really sorry that they're all complicit in this."

*Complicit.*

Amelia wrapped the word into her soul, then let it sit there for a while.

They were all complicit. It was all their fault. They all had something to do with it. Something to achieve through their actions. Which was to hurt her.

And they all had something they deserved to lose.

"Yes," Amelia said slowly, turning the thought over in her mind. "That's what I want. That's what I need."

"What?" asked Wendy.

"All of them are at fault. All of them need to be taught a lesson. I'm sick of escaping. It's their turn to listen to me ... And I know how I'll make them listen."

## 7

It took the better part of the day for Amelia to get the alcohol out of her system and finally be able to clean up and feel comfortable in her own skin again. No hangovers, no dehydration, no headaches, nothing of the sort.

And in all that time, she failed to develop any further ideas for her plan to exact revenge on her family.

"I'm not sure what you hope to do with them exactly," Wendy said after an extensive day of hanging out with her friend, chatting, and watching films. "Humiliate them? I wouldn't even know what would humiliate someone like Cara."

"It's not exactly intended to humiliate them, because in order for that to happen, she'd have to have the capability for humility." Amelia began assembling an idea in her head. "Every time they do these things to me, it works out for them perfectly. So, what if it didn't? What if Cara wanted to steal a guy, and she failed? What if ..." She trailed off.

Now that she was saying it out loud, the holes began to

show. What she was proposing was that she find herself a guy who was so desirable that Cara would immediately go after him. But also so humble and gentle and perfect that he would have the integrity to turn Cara down and remain with Amelia.

*And there is the problem*, she thought. Every partner she'd ever had ended up leaving her the minute Cara tried to seduce them. She didn't want to deny the possibility that the perfect guy—or, well, the perfect guy for her little plan—existed out in the world somewhere. That said, she had certainly never found one.

"It's a pretty good idea," Wendy said. "So you're looking for a guy specifically for the sole purpose of him rejecting Cara."

"Yeah, but if he's a guy Cara would want to steal, then he's probably the kind of guy who would ... well, want better than me."

"Please stop doing that to yourself." Wendy gave her a stern look. "There's nothing wrong with you. At all."

"You really think so? I have trouble believing it sometimes."

"I'm not surprised. Your parents don't exactly help you stand up for yourself or reinforce any reason for you to look kindly on yourself. If you were able to date a guy who would turn down Cara's advances, what do you think would happen?"

"Mom would have to justify her beloved daughter's failure somehow. And Cara would be angry and upset that the world wasn't working her way."

"So, then they could tear into each other for once instead of tearing into you," Wendy said. "Not bad, not bad. And your dad? What would he do?"

"I don't think he'd get involved. The point is, it wouldn't work. I would have to find a guy to cooperate. And how am I supposed to do that? Just come out with this plan to some guy? He'd think I was crazy, and I wouldn't blame him. Or I could get involved with a guy, introduce him to my sister, and hope he'd be different from all the others."

Wendy stared off into the middle distance, so Amelia kept talking.

"To be honest, I don't think I have it in me anymore. Am I really going to bring over somebody to trap my sister, or am I actually going to find a guy I want to spend time with only to risk losing him? I just got divorced. I don't think I can have my heart ripped open again."

"Hm," said Wendy, still staring.

"Are you even listening to me?"

"Oh! Yeah, yeah, I just—"

"Oh my God! Am I boring you?"

"No, Amelia! I was thinking about options."

"What options?"

Wendy took a big sip of her water, then set the glass down on the coffee table. She sat at the edge of her seat, her elbows on her knees, holding her hands together while pensively resting her chin on her thumbs.

Amelia knew that something was going on in her mind. She'd rarely seen her friend this serious before. Wendy looked confident but nervous and scared too.

"Amelia," Wendy started, "you know I love you, and, honestly, I always loved your marriage to Sam until he turned out to be a complete ass. And I always thought that you can be happy doing your own thing, and you should be. Everybody should be allowed to be happy."

"What are you talking about, girl?"

"For the longest time, I assumed that girls just marry boys, and they have babies, jobs, homes, and things just happened that way. Then, in high school, I figured out that there were a lot of people who live very differently. You were there, so you saw that I had a lot of fun figuring that out."

"You sure had your share of fun," Amelia agreed with a grin, "but sometimes that's just people getting it out of their system before they find the right one and—"

"But what if people don't?" Wendy interrupted. "What if some people realize that they don't want to do the whole marriage thing and just want to have fun?"

"No judgment. They should. As long as they don't hurt anybody."

"Yeah, but more than that," Wendy insisted, her voice animated. "What if I go out to a bar and find a guy, and we start getting frisky, and then we have very different ideas of where this is going to go? All of a sudden, he wants to see me more often, and, well, I just don't."

"Um ... consensual planning, setting boundaries early on, and—"

"Yeah, great, but I'm not talking about trying to find the 'right guy' by constantly going through a dozen or more wrong guys and dating them and wasting my time. I'm talking about knowing exactly what I want ... and knowing where to get it."

Amelia was silent for a moment. She thought she knew where Wendy was going with this. But she wasn't sure if she could believe it.

It sounded like some fake adolescent fantasy.

"Wendy." She finally spoke up. "You mean you find a guy exclusively for quick ... 'encounters,' and then you 'dismiss' him?"

"Basically."

Amelia paused before she asked, "Does he get paid for this?"

Wendy didn't answer. She just stared at Amelia with that look of pensive consideration and nervousness. She seemed to be putting all her trust in Amelia with her eyes.

"Wendy, that's prostitution. Where would you even ... I mean, men do that kind of thing?"

Another long pause. And then Wendy reached into her purse, pulled out her wallet, rifled through it, and finally removed a business card.

Amelia looked at it. "Sterling Escorts." There was no phone number. No email address. Just directions and a password.

"It's where I found what I wanted out of life," said Wendy. "And I think they might be able to help you too."

---

## 8

It had been five days since Wendy and Amelia had their conversation at her place. Six days since Amelia's birthday party.

The trauma of witnessing her sister and her ex-husband together, not to mention the trauma of her parents basically approving of the pairing, was still lingering; it wasn't going to go away anytime soon. That said, it was starting to get a little easier to handle the experience, thanks to Wendy.

Amelia had to admit that Wendy sure had a way of keeping her mind active. And there was a lot going on that Amelia couldn't quite believe.

Amelia and Wendy were walking a group of dogs through Central Park with Amelia's neighbor Mark, the professional dog watcher responsible for arranging this therapeutic puppy parade. The air was fresh, the sun was bright, and it was almost impossible to be in a sour mood when there were so many fluffy critters ready to either pull her around the park or jump on her and give her a hug and a lick. Amelia was laughing with joy whenever she wasn't panting at being pulled around by some rambunctious little guy. It had been ages since she felt this happy, this filled with life.

While Amelia was waiting for a Labrador puppy to finish sniffing a tree, she looked across the park to see Wendy chatting up Mark. They were too far away for Amelia to hear what they were talking about, but every now and then her eyes met with Wendy's as she glanced over and gave her friend a smile.

Amelia imagined that she was probably flirting her way into his good graces before suggesting they head over to some quiet hotel. It made sense now that Amelia knew all about Sterling Escorts.

Amelia had expressed to Wendy her desire to trap her sister and mother in a web of their own devising, by presenting Cara with an extremely attractive man who would then reject her. But Amelia realized it was a very conniving, adolescent plan. After all, how could all this work out exactly the way Amelia wanted? It sounded like some vengeful teenage fantasy.

But as it turned out, Wendy had somehow gotten involved with an escort service. Except not as a call girl. Rather as a client.

Which meant that she had an answer to Amelia's dilemma.

"They do have female sex workers as well," Wendy had told her. "Hard to imagine them staying in business if they didn't. Still, they've cornered the market when it comes to providing male partners for female clients; they're the go-to business for women who need that service."

"You talk about 'that service' as if they're landscape

gardeners or something," Amelia said, wide-eyed and shocked all over again. "It's prostitution!"

"It's ... that's not what they call it."

"Well, zippidy doodah for them; you're paying men to fuck you."

"The escort service provides men who fulfill every one of your wishes. Physically, but also everything leading up to that. They let you feel like you're appreciated, like you're loved. They focus on you, pay attention to your needs, and allow you to enjoy yourself and discover who you really are. Yes, obviously it's in exchange for money. It's a service, after all."

Wendy made a very compelling argument that the job of these escorts was to fulfill a woman's needs. The implication, of course, was that it would involve sex, but that wasn't necessarily the case. It could be something as simple as a casual date.

In this case, as Wendy suggested, a handsome man hired to allow Cara to attempt to seduce him, only for him then to reject her.

It was exactly what Amelia needed.

And it would be provided by a male "escort": from an agency specializing in sex work.

That was the clincher, Amelia thought as her leashed Labrador walked away from the tree and started heading back toward Mark. No matter how they tried to disguise it or jazz it up, it was a service designed to provide women with access to men in exchange for money. If sex wasn't implied, then there was no reason to be so skittish about it, now was there?

Obviously, there was sex implied. Obviously, it was a sex service.

Wendy was asking Amelia to cross that line. And if she did, it would always be a part of her. Even though she wasn't paying for sex, it was what people would think. Or at least what people who found out about it would think. So she would have to spend the rest of her life hiding it. Lying about it. Pretending it wasn't real.

She came back to Wendy and Mark, and after a few laughs, they proceeded to herd the dogs out of the park and back to Mark's van.

No, she thought. She wasn't going to do it. She was grateful to Wendy for offering the suggestion—and for giving her many nights of fantasy dreams about what this sexy naked male harem must look like—but it just wasn't her. She didn't do that kind of thing.

Wendy was insistent that Mark drop her off first, even though it was out of the way. Amelia didn't think that that was a very effective way to get Mark on her side if that really was what she was planning for him. But, then again, Mark was such a sweet and slightly airheaded guy that he probably wouldn't have even noticed.

Case in point, after they dropped off Wendy and drove back to their building, he was all smiles as he told her stories about his dogs.

Amelia helped bring the dogs up to Mark's apartment, then gave him a friendly hug as recompense for the wonderful afternoon. Then a quick walk over to her own door, and she was able to strip away her shoes, her overcoat, and settle into some comfy sweatpants for the rest of the afternoon.

She suddenly remembered that she hadn't taken her phone with her on their puppy adventure—it was almost out of juice, and besides, the only people who would've called her were either her parents or her agent. Her parents were the last people she wanted to talk to, and she didn't want to explain to her agent why she still had trouble painting anything of value. Why she couldn't dredge up her pain into something miraculous. Why she couldn't be like other artists.

She walked over to her phone to see if the charge was full yet ...

... and saw a message from Cara.

She knew it was going to be deliberately mean, and she didn't want to hear it.

Problem was, in order to erase it, she had to play it first. Even if only for a second.

*Fine*, she thought, she'd do it quickly.

She called her voicemail, and the automated voice told her she had one new message. Amelia pressed the button to hear it.

She was getting ready to delete it when she heard a man groaning.

Followed by a woman's heavy breathing.

Followed by rhythmic bouncing.

Amelia didn't erase the message now. She was too shocked. She listened to it intently. She had to know if it was her imagination, or if she was hearing what she thought she was.

And as she was trying to fathom it out, her sister's voice rang in, husky and urgent:

"Oh my God, Sam, you feel so good."

Amelia's eyes went wide, and she almost dropped her phone. This was actually happening. For real.

Her sister had recorded the sounds of her and Sam having sex. And that was what they'd sent her.

She could hear Sam's voice underneath Cara's. And then she heard his breath grow heavier, his voice get stronger, his grunts drop an octave deeper.

She'd slept with that man for close to a decade; she knew what he sounded like when he was about to orgasm.

His thrusting exhalation came at the same time as Cara's high-pitched moaning, followed by her laughter and exuberant complimenting of his amazing cock. This whole thing was probably real, Amelia thought. But even if they were faking noises into a phone, the very idea that they would record this and leave it on her voicemail was intolerable.

And for Cara to take pleasure, not in the act of it, but in knowing that Amelia was on the other end of the line. Listening.

She'd done nothing to instigate this. Amelia hadn't contacted her sister or her parents once since the birthday party. There was absolutely no point to this.

Cara had just decided to attack Amelia.

*Fuck it*, Amelia thought. Maybe somebody would find out that she called an escort service. Maybe someone would find out she was tracking down men for hire.

Amelia didn't care. She needed a win.

---

## 9

After being led around by phone instructions to multiple locations, only to be forwarded to another phone and another location, Amelia finally arrived at her meeting with the man evidently in charge of Sterling Escorts.

They met in a comfortable but otherwise desolate waiting room on the first floor of an upscale Long Island hotel. Amelia didn't know why he'd selected a simultaneously public and secluded location, and she ultimately decided that she didn't have to.

She was about to pay for a male sex worker. The less she knew, the better.

The man was about a generation older than Amelia, but he carried himself with great poise and masculine warmth. She guessed he was of Japanese heritage. He had slight graying at his temples and a few extra wrinkles on his forehead and under his eyes, though Amelia noticed that those were the only indicators of his age and maturity. In all other respects, he was a quite charming, enticing older man. He had a broad confident smile, which was dominant without being threatening. He had a glint in his eye that made Amelia feel that there was something dangerous about him, though she wasn't sure what. And his handshake felt assertive, but it wasn't overbearing. He exuded the feeling of being strong while also being welcoming.

"Good evening," he said with a polite, gruff voice behind his sweet smile. "My name is Nicolas Wan. You must be Amelia. It is such a pleasure to meet you."

"Likewise," Amelia answered, feeling a little warm.

"Would you like to sit down?" he continued, motioning to a pair of armchairs facing each other. "May I get you some coffee or tea?"

"I guess coffee with milk, please."

They took their seats as Nicolas motioned toward a young man in a waistcoat, who looked like they worked in the hotel. The only words out of his mouth were, "Coffee with milk." Otherwise, nothing was communicated between them. It was implied that everything else, like payment, was already arranged.

This man held a position of respect at this hotel.

"So, Amelia," Nicolas continued, "before you start feeling too embarrassed, let me assure you that virtually everybody who calls for the first time feels very bashful. So, please, there's nothing that you should feel embarrassed about.

"In order to provide you with the best service my company can provide, I need to know what your goals are. If you wouldn't mind, I'd like to get to know you a little better."

For the first time since she met him, Amelia felt awkward. "I thought I explained over the phone. I just need to ... well, see if a man would be my date for a night, maybe more. Nothing special. Maybe a nice man to go with me somewhere. And it doesn't have to involve sex." She realized how ridiculous all of that sounded. Particularly the last part. She felt like a fool.

Nicolas gave her a reassuring smile. "You've said over the phone, much as you've told me now, that you are looking for an escort for a nonsexual experience, and your priority is that he is an exceptional man. You're not overly specific about what it is that makes him exceptional other than that you feel it should be a combination of physicality and gravitas."

Amelia found herself relaxing at last; comforted by his smooth tones, she found herself hanging off his every gentle word. She was so enraptured that she scarcely noticed that somebody had provided her with her coffee, which was now resting next to her.

"Now, you know what you want," Nicolas continued. "You have a goal in mind. It's a goal that drove you to seek out my help. I, however, do not know your goal beyond the most generic outline. But if you are willing to share with me what has been draining the smile from your face lately, I promise I will find you somebody who will make you feel exceptional and give you exactly what you want. And wouldn't it be wonderful to take the chance? All it takes is to be bold with what you have to say."

Amelia felt relaxed, soothed, like silky milk running through brilliant coffee. She'd already found herself in an expensive hotel lobby, sitting across from a man willing to provide her with many, many other men. What did she really have to lose by hiding herself?

"My goal is to find an extremely gorgeous man," she said, "in order to take revenge."

Nicolas looked intrigued. "Revenge upon whom?"

"My sister, Cara. My entire life, she's been stealing my boyfriends from me. I always thought that maybe it would stop, or someday it wouldn't affect me anymore. But recently, I got divorced from my husband of ten years. And then I found out that he left me for my sister."

"How did you find out?"

"They waited until my birthday to flaunt their relationship in front of me. It was specifically timed to hurt the most."

"Was it an unhappy marriage?" Nicolas asked, his tone gentle. "Why would your ex-husband participate in this?"

"It was a marriage that had been fading into nonexistence. After a while, we didn't really have anything in common anymore. Cara has flirted with him over the years, but as far as I was aware, he'd always laughed it off. But now, it looks as though he went to her so as to hurt me. He's doing this because she's enticed him into it. Or maybe he hated me more than I thought."

"Did you have any other male lovers during your marriage?"

"No! Why?"

"So for the past ten years, your sister never had an opportunity to destroy a relationship except the one with your husband?"

"I suppose that is true."

"After a decade of receiving nothing from him, she finally stole him when things were going badly between the two of you. It shows her desire to do this to you despite all other odds. Even after years of respite, she still wishes to hurt you instead of move on."

"Yes."

"Have you ever wondered why?"

"I guess I always have wondered, but I haven't ever figured out what I did to cause her to do this to me," she said.

Nicolas remained quiet for a moment, nodding slowly. "It seems to me that if you were to present a wonderful example of a man to your sister, she would be psychologically forced into attacking you again. Regardless of whether she's now associated with your ex-husband or not. The temptation to repeat her assault upon you would be too great; she would not pass up an opportunity to steal another man."

"Yes! That's what I was thinking."

"So what you need is a man who would appear to love you in order to seduce your sister. And then let her down rather sternly."

"You can ... can you do that?"

"Women request the services of a host for a great many reasons. A false relationship, with the intention of it being false despite it being respectful, doesn't come up every day, but it's also nothing new. I can assure you that you'll be able to give your sister a feeling of rejection so complete that you will feel as if you have actually struck back at those who have been beating you your entire life."

"You make it sound so violent. I never wanted to think of myself as this kind of person."

"It's one of the most fascinating, and saddest, talents of an abuser: you interpret yourself as 'violent,' where most people would interpret you as acting in self-defense. You have every right to strike back, Amelia. I want to give you the strength to be happy."

He was very good, Amelia thought. She almost had to remind herself that he wasn't actually the reason why she was here. Especially considering how charming he had become in only one conversation.

Fortunately, and in part thanks to Nicolas, she could focus on her goal.

"You have someone in mind?" she said.

Nicolas turned his attention to his phone and quickly sent out a text. "I have the perfect man for your needs. Damon Chase is a former stage actor who has extensive experience in creating characters. His theatrical roles have not given him the financial life he wished for, so he works for me now. I feel that he would be overjoyed at the idea of performing a role again."

"Well ... cool."

"Yes. Although, obviously, I could ask you to pay and be on your way, but then I wouldn't be anything even remotely similar to a professional, now, would I?"

"Meaning?"

"At the end of the day, emotions are not a light switch that you can flick on and off. For you to get your money's worth and for your plan to work, you have to believe in your date. Thus, the second part of your meeting tonight. Just now, I asked Damon to join us. I would like you to get to know him and see if he 'clicks.'" Nicolas looked over her shoulder and gave a polite smile and nod.

Amelia turned her head and found herself staring at a very powerful torso. Her eyes followed him up to his strong chest, broad shoulders, muscular arms and neck, until she was looking into the eyes of the kind of man she'd only ever seen on television or in magazines. Exquisite. A heartthrob. The stuff of dreams.

He smiled at her.

After which, she couldn't remember anything else.

## 10

Damon was dressed in black suit pants, a black suit jacket over a white shirt, with no tie, and the collar undone. His black dress shoes were polished to the point where they could show a person's reflection. He had a square jawline, dimples, and bright blue eyes. He wore his blond hair a little long. It was simultaneously sexy and slightly boyish, a look that he wore well despite the fact that he was clearly in his forties. Everything about him was perfect.

He gazed at her intensely. It was intimidating, but Amelia didn't feel threatened because his eyes were like pools of crystal-clear California water. The only time she looked away from them was out of shy coyness, and then glancing away, she could see those dimples, that jawline, that smile.

She understood why Damon had a career as an actor in his past. He certainly had the looks for it. She kind of expected him to be some sort of suave character from a melodrama, standing around and looking enticing while being told that his evil twin and his vixen sidekick just infiltrated a children's hospital, or whatever crap they come up with on those shows.

Amelia felt herself becoming very hot and uncomfortable. She had to remind herself that she wasn't genuinely trying to pick him up. She simply had an arrangement with his employer. The fact that he was an exceptionally, intensely dreamy man was proof that she was going to make the right decision by paying to get him involved. This was the kind of man she needed for her purposes.

For revenge.

"It is a pleasure to meet you, Amelia," he finally said. "And please don't get me wrong, I would enjoy spending the evening gazing at a beautiful woman such as you, but I'm forced to assume that you asked me to come down here for a different reason."

Indeed, Amelia thought, snapping out of it. Nicolas had gone across the room to get himself a drink at the bar, leaving Amelia and Damon to speak privately. That must've been about two or so minutes ago, Amelia realized. In fact, she wasn't sure how much time had passed. All she knew was that she had spent an inordinate amount of time just silently staring at a guy she'd never expected to give her the time of day.

At least, not when her sister was around because before he could, Cara would steal him away.

"Right, of course," Amelia finally said. "I need some help. I don't know how much Nicolas told you—"

"I only received a text from Nicolas asking me to come down here and meet you for a special job."

"Ah. Well then, it's different from usual, I guess," Amelia said as she explained the situation. "So I don't even know if this is going to work, but my plan is for me to be with a new guy, and then, when my sister, Cara, tries to seduce him, he rejects her."

"And?" Damon raised one perfect eyebrow at her.

Amelia frowned. "And what?"

"After I turn her down, do you think she's going to quit? Or do you think she'll keep coming after me?"

"I'm not sure. I don't think she's ever had a relationship for longer than a few weeks. And they've always been about sex. Come to think of it, I don't think she's ever had a real boyfriend."

"So it really is about control."

"Very much so. Dominance over me, to be specific."

"After I turn her down, she's going to need to maintain her definition of who she is. Which means she won't stop trying to become involved with me. It will frustrate her, which I'm sure is your goal. But you may have to be prepared for the idea that she's going to be hunting me for a long time."

"Will that be a problem?"

"It could be for you," Damon said thoughtfully. "The most logical method for your sister to get to me is through you. Which means she's going to be entwined in your life considerably more. And, secondly, well, I hope you'll forgive me for being blunt, but it would cost you more to keep me on assignment longer."

"Yes, that's true." Amelia nodded her understanding.

"Of course, if you can't pay me after a certain time, then I won't come back, and she'll never find me again."

"But if she did track you down and paid for you, would you 'accept' her?"

"Well," Damon murmured, thinking the situation through, "then it would be an entirely new arrangement.

Since at that point she would know you and I weren't an item, she might lose interest. And," he added, "even if she did sleep with me, it would accomplish nothing."

Then, after a moment in which Amelia sipped her coffee, Damon continued, "That said, if I ever did run into her again, I wouldn't mind helping you out. You look like you've been hurt a lot, and I don't like leaving women feeling hurt."

Amelia smiled a little. That was sweet. "Would it bother you to hurt Cara?"

"I said women." He tilted his head at her. "Not bitch sisters."

Amelia liked his attitude and his insightfulness. This was starting to seem like it would really work. "Mr. Chase, I don't—"

"Call me Damon. Get used to it, particularly if you want to make this real. I certainly do."

"Damon, I don't know the next time I'm going to see my sister. Do you feel comfortable about the idea of being on call?"

"Yes, as long as you're willing to fund my services."

Amelia reached into her purse and pulled out several large bills, earned from selling some of her personal items through online marketplaces. It would be complicated if she used her mother's money—especially considering the possibility that there wasn't going to be any more money from her mother soon. She wondered how her life had gotten to this point. She was making money selling her stuff to strangers. She was visiting an escort service, talking to one of the most attractive men she'd ever met about hiring his "services."

Her family was effectively dead to her.

"Why are you helping me?" Amelia asked as she handed him the money.

Damon accepted the bills. "I have my own experiences. And I don't appreciate when people are forbidden from living their lives. Torn apart, harmed. Nobody should have to live that way. Especially somebody who's never caused harm to anyone. You don't deserve this. When I look back on this job, I'll feel like I've really accomplished something. Really done some good in the world."

"Thank you." Amelia smiled at him. "I'm grateful we're on the same wavelength."

"Likewise."

"But just so we're clear, there are no 'benefits' involved in this job. No sex. It's strictly business."

"Of course, Amelia. Strictly business."

## 11

Amelia stood in a large hall of one of the most exquisite art galleries in New York City, admiring the works of nineteenth-century classical painters. She stopped in front of a painting truly eye-opening in its depiction of horror. It actually wasn't very grotesque or revolting. Frankly, it was pretty colorful and well done. It just gave off an uneasy sense of something hiding in the background.

"This looks familiar," Damon said from somewhere behind her.

She turned and met his gaze. Damon had been accompanying her throughout the entire gallery and seemed genuinely interested in a lot of the paintings. "You ever heard of Edvard Munch?"

"Oh, yeah, I think so. *Scream* guy, right?"

"Yes, the painter of *The Scream*. He also did this one."

"Ah."

"Obviously, not as famous in pop culture as *The Scream*, but it's nice to remind people that famous painters create more than just one image during their entire lives—lives that are long and rich overall."

"What's this one called?"

Amelia didn't have to look at the note on the wall next to the painting. "*Ashes*."

"Looks ... morbid."

"Well, he had a lot going on."

They both smiled and snickered.

If she wasn't careful, this would no longer be strictly business.

This was the third time that Damon and Amelia had gone out to do something together. Curiously enough, it ended up being relevant to Amelia's life as a painter. These days, she rarely went out to do something relaxing, like spending time at an art gallery, looking at the works of the masters.

It was a way of reminding herself that if she didn't get back to work, no one would ever appreciate her work the same way she appreciated theirs.

She still hadn't been able to get out of her funk, hadn't been able to pick up a brush and create something more substantial than simply painting whatever was in front of her without any emotional attachment. Even that hadn't occurred in quite a while. Even the straightforward act of painting ordinary still lifes had been put on the back burner. She hadn't had the energy or the opportunity to work, considering everything else that had been going on in her life recently. In a way, her passion for her career had been shoved off into the background.

Additionally, there was always the issue of money. She hadn't been in touch with her mother since her birthday, and she couldn't help but notice that her mother's regular deposits to her account had stopped coming in. Which became a particularly unnerving experience when her landlord pointed out that her monthly rent was overdue. Other than the money she received from her parents, she had an extensive savings account, largely made up of family money. She held on to it precisely for when things like this happened.

Now, thanks to this month's rent payment, it was a slightly smaller account. Next month, it would be smaller still. Particularly if she had to use it to buy groceries in the meantime. She wondered how long that savings account would last.

It was that anxiety that led to her decision not to use any of her savings to pay for Damon's services, instead choosing to sell off some of her old things she didn't need anymore. She needed to stretch her money as much as possible.

Damon seemed to understand this as well, which was why, she assumed, he offered to make this museum day trip a free-of-charge experience.

"Don't worry about it," he told her when she expressed reservations about him doing something for her for free. "I have my own life too. And I can spend my own time however I see fit. And, in all honesty, I don't think I've ever been to this gallery before."

It was a nice gesture. The other times that the two of them got together, it had been paid for out of Amelia's pocket, using some extra money left over from her online selling. Her outings with Damon weren't really expensive, but it didn't change the fact that it was an expense she hadn't been planning on only a few weeks ago.

Of course, having her birthday ruined by her sister and ex-husband had changed her perspective.

Effectively, what was happening now had been arranged by Damon. He pointed out that, for her plan to ruin her sister to work, they had to make sure Cara wouldn't be able to see through it and realize that Amelia was trying to entrap her.

"When she sees us together, she needs to feel that there's a genuine connection here," Damon told her. "We need to give her something to destroy. Or, well, try to destroy, anyway."

As far as Damon was concerned, that meant dates. Lots of dates. Social, intimate dates.

Which, in Amelia's mind, just meant spending more money.

Not that she didn't mind the experience itself. After her marriage to Sam collapsed, it had been quite a while since she'd spent time casually, easily with a man.

And so, for the first time in as long as she could remember, Amelia was enjoying a nice little date with a very handsome man. No fear of being harmed or humiliated. No fear of being left alone or abandoned.

It was a different feeling, she thought. It was ... nice.

Heading to the end of the gallery tour, they returned to the front desk, where Amelia stopped in her tracks. She was fully aware that this was the gallery that Wendy worked at, yet, somehow, as she'd been strolling through with Damon, she had forgotten about it.

But now, there she was, sitting behind a desk, selling tickets and answering questions. Sometime during their visit, her shift must've started.

Amelia wasn't expecting to see a familiar face, much less one that she would have to explain herself to. Still, Wendy had put her in touch with Sterling Escorts. If she saw her with an extremely handsome man, she would quickly put two and two together.

"Everything all right?" Damon asked.

Amelia nodded and proceeded toward Wendy. Nothing for it, she thought. At the very least, she didn't have any reason to feel embarrassed or hide anything. After all, this was Wendy's idea.

Wendy looked up at Amelia, then glanced at Damon. "Oh, hey!" she drawled.

Amelia rolled her eyes. She did not need that.

"Damon," he answered politely as he reached out and took Wendy's hand.

"Hi, I'm Wendy," she said with a smile. "I know Nicolas. Nicolas Wan." She winked. "I'm the one who suggested Sterling to Amelia."

"Ah," Damon replied knowingly. "Well, it's a pleasure." He then turned to Amelia and said, "I can get the car started if you want to talk to your friend a little longer."

"Yeah, thanks," said Amelia, warmly.

Damon smiled and walked away.

Wendy turned sharply back to her friend. "Freaking fuck," she whispered excitedly. "I know you want to make your sister jealous, but hot damn!"

"It's not like I had a catalogue to look through or anything. It just happened."

"I hope it works out. He's perfect," she gushed.

"I'm sure you can rent him later."

"Oh, ew, skeezy!"

"Well, I mean, it *is* his job."

"Yeah, but I'm not going after your guy once you're done with him. I'm not that much of a bitch."

"He's ... not my guy."

"Too bad for you." Wendy went a little wide-eyed. "You should consider making an arrangement every now and then after you're done with the Cara project. It all seems to be working out so far."

"It sure feels nice," agreed Amelia with a smile. Wendy's statement about "your guy" would obviously never come true, seeing as how Amelia never attracted the attention of men like Damon.

But still, the thought of it gave her a warm feeling.

## 12

---

"Breathe," Damon said. "Now continue breathing and imagine that the world underneath is breathing in the same way."

Damon was leading Amelia through an exercise that was meant to combat anxiety and encourage relaxation. They had already done several of these exercises, in which Damon taught Amelia about focusing on her breath, creating a rhythmic pattern that she could trust and rely on. He also taught her about closing her eyes and imagining herself in a far-off, comfortable location. The typical one that tended to come up was to imagine herself on the beach on some tropical island.

But this time, Damon asked her to lie down on the floor and feel the coolness of the contact between her skin and the hardwood floor of her apartment.

Making herself so vulnerable was a very different experience. Lying down on her back, with her arms and legs splayed, she couldn't help but feel that she was displaying herself. Her eyes closed, her body unprepared, she had to trust that Damon wouldn't try anything as she lay there.

He was a professional, of course. And a gentleman. Over the several weeks that they had gotten to know each other, Amelia had come to trust that if she made herself vulnerable around him, he wouldn't try anything. It was nice to feel that way around somebody again.

She realized that this was the first time she'd had a strange man in her apartment since her divorce.

"You can feel the seashore underneath your fingers," Damon continued, "underneath your heels, on the back of your head. As you breathe in, feel the world beneath you closing in behind. As you breathe out, feel the world underneath you stretching out. So, Amelia, it's like you can feel the world moving with every breath. Breathe in ... Breathe out."

Amelia did as he said, breathing in and out deeply, slowly, steadily.

"Don't open your eyes, but look up and see the clouds moving in the sky above you. There's so few of them, they don't block out the sun. They're gentle in the breeze. The only sound is from the tide lapping up against the shore. And it's so quiet, so gentle, it's barely there. Keep breathing; breathe in ... Breathe out."

Amelia could picture every detail, every change in temperature, as if she really were reclining on that magical island beach. Everything relaxed. The sound of Damon's voice was present and protective. She wanted it to be always there, to make her feel right.

"Continue breathing. Steadily, just breathe in. Breathe out. You don't have to say anything. You don't have to think about anything. Simply continue breathing and watch the world around you live on peacefully. And just ... rest here for a little while longer."

Somewhere, in the depths of her memories, Amelia remembered that she had a sister. That she had a mother. That she had an ex-husband. But they might as well have been miles away, in some foreign country. Here, on her private island, there was nothing else except the seashore, the sparkling beach, and the blue sky. There were no animals, no people. No money, no job, no responsibility, no problems. Everything was taken care of. The world was innocent and pleasant.

All she had to do was lie back on the sandy shore and let the world pass her by. Somewhere, something was happening. Here, she could continue breathing; she could feel the shape of her chest, her lungs, her heart. And she could soothingly lie here enjoying the sun and the sand forever. It was pure bliss.

It was everything she ever wanted.

"And now," Damon's voice softly interrupted, "you can slowly start coming back. Focus again on your breathing, feel your breath, feel where it's going. Feel how it's coming back through your body. Breathe in deeply enough to fill your belly. Fill your arms; fill your legs. And when you start feeling the ground beneath you again, start to blink open your eyes. And look at the world around you again."

She followed every instruction. When she finally opened her eyes, she knew she was lying on a hardwood floor in her apartment. She could see the stucco white drop design of her ceiling and feel the golden rays of the sun passing through her window, shining and warm upon her face. It was like it was the only recollection from her beachside travels in her mind: the warmth of the sun, still tickling her skin.

Back in the real world, Amelia took a deep breath and exhaled loudly. "Whoo," she said to Damon, trying to break the tension.

He smiled at her and gave a little laugh along with her exaltation. Then he reached down and offered her a hand to help lift her off the ground.

So powerful was the relaxation of Damon's meditative techniques that she felt like nothing could ever hurt her again. And in this most vulnerable and innocent of reawakenings, she could see him standing over her, welcoming her back. A constant presence of safety and kindness. If nothing else, these past weeks had been an extremely therapeutic experience for her. She was eternally grateful for her ability now to control her frustrations. Let go of her anger.

And how Damon helped her to get there.

She also appreciated the fact that she could trust him implicitly. It was nice that she had made such a friend.

But she regretted that the whole reason why she'd hired him in the first place had never really come to fruition.

That was, until a few days ago.

Part of the reason why she needed help with her anxiety now more than ever was because she'd finally got a phone call from her mother to remind her about the upcoming Christmas party at the family home in Connecticut.

Amelia had been filled with a sense of panic. There was going to be a social event to which Amelia knew Cara would bring Sam because she was still attempting to hurt her. That was an extremely sore sticking point. Aside from the fact that her marriage was ruined, the Christmas party would now act as an additional reminder of the last time Cara brought her ex-husband along to ruin everything in Amelia's life. It felt like a continual stabbing of her soul.

For the first time in her life, Amelia had the power to take revenge. All she had to do was actually go through with it.

And the thought of Damon's involvement in everything becoming real led her into a panic attack.

Which, thankfully, was a pattern that Damon had been working on for quite some time.

Thanks to his presence in her life, she'd learned how to relax, how to breathe through the hard times. She'd learned how to have fun on a date, and how to be comfortable with a man. Amelia felt confident that, if they had to make out in front of her sister, then it wouldn't get really weird. She knew she could count on Damon to take it in his stride, treat it as another essential part of their plan.

As Amelia headed off to the kitchen to get some sparkling water for her and Damon, she heard him call out behind her, "By the way, I've got something for you."

"What?"

"I was thinking about what you said, about the Christmas party with your family? A part of your plan has been neglected this whole time."

"Oh, God. What did I miss?"

"Don't worry, nothing that will ruin it. I'm just saying, your plan is to make your sister extremely jealous that you have this wonderful man with you. But delving more deeply into that, your plan also involves proving to your sister that, by virtue of this man in your life, your life has become far better. You have to give her something to ruin, right?"

"Well, here's hoping otherwise," Amelia said, pouring out two sparkling waters.

"But you know what I mean. It's not just that I have to be there, but *you* need to be the most brilliant and exemplary version of you possible. You have to make your sister feel as if she's really missed out on an opportunity. So I was thinking of how to make you a little more exquisite. I was hoping you'd take a look at this."

Coming back into the main living room, Amelia saw what it was that Damon wanted her to see. And her eyes went so wide, and her mind became so clear, that she almost dropped the drinks in her hands.

Damon had opened a package, revealing a floor-length red dress with a low back and narrow spaghetti straps over the shoulder and around the neck. It was the most brilliant, breathtaking dress she had ever seen.

Considering how she always dressed so modestly, so relaxed, it was safe to say that this dress was entirely different from anything she had ever owned. It was revealing, bold, sophisticated. It was very strong and very independent.

This dress wasn't her.

"Damon, I can't wear this. It's far too revealing."

"I can understand that," he replied. "But I encourage you to consider that you don't want to give your sister any ammunition. Looking like you've completely turned your life around, whether it's with a new man or with a new dress or with a new outlook, will lead her to believe that she's got to come after you again. And to let her down after you've risen so high ... after this party is over, I promise you, you'll walk away feeling incredible. Like you really won in life."

It was everything she ever wanted, Amelia thought. She wanted to be exquisite; she wanted to be a winner.

She wanted to wear a dress like this stunning red gown

and not have it become an event. That it would just be clothing. Clothing that she could wear with confidence.

She took a deep breath, focused on it moving through her.

Calm, playing.

Like the gentle wind upon the ocean.

Amelia just wanted, finally, to relax.

# 13

---

Amelia breathed in. Amelia breathed out.

The winter air was cool in her lungs, yet it felt smooth, as if she had floated away into the most serene, comfortable environment in the world.

She needed it. She needed a calm strength right now.

Putting her arm through Damon's certainly helped.

Amelia buzzed the doorbell.

After a moment, her mother opened the door. "There you—" she began before stopping herself when she realized that someone else was there. Her eyes lingered on Damon. "Oh!" she said after a long pause, as if having trouble believing that such a handsome man was with her oldest daughter. "Hello! I didn't ... and, and you are?"

"Damon Chase," he replied, taking her hand and kissing it gently. "It is a pleasure to meet you finally, Mrs. Gray. I now see where Amelia gets her beauty."

Damon and Amelia entered the house, attempting to look nonchalant, while Amelia watched her mother trying to wrap her head around what just happened.

Over her mother's shoulder, farther into the house, Amelia caught sight of Cara moving close to Sam, grabbing his butt, cramming her tongue down his throat, obviously trying to time the moment perfectly so that this PDA would be the first thing Amelia saw when she entered.

Cara stopped dead when she realized somebody else was there. The moment ruined. For her at least.

The expression on her face, Amelia thought with glee. Cara looked as if she were witnessing something that was simply impossible, a fantasy that shouldn't be capable of manifesting in the real world. She didn't know how to wrap her head around it. Except, unlike their mother, she wasn't pleased.

Amelia noticed that Sam wasn't pleased either, for entirely different reasons: he was fully expecting to get right up in Cara's personal space, only to be confused as to why Cara suddenly couldn't be bothered with holding onto him. Why wasn't he the center of her attention?

He looked confused. And hurt.

*Good*, Amelia thought.

Amelia and Damon took off their coats and politely chatted everyone up.

Her mother was still unable to articulate a proper sentence as she struggled to make sense of the fact that Amelia had arrived in a dress that appeared to be more lavish than anything she had in her own closet. Which was fine with Amelia, given that she really didn't want to hear anything her mother had to say, but was very pleased with the attention and looks of admiration.

For his part, Damon was extremely amicable and sociable with everybody he encountered. He was very charming, and knowledgeable about theater craft and professional acting, subjects that were rather alien and curious to anybody in this house. He held everybody's attention and made himself desirable to anybody who had a moment to speak to him.

Amelia smiled and laughed. She couldn't help but notice that most people wanted to talk to her date rather than to her, but she didn't care. From a distance, she caught sight of partygoers looking over at them, whispering. Not with laughter, but with surprised adulation. Everybody was impressed; everybody saw her as a lucky one.

And she had to admit, that feeling started to rub off on her. She couldn't stop smiling.

Then, for the first time in an hour, Amelia and Damon had a moment alone together, still in the same room as everybody else at the party, but at least out of earshot.

Damon smiled, showing off his brilliant white teeth, and he came over close to Amelia's ear, as if he were going to murmur sweet nothings. "It's working," he whispered.

"No, it's not," she whispered back. "Cara hasn't approached you at all."

"I think she wants to stab you in the back. But she doesn't want to do it to your face just yet. This won't work if you're next to me all the time."

Amelia had to admit that he was right. Which was disappointing, because she really wanted to see what would happen if Cara approached him now. But, priorities, she thought. She needed to make it happen, and that wouldn't happen if she was around.

Feigning some flimsy lie about going to get hors d'oeuvres, Amelia gave Damon a gentle stroke on his arm and went off to the dining room, where the Christmas buffet was on magnificent display. She looked around, saw some distant family members, all of whom had come over to talk to Damon, and now didn't have any interest in her at all.

It took Amelia a moment to realize that she hadn't seen her father yet.

Looking around, she couldn't spot him, but she did see what she had come for: at that moment, Cara crossed the room and began talking sweetly with Damon. She was looking very voluptuous but seemed to be playing coy. Amelia was too far away to hear what Cara was saying, but she generally knew the act by now. She watched her sister perform it well.

And then she watched as it took her sister a moment to realize that Damon didn't seem to hear her. Both Amelia and her accomplice knew, of course, that he definitely did hear her. But they had discussed this scenario ahead of time: he was pretending not to at first.

When Cara became aware that she had just exerted a large amount of energy chitchatting to someone who didn't appear to notice her, she tugged on his jacket. Finally, Damon turned to her as if he'd just noticed her for the first time. Amelia then watched as Cara basically repeated her whole routine.

"Hi, Amelia?"

She was so focused on her sister's efforts to steal her new man that Amelia hadn't even noticed that a man had come up to her as well. Startled out of her focus, she suddenly realized that it was Sam.

It was literally the first time he had said anything to her since their divorce. He hadn't even said anything to her at her birthday party.

"Hello. I hope you're doing well," he tried now. "It's good to see you."

"Fuck off." Amelia didn't say that with rage or even with tears. After all the meditative work she'd done with Damon recently, she'd learned how to say it nonchalantly, impassively.

It certainly wiped the smile off Sam's face. "What?" he said, genuinely taken aback.

Amelia had waited for this for months. "You don't hope I'm doing well, Sam. Otherwise, you wouldn't have cheated on me, and you wouldn't have acted the way you have been, with my sister's hand down your pants right in front of me. This is a waste of my time."

"Then ... Amelia, I'm trying to be polite here."

"No, you're trying to fill up time because your current woman, the one you cheated on me with, is cheating on you. Whatever." And with that, she walked away, feeling warm and pleased and wondering if Sam was actually hurt, or if his little brain was still processing the grammar of her statement. Was he even aware of what Cara was doing right now?

Case in point, she looked over at Damon and Cara again and was happy to see that Damon was looking generically polite, but overall kind of bored and dismissive. Cara seemed increasingly irate. She wasn't happy at the way this conversation was going, evidently.

And then, the magic moment: as Cara made a last-ditch effort by trying to grab onto Damon's arm, he slid himself out of her grip, but then, without even looking at her, he waved his hand in her face as if brushing away a pesky fly. Right before striding away from her and tracking down Amelia again.

Cara looked confused, but also offended, as if she didn't understand why her favorite toy was breaking down and going horribly, horribly wrong. Her face gave the impression that she felt as if she was personally being attacked.

Because she was, Amelia realized.

Damon came over to Amelia and leaned in, looking as if he was about to kiss her, when in fact he whispered into her ear, "Do you want me to tell you all the details?"

"Maybe later. Looked good from a distance," she replied.

They laughed together, like a happy couple at a Christmas party. From the corner of her eye, Amelia could see Sam crumbling, as if everything he'd ever labored for had begun to fall apart. Off in the distance, Cara looked like a bratty child who was about to cry.

And Amelia stood, quite beautiful in her red evening dress, holding a delicious pâté snack while her mother pointed at her and talked about her to her friends, smiling.

Amelia couldn't remember the last time she'd had such a wonderful Christmas.

## 14

Amelia played the next message on her cell phone.

"Uh, hey," came Cara's warbling voice, sounding a little nervous. "So, listen, I think I may have, uh, dropped a ring at the Christmas party near your new boyfriend, Damon, was it? I just wanted to get in touch with him and see if maybe he picked it up. So if you could just text me his number, I'll take care of the rest. So ... yeah ... let me know."

It was not the first message from Cara on her machine. It was noon on the day after the Christmas party. Amelia and Damon hadn't even left until about 1:30 a.m. And her message service was already flooded with calls. She didn't want to think about how quickly after they'd left the party that Cara had started calling.

Amelia, smiling, left the phone on loudspeaker on the armrest of her couch. She walked over to the kitchenette, to grab a glass of wine and pull out some macaroni and cheese in Tupperware from the fridge, then pop it into the microwave.

Somewhere behind her, the automated voice said, "End of sixth message. Playing the next new message."

"Hey, it's, it's me," came Cara's voice again. "Listen, I've been thinking, we never really make an effort to connect, you know? Maybe we should hang out more. Like ... I don't know, what do you even do?"

It was strange, Amelia thought while turning on the microwave, what a dichotomy there was in this current message. Almost all of it sounded like bullshit, and then the last sentence—where Cara admitted she didn't know jack shit about Amelia—sounded honest.

"Sorry," Cara continued, "I mean, we should hang out more and, like, get to know each other better. So, I was thinking, maybe we could do a double date. I'll come with Sam, and you come with Damon—"

The message suddenly cut out, and Amelia could hear the machine voice again: "Sorry, but that message reached the end of its recording time. End of seventh message. Playing the next new message."

There was a beep and then ...

"Fucking bitch, answer me! Pick up! What is wrong with you? Who the fuck is Damon?"

Then there was a loud crash, followed by a sharp electrical signal and a beep. Amelia wasn't sure, but her assumption was that Cara threw her phone and broke it.

The microwave pinged, and Amelia pulled the bowl of mac and cheese out and set it down on the counter to cool.

"End of eighth message," came the answering machine voice. "Playing the next new message."

"Hey, uh, me again," Sam said. It was his third message. This time, he sounded tired. Maybe even a little gloomy.

*Good*, Amelia thought.

"Listen," continued Sam, sounding reserved. "I feel it's important for me to fix the mistakes in my past. One of my biggest mistakes was the way I've treated you. Maybe we should reconnect and see if we can make amends. Could you call me back? Maybe we can arrange a time to meet, and I can explain myself better?"

Amelia checked the temperature of her mac and cheese bowl; it was cool enough now that she could hold it in her hand. She grabbed it, poured a glass of wine, then went back to the couch.

Maybe Sam's call would've affected her if this was seven months ago and she was still a distraught emotional mess. Or maybe, just maybe, it would've affected her if it hadn't come just a few messages after Cara had left something equally blithering. After all, both his messages were vague indictments of past transgressions, negative circumstances, and wronged wrongs of no discernible specificity. They were just saying that they did "something" wrong, and they wanted to make "amends," without taking any kind of real responsibility for what they actually did.

Amelia wasn't stupid. And she had no interest in being emotionally manipulated anymore. Not after so many months. Not after so much time had passed.

The truth was that Sam wasn't about to take any kind of responsibility for his actions. Largely because he wasn't aware that he had taken any actions for which he had to take responsibility. He had no idea how much pain he'd caused, because such awareness wasn't part of his programming. He didn't care. He was just having fun.

The real reason he was trying to make amends was because he felt bad now. He had been having fun, and then his fun caused him to hurt, and he wanted Amelia's permission to stop hurting. That was really all it was. He hadn't matured, he hadn't grown—he was forty years old, for God's sake, Amelia thought—he just wanted to know that he was allowed to stop feeling bad for being a bad boy.

Funnily enough, she thought, swirling the wine in her glass, it gave him something in common with Cara. It was sick and sad, but it made them a pretty good couple.

"End of ninth message," said the answer machine. "Playing the next new message."

At first, she wasn't sure what she was hearing, because it just sounded like some heavy breathing. Then, based on its rhythmic pattern, Amelia thought it sounded like crying.

And then came Cara's voice, which definitely sounded like she was crying.

"I just want ..." she drawled out before sounding like she was weeping again. It was a kind of silent weeping, but one that was constantly interrupted by Cara trying to breathe.

It was a little sad, Amelia admitted. She wanted to think of it as pathetic. This was Cara, after all.

"I don't know what's wrong with me," she continued. "It was so easy. I just wanted to have fun and be somebody. I wanted boys to love me, and ... God, what's wrong with me?"

"Sorry," came the voice, "the message reached the end of its recording time. Your mailbox is full—"

Amelia turned off her voicemail. With her other hand, she continued gobbling up the mac and cheese. She thought that she would be more than happy to erase some of those old messages, since they were composed entirely of Cara screaming or Sam begging.

Then she caught a glimpse of her text messages. Thankfully, she only had the one new text.

And it was from Damon.

Hey, let's reconvene after last night. Touch base about the plan and its results. What do you say? Café in the park?

Amelia smiled. They had visited several cafés and parks over the last few weeks. But "café in the park" signified a very particular one, where they'd really had one hell of a laugh. It was sort of a secret code between the two of them. She knew exactly what he meant and where to go.

She finished up her breakfast, then sloshed it down with wine before getting dressed and heading off to the café. She made sure to text him to let him know that she'd be there.

Even though she arrived quickly, he was already waiting for her, pulling out a chair at their table for her.

"Great to see you," he said, giving her a warm hug. "Please sit down. May I get you anything?"

"No, it's all right," she replied. "I wasn't planning on staying for very long."

"Oh, no, please. We should celebrate. I mean, we've been working at this for so long, and now it's worked. We should absolutely take a victory lap."

"I'm afraid I beat you to it." She laughed. "I had wine for breakfast. With mac and cheese."

"Oh! Bold! That's a helluva way to wake up."

"Not how I prefer to do it. But like I said, celebratory drinks."

"Next time, we should consider having some of those in the evening. And preferably not alone."

"I'll keep that in mind. And I'll take you up on that. But for now, God, I just want to bask! I feel like the world's opened up to me. Like I'm allowed to feel good about things again."

"Do you feel like somebody's had you tied up in a sheet of anxiety and misery, and they just finally tore it off, and you can feel the warmth of the sun again?"

"Yes, that's it exactly. I feel like the sunlight is shining on me for the first time. And colors are more radiant today. I guess it's perfect that it's the Christmas season, you know? So many red, blue, white, and green bubbles, so many lights, so many stupid Christmas songs playing everywhere. Festivity feels festive to me again. I couldn't have picked a better time to feel great about all this. Thank you, Damon. Thanks for giving me one hell of a Christmas present."

"I should be thanking you." He grinned at her, his teeth dazzling. "This has been one of the most fascinating experiences I've ever had in helping out a friend. It was a real adventure, and it worked. I feel like I gave you back a piece of your life that was stolen from you. I feel like I helped to heal you from an old wound. Like, some life has managed to reawaken here. I don't know if that makes sense to you; I'm just really proud I could be a part of it."

Amelia smiled. It was a sappy way of putting it and a touch weird. But she understood that he was trying to give her a fond wish of happiness. And it was nice to see that he had an awkward side about him. It made him more human, made her almost feel like she could forget that he was a playboy for hire.

That idea of him being a playboy for hire jogged something in her memory. "Oh! Before I forget, I'd better make sure I don't get you into any more trouble." She reached into her purse for the rest of his pay and handed it to him.

Damon stared at it, looking a bit unsure before politely nodding and pocketing the money. "If you hadn't reminded me, I probably wouldn't have brought it up. In all honesty, I had a wonderful time working with you. And if I may say so, if you're ever in the mood, I'll be more than happy to work with you again."

"I would like that," she said, staring at his cute smile just above his perfect jawline. She pictured his tongue behind those lips and had to stop herself from having some rather interesting thoughts.

"What's next for you?" Damon continued. "You've said you haven't been able to paint for some time. I noticed when I was at your place, your easel was still empty. Are you going to get back into that?"

"I don't know. Maybe."

"Well, you should. The way you express yourself, the way you make people feel, I have every confidence that you're an exquisite artist. I think you'll be able to create something beautiful."

"That's really thoughtful, thank you." She flushed slightly in pleasure at his compliment. "Ever since my divorce ... Do you know what? Forget it. That doesn't matter. I'll just paint. I'll just do what I've always wanted to do."

"I'm overjoyed to hear it. I would love to check in on you in the future and see all the amazing things you've painted by then."

"I hope so," Amelia replied, staring down at the table. Looking at the way the light bounced off it, the way the little bit of snow glittered up from the floor. She loved the way the light worked with the shade. She found herself inspired again.

After a quick and polite salutation, she headed to the door—Damon accompanied her, holding the door open for her. *So sweet*, she thought as she continued down the sidewalk back to her home.

She'd had such a wonderful meeting and only regretted that it was so brief. She wanted to find more excuses to call him up and see him again.

It occurred to Amelia that, given his occupation, she could, hypothetically, call Damon up anytime she wanted, pay him, and see him all she wanted.

But then, she asked herself, would that really make her happy?

What, Amelia wondered, was it that she actually wanted?

---

## 15

I t was the first time in a very long time that Amelia felt like she had actually discovered something inspirational.

She moved her hand ever so carefully in a straight line. The brush she was holding glided the precise, gentle touch of magenta over the canvas. Based on the way she was moving her arm—in a straight line and very slowly—she fully expected that she would've made one of the straightest lines across the canvas.

She knew she could always get out a straight edge and just paint alongside that. Except Amelia wanted her line to appear human. At first glance, it would've looked like a perfectly straight line. Upon closer observation, somebody would be able to notice that there were ever so slight waves and blobs.

After finishing her magenta line, she stepped back and assessed the progress of her painting. There was a bull's-eye center, a white dot that, the more she painted, the smaller it got, as the artwork became fuller with more colors. And the colors were the pinpoint commencements of various lines that shot out from the middle of the canvas, all the way out to the edges. All different colors, different shades. She had even blended some of her pink paint with regular over-the-counter glitter paint, giving it a kind of childish sparkle.

Her new work was really starting to come together, but she was only about two-thirds of the way done. And she had already painted well over two hundred lines. It was taking a long time because she wasn't exactly sure how to deal with the lines toward the edges of the canvas. At this stage, she was still being too technical about it. She just wanted to enjoy the idea of something bursting forth with color and radiance.

She was about to approach the canvas again when there was a knock at the door. Somehow, she had lost track of time and had forgotten that she had already agreed to celebrate with Wendy. With a frustrated sigh, Amelia put away her colors and laid a protective sheet over her work.

After the celebratory drinks she'd had with Damon, Amelia had determined that Wendy deserved some of the credit for the part she'd played in this as well. She was, after all, always there for Amelia, through the horrible emotions and the tough times. And she was the one who'd directed Amelia to an escort service in the first place, which had led her to Damon.

Amelia flung open the door and saw Wendy there, bottle of champagne in hand. Amelia knew that Wendy was pleased with any excuse to drink in the afternoon, but she could also detect genuine radiance when she felt it: Wendy was ecstatic for Amelia. She was finally free.

Amelia certainly felt free these days.

Wendy gave her a big hug and a couple of kisses on her way in.

Amelia ran over to her cabinet to grab a platter of cheese and bread while Wendy went over to the living room to place the bottle of champagne down on her coffee table. "Whoa," she said. "What's that?"

Amelia looked over and saw what she was referring to. "New painting," she said offhandedly. "It's not done."

When Amelia got back to the coffee table with champagne glasses and some cheese, she noticed that Wendy had lifted the covering and couldn't stop staring at the new painting. "I don't know what it means," Wendy finally said. "I just know I love looking at it."

Amelia smiled. "Funnily enough, I also don't have a damn clue what it means, and I also love looking at it."

"Oh! Well, there you go. Maybe everyone else will feel the same way."

"Fair enough," Amelia replied, pouring the champagne. "Maybe that's what I'll go for. Maybe I'm trying to depict joy. I mean, you just described it perfectly."

"You know," Wendy said, grabbing the full champagne glass from Amelia, "if we keep discussing paintings like this while holding drinks, you're gonna make me feel like I'm at work, and I don't want to feel like I'm at work. Sit down and tell me what Damon looks like with his shirt off."

They went on talking—and getting more and more drunk. Most of the laughter was due to the fact that Amelia was rather unsuccessful in convincing Wendy that she'd never actually had sex with Damon. Amelia understood Wendy's surprise: the more she thought about it in her own head, the weirder it sounded to her as well. She had, for all intents and purposes, rented the services of a male prostitute. And she'd never had sex with him, not even once. If the roles were reversed, Amelia wouldn't have believed it either.

"So the most you got out of him," Wendy said, trying to restrain the laughter that wanted to escape through her tipsy mind, "was a fancy warmed-up avocado sandwich from a fancy café. Like, all the money you spent on him, it never even crossed your mind to get the most out of him?"

"You make him sound like a product."

"His career is to make himself a product. It's not like he's naïve about what he does. And it's not like he wouldn't be having fun."

"It really did seem like he was having fun anyway," Amelia said, swirling what little was left of her champagne. "Sometimes, he insisted that I not pay. But he'd pay for me. It made it feel more like a date."

"What? Like when?"

"When we went to the art gallery, he bought his own ticket."

"Oh, well, that's how much—"

"And I didn't pay for that day. And it's never come up again."

"So he worked for free."

"That day, yeah," Amelia replied. Then she stopped and wondered: How many days had he worked for free? It seemed like a lot. Amelia didn't bring it up because, well, paying a man for his services wasn't something she did frequently. So, in all honesty, she tended to forget. She was expecting him to remind her. He didn't, though. And when she finally paid him for his last day, he seemed surprised. Like he had forgotten as well.

"Jeez," Wendy replied. "I couldn't even imagine working my job for free. And I like my job. But I'd still be like, 'Hey, paycheck bounced, give me my cash, or I start burning Van Goghs.'"

"I can believe that," Amelia answered, laughing. "Maybe it was because I was paying him to mess with my sister. I wasn't paying him to go out with me, and ... a lot of what we did kind of felt like dating. Maybe he let that slide because, well, he just wanted to date."

"Sounds like he gave up on a lot of money. Which doesn't sound sensible, given what he does."

"Well, sometimes I wondered, I mean, getting aroused and pumping away isn't, y'know, an automatic thing for guys ..."

"Depends on the guy. Watch out for college boys."

"Thanks for the image. I'm just saying, given what he does for a living, maybe he appreciated being with a woman who wanted to give him a break. Let him just hang out in a fancy café and walk around an art gallery for a couple of hours."

"Fair enough. But that doesn't excuse good common business sense. He was still on the clock. My best guess is maybe he really liked you."

"Oh, fuck you." Amelia batted her friend's idea away.

"No, really. Maybe he was stupid enough to save you a couple of dollars and see if he could get into your pants."

"You find a way to make it sound nice; then you immediately find a way to ruin it. That really takes skill; thank you, Wendy."

"Cheers," Wendy replied, raising her glass in a toast. "Anytime, honey!"

After the bottle was finished, Amelia brought out one of her own, and soon they'd finished that one off as well.

Eventually, Wendy remembered—with some difficulty—

that she had to work the next day, and showing up hungover was probably not the best idea. Amelia insisted on making her a cup of coffee, so they finished off one of those each too before Wendy set off for the road.

Amelia walked Wendy out to the street, and they gave each other another kiss on the cheek. Then Wendy wobbled off into the night, heading off to her place.

Watching her leave, Amelia realized that she had basically lost the day. She'd really felt like she wanted to get some work done, and her best friend had robbed her of that. But she didn't care. It had been a wonderful evening, full of drinks and laughter. And it was riding on the high of everything going very well for her recently. She needed to remind her friend that she loved her, and she was eternally grateful for everything that she'd brought into her life. If she never painted again, she thought innocently enough, at least she was happy that she had her friend with her.

A friend who was stupid enough to imply that a man like Damon would be willing to fork out money in exchange for spending time with someone like Amelia, but a friend all the same.

Giggling to herself at the thought of it, Amelia looked over toward the end of the street, where she was absolutely certain that she saw Damon's car driving away. Which was weird, considering that her professional relationship with Damon was over.

*Well, that's just perfect*, Amelia thought. *Now, thanks to Wendy, I'm imagining Damon everywhere.*

*At least I hope I'm imagining him.*

# 16

In addition to being extremely successful in terms of what was going on between Amelia and Cara, Damon's presence also effected a marked improvement in Amelia's relationship with her mother.

Amelia was in her mother's good graces. Gaining her mother's approval felt like lifting a horrible weight off her shoulders that she didn't even know was there until it was gone. And finally being treated like a normal daughter was a gratifying experience. Suddenly, another aspect of her life became mundane, even pleasant. She wanted this. She wanted a normal family life.

And once her mother started feeling happier, she not only provided Amelia with enough funds to pay her January rent, she also provided her with the money she had obviously been withholding for December.

For the first time ever, her mother had invited Amelia to the family's New Year's Eve party. She'd invited Damon too, so Amelia had called Sterling Escorts and requested him by name. Evidently, the job was not yet over.

The evening of the party, Amelia took great pleasure in watching from a distance as Cara got yelled at by their mother. Receiving her own mother's approval was like icing on the cake, but simultaneously watching Cara gain their mother's disapproval was like the cake itself.

It was truly an unbelievable sight. Cara was basically begging their mother to intervene in her attempt to seduce Damon. Not in those exact words, of course. But after several attempts to encourage Damon to talk to her, look at her, even acknowledge her, which simply weren't working, Cara was finally pulled aside by her mother and reprimanded for being a nuisance.

"Look, they'll talk to you," Cara told her mother. "They'll listen to you. Can't you just make them talk to me?"

"Oh, stop being a damn baby," her mother replied in exasperation. "You're supposed to be better than this. What about your current partner? You know, Sam?"

"I don't want him. I want Damon."

Cara said it loud enough that other people had to have heard it. Certainly, Amelia was eavesdropping, but she'd be surprised if Damon hadn't heard it as well. Maybe, fingers crossed, there was a possibility that Sam had too.

Her mother was obviously concerned that the whole world heard it, so she grabbed Cara by the arm and dragged her into the next room.

Maybe there really was a Santa Claus.

Amelia did her best not to laugh at the sight of it.

Damon came over. "So?" he asked. "Best night of your life right now, or was that still Christmas?"

"Damon, at a certain point," Amelia replied, "it's not really about quantity as much as it is about quality."

There was an awkward pause before Damon blurted out, "What?"

"Um ... in the sense that, well, measuring which day is better on a numerical scale ... You know what, it made sense in my head."

Damon grinned. "How many of those have you had?" he said, gently tapping Amelia's champagne glass.

"More than I should've had," she replied, smiling, "but less than is necessary for family."

"I understand that," Damon said, nodding and looking off into space. "Well, be careful; you don't want to ruin our evening by losing control. Everything is going so well."

"Well, as long as I've got you here to watch me, I'm sure I'll be fine."

"Really? ... You know, you keep talking like that, I may just have to invite you back to my place."

"You keep pouring me more champagne, I may forget myself and take you up on that."

"As charming as that is, I'm sure you would've said the same no matter how much champagne I was pouring."

Amelia laughed, and as she did so, she suddenly noticed that Sam was trying to work up the courage to talk to her. He clearly wasn't going to do it as long as Damon was within earshot, so she shoved Damon away. "Go!" she said urgently. "Go over there!"

At first, Damon looked as if he didn't understand.

Amelia gestured toward Sam by tilting her head slightly to the side.

"Ah, right, I'll just be over there." Damon leaned in and kissed her cheek before moving off toward the punch bowl.

Amelia knew she could trust Damon to give her the moment she was waiting for. She strolled leisurely over to a different corner of the room, farther away from where Damon had gone.

And quite expectedly, Sam immediately marched over to her. "Hi," he said.

"What do you want?" she replied.

"I don't know if you got any of my phone messages."

"Got all of them. Had to keep getting rid of them. You sent far too many, and they took up space. Kind of like most of your stuff."

Sam started to laugh before realizing it wasn't a joke. "So," he started again, "how are things going between you and, well, your new guy?"

"'New guy?' Didn't Cara tell you his name? She seems rather focused on him; you'd think she would've told you by now."

"We haven't been talking much these days."

"Oh, but you seemed so perfect for each other. Like you threw off some old piece of shit just to be with her. I'm sure it was so worth it, yes?"

There was a silence before Sam picked up on her meaning. "Oh," he replied.

"Not having a winning night, it seems," said Amelia.

"Look, I really hate that we're talking like this. Obviously, I didn't want us to end up this way."

"What do you mean? You divorced me by phone. You told me the reason for our divorce was because you wanted to hook up with a younger woman for more sex. Better sex."

"I was an idiot."

"I don't care."

"I know I did wrong, but after ten years of marriage, isn't there any part of you that, well, still wishes that things could've turned out better?"

"You know, Sam, I might've considered it if you hadn't shown me exactly how happy you were to follow every one of Cara's instructions on how to hurt me. But you not only cheated on your wife, you then deliberately went out of your way to tell me how much you loved it. It was premeditated; it was a pleasure for you. Whatever hope there was is gone; you did everything in your power to destroy it. I mean, what the hell did you expect my reaction would be?"

There was a long pause, in which Amelia finished off the rest of her champagne and started looking around for a fresh glass within arm's reach.

Sam spoke up again. "Wait, so you might've considered forgiving me, you said?"

Amelia wanted to smash the champagne glass in her balled fist.

"Did your brain switch off after the first sentence? Halfway through it? Did you just not listen at all?"

"I'm just saying ... Don't you miss me the way I miss you?"

"Can you please, *please* fuck off before I go and suck my new boyfriend's dick? I mean, he tastes so much better, just so you know."

And with that, she stumbled her way as elegantly as she could over to Damon. If for no other reason than it would keep Sam as far away from her as possible.

As soon as she looked up at Damon, he was attentive. He was already watching her.

She wondered if he had been watching her the entire time she was with her ex-husband.

That was a little overprotective, she thought. And if she were being honest, a little sweet.

## 17

"The original idea behind a poodle was that it was going to be a game-hunting dog," Mark explained, "so it would splash into ponds and lakes to catch ducks and other things like that. Its hair gets very fluffy and matted to keep it warm in northern European environments during hunting season. The idea of it being a pampered and groomed dog came much later. By its nature, it's a very athletic, intelligent dog."

Amelia didn't need to be told twice, or at all, she thought, as the poodle she was trying to control suddenly raced off and caused her to desperately chase after it while trying to keep from tripping.

She'd been spending a lot of time with Mark and Wendy —Wendy was always insistent that Amelia join them on their excursions. Amelia was starting to think that Wendy was developing a serious crush on the guy and was simply nervous to be alone with him.

She'd started to learn a lot about dogs from Mark. Stuff she never expected to know or even care about, as she never really saw herself as much of a pet person. Frankly, Mark wouldn't shut up about dogs. It was a charming quality, at the right time of day. Typically, when walking through a park, enjoying the fresh air, trying not to get exhausted from laughing and having to control all these mischief-making little creatures.

If Wendy really did have a crush on this guy, Amelia thought, she certainly picked a good one. He was a very loving, very smart character.

Amelia liked going out with her friends, but also appreciated the benefits of being single, for the first time in a decade. It gave her a lot of time to stop worrying about making a happy home life and start thinking about whatever the hell she felt like doing at any particular moment.

Especially in her art. Her explosive linework piece— eventually, she named it *Joy*—was only the start of her inspiration, as it turned out. She liked that piece, but also wanted to experiment with more than straight lines. She started taking several canvases and decorating them with patterns and colors that enriched the gaze when looking upon them. Some of them swirled; some of them seemed to cave in. But ultimately, every single piece she did encouraged the eye to move in a certain direction, scanning the plethora of sites and sparks along the way. Sometimes, when she looked at the designs and patterns and colors of her own works, she could almost imagine that she knew what they sounded like. It created a hallucinatory quality, like tripping without the drugs.

Over the course of nine different paintings, she had created an impressive abundance of colorful movement. She kept naming them using words that she felt adequately represented the sensation brought on by what caused her to make each piece. Words like *Spellbound* or *Energy*. These were beautiful, exhilarating paintings.

At least, her agent, Margo, thought so. After Amelia's long hiatus, she was not only happy to see her talent back at work, but also happy to see that Amelia was creating art that had the potential to be both aesthetically inspiring while offering a certain nod to pop culture; these new pieces were *marketable* and *cool*, as she put it. Margo told Amelia that if she could continue in this direction, they might even be able to hold a gala.

Every time Amelia looked down at her fingers and saw the little spots of paint that she wasn't able to wash off, she thought of that moment. And how far she'd come to earn it.

As she ran ideas for her next painting—*Verve*, perhaps? —through her mind, it occurred to her that she hadn't heard her phone ring for quite some time. Now that the poodle she was watching had finally arrived at its destination—apparently, it just had to sniff a very interesting rock—she had a moment to check it.

No wonder it wasn't ringing or vibrating. Her voicemail was full again.

However, the call display indicated that it was Sam filling up her inbox. No doubt filling it with demands for her obedience, poorly disguised as pleas for reconnection, which themselves were poorly disguised as casual chitchat. It would be sad, tragic even, if it wasn't kind of funny.

Well, at least one of the benefits of having her ex-husband flood her voicemail was that, somewhere out in the world, Sam was probably trying to call her, only to receive the automated message to say that the phone was unavailable. Over and over again.

Amelia was starting to wonder if she was inheriting some

of her mother's more sadistic tendencies. In truth, she never wanted to be quite so happy to think of Sam in such a state.

Then again, he'd never tried to stop Cara from sending a recording of the two of them banging. So there was that.

Now that the poodle had sufficiently confirmed the rock to be a rock, she seemed more than eager to continue on with her wandering around, followed obediently by Amelia, who looked across the park to see Mark and Wendy waving at her. Amelia waved back at them.

And then she saw somebody step out from behind a tree.

Amelia gasped, but he simply gave her a little wave.

It was Damon.

The surprise was enough to put a stop to her waving. She wondered if she was actually seeing the man, or if she was just becoming exhausted from running around in the snowy park for so long.

"Hey," Damon said as he approached her. He wore gloves, a woolly hat, and a winter jacket, but he still managed to exude a very real kind of sexiness. "Long time no see."

"Hi," Amelia replied. "Didn't we see each other yesterday, though?"

"Huh?"

"I was coming back from my agent's place, and we ran into each other as I was rounding a corner."

"Oh, yeah! No, you're right, my bad."

"Hardly bad," she said before she could stop herself. That was starting to be a little on the nose, she thought, and she didn't really have much of an excuse for it. "I mean, it's always a pleasure to see my partner in crime."

"You keep calling me that." He arched a brow teasingly. "I'm starting to wonder if you think of what we're doing as illegal."

"No! I mean, not illegal per se. Maybe a little devious. I mean, I imagine my parents and my sister wouldn't be entirely pleased. Oh! I can tell you right now that my ex certainly isn't. Here." She pulled out her phone and showed him her screen, indicating all the calls she'd been receiving from Sam.

"You joke," Damon replied sternly, "but that definitely could be interpreted as criminal activity. Stalking. Harassing. You shouldn't have to put up with all those calls. If you want, we could do something about that."

Amelia smiled and shook her head. "If I wanted him to stop, I could easily block him. But then I wouldn't get to hear his desperate pleading in all those millions of phone calls, now, would I?"

It took Damon a moment to wipe his grimace off his face and force a smile. "Well, I can't say you haven't earned the right to a little satisfaction," he finally admitted. "That said, if you ever need somebody to help you handle the situation, you know how to reach me."

"Yeah ... what are you doing here, anyway?"

"Hm?"

"In the park."

"Just, well, exercise. It's a nice day today. You?"

"Helping a friend with their dogs. I think I like dogs now."

"Really?"

"Yeah," Amelia replied, then turned to motion toward Wendy and Mark. "Mostly, I think there's a thing going on between those two as well."

Damon looked over and shrugged. "Well, all right," he said. "Want to go do something? We can have a nice cup of coffee if you like."

Amelia smiled. "No, I'm already committed to trying to get this little bitch under control. Both literally and figuratively, it's a girl dog who's kind of a jerk. Plus, I've got to save up cash, for now. At least, until after I get my new gala up."

"Wow! New gala? You've got a show coming up?"

"Yeah! First one in ages. I can't believe I actually made enough material for one."

"Your work is brilliant. I'm sure you're going to make everyone there buy up everything you have. Or at least, judge you fairly."

"Preferably both, more the former."

"Wait, why do you need to save up money?"

"Well, I really wouldn't be able to easily pay you for your time. Plus, there aren't any family gatherings coming up for a bit. My dad's birthday is next, but I'm not even sure I'll go."

"Oh, you don't have to … I mean, it was my idea; we could just go get coffee."

"No, no, it's all right. I've got to get this dog back to my friends. Thanks though." And with a smile and a wave, she was off, following her poodle back over to Wendy.

By the time she got back, Mark was finishing his struggle to gather up the leashes of twelve dogs. Wendy was doing what she could to control two.

"Hey," Wendy said, greeting her; then she squinted and looked over Amelia's shoulder.

When Amelia looked behind her, she noticed that Damon was still in the same part of the park, waving back to her. Amelia smiled and nodded.

"Is that Damon?" Wendy asked.

"Yeah, just ran into him."

"Cool. Did you say you'd meet him?"

"No, he's just out to take some exercise."

Wendy grinned. "Not surprised, with a body like that. He must go for a lot of walks."

Amelia rolled her eyes. Wendy had no shame, openly lusting after one guy while on a date with another. Instead, she focused on controlling her one little poodle. Looking over her shoulder again, Damon was still there, watching her.

Clearly, he wasn't doing a lot of walking at the moment despite his professed need for exercise.

He certainly walks around a lot, she thought, given that she'd run into him just yesterday too.

The more she thought about it, the more Amelia realized that she tended to run into him quite often. Not that she was interested in how many women he had sex with for money, of course, but when *did* he actually work?

## 18

A melia turned on her computer and logged on to double-check her bank account.

There it was: a deposit from her agent.

Doing the math in her head, Amelia realized that the figure was larger than what she'd expected. She quickly scrolled down through her email and opened the email from her agent, explaining the situation.

Indeed, she had sold two paintings at her gala. She'd had twenty-five paintings there in total, so it wasn't exactly anything to go crazy about. But considering that she hadn't sold anything in the nine months prior, the fact that she'd sold any amount of her artwork, as a young, relatively new artist in the New York scene, was an achievement. Her agent had also had prints made of her paintings, and she had been able to sell a few of those to the more casual art fans.

But the real income, as the email described, came from a very sudden surprise purchase. Her agent had noticed that some of the postcard prints were being purchased by teenagers and young adults, and apparently, that helped solidify her theory that Amelia's most recent line of work had pop-culture potential. She took the initiative to contact a printing company who made a side gig of selling posters to college kids.

The volume of the print postcard sales convinced the company to agree to a licensing deal: they paid a hefty sum to acquire the legal rights to print images of Amelia's artwork onto poster paper and sell them to nineteen-year-olds with too much of their parents' money.

Amelia honestly didn't know how to feel about that. It seemed a little crass. But she did love the idea that her work was worthy of being treated in such a commercial manner. After all, no one paid to license work that they didn't want; people were obviously gobbling it up. Her colorful spectrums were becoming something of a psychedelic, emotionally charged hit.

And to be perfectly blunt, in a capitalist world, the advance that Amelia saw in her bank account didn't hurt either.

She couldn't be happier, she realized. She started literally jumping for joy in her apartment. Amelia realized that she didn't really need the money her mother had given her for January's rent. She wouldn't need money for February's rent either, at this rate. The real question now was whether to take more of her parents' money and use it to start fattening up her dwindling bank account. Or whether to tell her mother to keep the money and experience the joy of watching her mother's face as she realized she wasn't allowed to talk to her in a hurtful way anymore.

Amelia started to get worried about how comfortable she was with such thoughts. They felt almost like a comfortable dress. She just slipped it on and knew how happy she was going to be to teach somebody a lesson they deserved.

In actuality, Amelia thought, it was somewhat tiring. Constantly having to fight against somebody, put them down, teach them a harsh life lesson in reality. In retrospect, she wondered how Cara could've done it all those years, completely devoting herself to harming a single person for so many years. Seemed exhausting, really.

She must've been really driven, Amelia thought. Admittedly, she decided, she simply didn't have that kind of drive.

Still, though, there were the last little details to deal with. By all accounts, Cara was still angry and vengeful. She still had Amelia's ex-husband to fall back on, and she still hadn't gotten it through her thick skull that Damon just wasn't interested. If Amelia let up now, she knew that Cara might notice, and she might be galvanized at the sight of Amelia without a current boyfriend. Hell, if Amelia cut her time spent with Damon in half, he'd lose a significant chunk of income, and he wouldn't have any reason to work with her plan, financially speaking anyway. If Cara ever tracked him down, she might even hire his "services," and he would have no reason to balk at the idea.

No, she thought. She wasn't done yet. She had to see it through. Just for a little while longer, fingers crossed.

Case in point, her father's birthday. Her mother—not her father, definitely not—had invited the "happy couple" over to celebrate with the family and eat some cake. Her mother had certainly taken to Damon. Amelia still wasn't sure if she was in love with this young man, or if she just loved the idea of her daughter finally being something other than a misfit. Either way, she was a sad old delusional woman. Something else Amelia didn't want to take any pleasure in.

Well, all the same, she decided that she was going to go. If she had to keep up this relationship with Damon, she would need funds, meaning her parents' money would help with that, meaning not pissing off her mom. Plus, she wasn't going to deny that she liked the attention from such a dashing, handsome man.

---

ON THE EVENING of the party, Amelia dressed in a sparkling dark blue dress that Damon had recently purchased for her. He'd made a valid point that her mother and her sister wouldn't be impressed with her showing up in the same dress to every party over and over again. But Amelia was becoming worried at how often he kept buying her sexy clothing.

There was a knock on the door.

She smoothed her dress, then went to the door and opened it. "Hey, how are—" She stopped dead in her tracks.

Damon stood there with a bouquet of roses.

"What's this?" she asked.

"Flowers," Damon replied as he held the bouquet out to her. "I thought, if you put them in a vase, they would look beautiful."

"For who, though?"

"What do you mean, 'for who'? For you! Who else?"

"Well, we're not bringing a vase with us."

"No, they're for your apartment."

"Why?"

"To ... look nice. Look, this is supposed to have been far more straightforward than it's turning out to be; I just wanted to get you some flowers. I thought you'd like them."

Amelia didn't bother trying to hide the confused expression on her face. It seemed prudent to let him know how she felt. "This was unnecessary, Damon," she replied. Seriously, she thought, what the hell was she supposed to do with these things now?

"Wow," Damon replied, putting the flowers down on a countertop next to the door. "That's a bit cold."

"No, it's just—" Amelia started to say, wanting to brush the entire experience out of her mind. This was supposed to be a happy moment; she had a new source of income and could finally put an end to this nonsense with Cara. She wasn't going to let some social flub ruin it for her. "Never mind, we'll take them with us. We can give them to my mom or something."

Damon stared at her silently for a moment before picking up the flowers and half-heartedly replying, "Okay."

And then they were in Damon's car and driving up to Connecticut. Along the way, Amelia really did start to pay attention to all the details of his car. She had a nagging feeling she'd seen it a while back when Wendy was leaving her apartment.

She was just ... she really had a suspicion about it.

Before long, they were at her parents' house in New Haven. Unsurprisingly, when Damon—with some prodding from Amelia—offered her mother the bouquet of roses, she was simply overjoyed at being treated so kindly by such a "close, dear friend" in her words. Her mother, of course, immediately arranged the flowers into a vase.

They entered the lavish house, where other family members mingled, now becoming an all-too-familiar sight. Various servers were preparing slices of cake and pots of hot tea. Funnily enough, when Amelia looked around to see if her father had gotten any cake, she found she couldn't find the old man anywhere at all.

She did, however, see Cara. She was sitting in a luxuriant wooden chair, propped up against the wall. Just staring bitterly into the room.

And she was on her own.

Amelia didn't see Sam anywhere. Cara hadn't brought him.

To be honest, the only reason Cara had ever brought Sam to family gatherings was to make Amelia feel bad. So maybe Cara had finally started to hear from Sam about how happy Amelia was to have him out of her life. Or, more realistically, Cara didn't say a word to Sam at all and was just sick of him.

It didn't matter. The point was, Cara had experienced a setback. She was losing.

Instead of feeling even remotely bad about it, Amelia grabbed a piece of cake. Nobody was supposed to have started eating yet, but at this point, she simply didn't care. She wanted the night to taste even sweeter.

And it was only going to get better from here, she realized, when she turned back to see Damon, and saw that Cara had finally left her seat to approach him while Amelia was occupied with the cake.

"Look," Cara said, with frustration in her voice, "all I'm saying is, if you want to give me just fifteen minutes of your time, I promise you I could show you exactly what you're missing out on."

Amelia had never heard her sister talk this way. Grace and flirtation had largely gone out the window by this point. Her sister was desperate.

Amelia was still pleased to see it, in a way. But even she had to acknowledge that this was starting to get kind of sad.

"No, thank you," Damon replied offhandedly.

"Fifteen minutes, just fifteen minutes."

"No, thank you."

"Look, just, let's talk about it somewhere more private; we'll just talk! I could—"

"No!" Damon replied sternly.

Amelia approached them, wondering where this was going to go. Damon was still maintaining his aloof nature, as was expected. Cara, for her part, hadn't even noticed Amelia getting closer. And she looked like she was starting to shake. Like something inside her was about to break down.

"Please," Cara begged, almost at a whisper. "I will let you do … *anything* to me. Come on, please."

All of a sudden, Damon exhaled strongly, as if finally letting everything go that he was holding in. He placed his hors d'oeuvre plate down safely on the countertop. "Do you want to see what you're missing out on?" he asked Cara.

Before Amelia even knew what was happening, Damon reached out, pulled her to him, slid his fingers through the hair behind her head, pulled her in closer, and kissed her passionately.

Amelia was so startled. She had been picked up off the floor and had to regain her balance. Damon's tongue was in her throat. Her instincts told her to start pummeling her assaulter, not that she could really move in his strong embrace.

Somewhere behind her, she heard mostly silence, but a few gasps, and maybe one or two people hooting and hollering softly. She suddenly remembered where she was.

She remembered what she was here for.

Attacking Damon now would've broken the illusion, she knew, so instead, she relaxed in his arms and finally was able to slide her arms around his shoulders and hold on tight as she held her lips open and allowed him to do anything he wanted with his tongue. She even moved her own lips a little, trying to mimic what she imagined it would look like if she were returning the kiss.

It felt laborious.

It felt wrong.

Amelia softly opened one eye and glanced over at Cara, to see that her sister was right up in their faces with pure rage and anguish. She was visibly shaking, balling her fists up, ready to pummel the both of them.

Cara turned to leave the room; she moved so quickly and jerkily that she pelted into a glass cabinet full of their mother's fine china. The noise caused Amelia to break the kiss in surprise. Cara began crying as the glass of the cabinet and the array of china within fell to the floor in a deafening clatter. She wailed loudly as some of the servers moved in to help take her from the room. Amelia's mother gave her and Damon a very nasty look before following Cara and the help out of the room as well.

Only when they were gone did Damon finally let Amelia go.

"Why did you do that?" Amelia whispered. "Why did you kiss me?"

"Amelia, darling," he replied, "I know what we set out to do here, but frankly, I have taken a lot from that woman. Like, she wouldn't let it go. It was just too damn much. I had to stop it. I figured kissing you was the most direct way to get the message into her thick skull."

"I just wish you had told me you were going to do that."

"I didn't know I was going to do that either. It was a moment of inspiration. And, well, you have to admit, it worked. And it was nice."

"What?"

"Well, you know. Watching your sister get dragged out of here. It was everything you wanted, wasn't it?"

The money, the successful painting career, the friends, the cute dog walks in the park. No more Sam. No more Cara.

It seemed like it was all that she wanted. Amelia couldn't understand why it didn't feel that way anymore.

melia rarely used the subway system, but as she left her apartment building that day, she made a beeline for the nearest subway station. She'd planned her route out ahead of time so that she would have to spend a minimum amount of time in the station looking around at maps and train numbers. She wanted to be in and out.

She needed to test a theory.

And then she met up with Wendy at a café in Brooklyn. Brooklyn was out of the way for both of them, so they didn't really know the area. Amelia chose this café—again, to test a theory. If she didn't know anything about it, then neither would anybody who knew her. Which increased the likelihood that she could go there without anybody knowing.

Once they'd ordered their drinks and sat down, Amelia told Wendy everything that had happened at her father's birthday party. Including the most important detail. The fact that Damon had grabbed Amelia and passionately kissed her in order to get Cara off his back.

"Did you know he was going to do that?" Wendy asked.

"No, I didn't," Amelia said. "In fact, we'd never discussed it."

"I mean, you did say you'd set some kind of boundaries, right?"

Amelia leaned back in her chair. "In a way, I guess," she replied. "Specifically, I'd discussed with him the fact that this entanglement was supposed to be fake. We were supposed to look very happy together, with the express purpose of making Cara jealous. But anything beyond that, I told him that ours was strictly a professional engagement. We weren't supposed to go far or to do anything, really. If anything, the majority of the responsibility was going to end up falling on his shoulders. What he had to do, more than anything else, was constantly reject my sister."

"Yeah, but you never actually told him he wasn't allowed to get in your personal space, right?"

"Should I have?"

Wendy started to shake her head, as if unsure of how to proceed. "Okay, it's not that simple," she finally said. "Yes, you should've set boundaries. Yes, you should have made it clear how much you wanted him to do, or how close you wanted him to get. Now, that said ... what he did was flat-out wrong. You gave him explicit instructions about what you wanted in regard to his role with your sister. The further he deviates from that, the further he's just coming up with his own shit. And that's not his job."

"Right, makes sense," said Amelia, staring into her coffee. She was doing everything in her power to try to recall any conversation she had with Damon, all the way back to when they first met at the hotel. She was wondering if there was any kind of mistake she might have made, or miscommunication she might have caused, that would've resulted in such a terrible lapse in judgment on his part.

"And," continued Wendy, "maybe this is just rehashing it, but you don't act in a way that you wouldn't normally act. It doesn't give you permission to do anything differently!"

"When you," Amelia started slowly, not quite sure how to bring it up. "When you meet up with men through the service ... Do you talk with them explicitly about what you want?"

Now it was Wendy's turn to lean back in her chair and think long and hard about her answer. "Even if I dress it up, I make it clear what I want. Because it's not really a date. It's not a relationship other than a working relationship. It's a service. You make it clear up front, or you make it difficult on yourself."

"I know what you're driving at," replied Amelia. "I don't really feel that I gave any information that could be misconstrued as something else, you know? I thought I was pretty direct about everything I wanted and expected. I keep trying to think of what I may have missed."

"Well," Wendy said, "it doesn't sound like you missed anything. You told him what the intention was between you and your sister and your mother and Sam. And he fulfilled that. And then you kept his services going so that you could continue fulfilling that to its logical and natural conclusion. And then ... well ..."

"He kissed me."

"Just like that."

"Just like that."

Wendy scratched her head and leaned in on the table. "It could be as simple as an exceptionally poor lapse in judgment. But if I were you, it's not the kind of thing I would forgive. I mean, it's not like he can't go back to Sterling and earn his living with other clients, but I wouldn't hire him again. At a certain point, you have to know if you can be safe with the person, and if he acts out of the blue like that, then carrying on with him might be asking for more trouble than it's worth."

"Fair enough," replied Amelia. "But, to be truthful, I'm starting to wonder if it really was just a single error in judgment."

"He's kissed you before?"

"No, no, not exactly. It's just that, when we had to go to the birthday party, he, well, he brought me a bouquet of roses."

Wendy's eyes went wide, and her jaw dropped a little. "A bouquet of roses?"

"Yeah, I know," said Amelia. "Kind of weirded me out."

"No, dude, that would send me into a damn panic. I would've slammed the door in his face."

"Really? Over flowers?"

"A romantic bouquet from an escort? That's just off."

"I thought so."

"Also, think about your relationship. You pay him for everything. You didn't buy those flowers; he bought those flowers with his own money. Nobody ordered him to. Did he buy them for your mother? Did he buy them to present them to you in front of your sister? No, he bought them for you, right?"

Amelia thought back to the experience, how Damon had wanted her to put them in a vase immediately. "Yeah," she answered. "That's exactly what happened."

"Right. That indicates his decision about what he was going to do with you. That's completely unrelated to the reason why you hired him. Weird." Wendy took a sip of her coffee and sort of stared off to the side.

"You know," Amelia said, hesitating, "he also bought me two dresses ..."

"What?"

"At Christmas and then again for the birthday party. He bought them."

Wendy looked really worried now. "You said you ran into him at the park when we were walking those dogs, remember?"

"Yeah," came Amelia's reply. "Why?"

"Was that the only time he just *showed up*?"

"Well, no. The day before, I ran into him as I was coming back from a meeting with my agent."

"Really?" Wendy gave Amelia a hard stare.

And that was enough for the floodgates to burst. Amelia started thinking about all the instances when she'd bumped into Damon outside of their professional relationship. When they met on the sidewalk. When they met coming out of a store. She had been running into Damon constantly.

It always seemed to happen randomly.

And more to the point, it only started happening after they started working together. She would have noticed a man like him if he'd been around before that.

Amelia thought about that. She'd hired Damon after meeting him at the hotel. They'd had a few practice date sessions to get her loosened up for the big job. And then she'd started asking him for fewer sessions.

And that was when it started.

Damon just kind of started ... always being around.

She turned to Wendy, her jaw growing slack. "He's

always just around," she answered. "I mean, just everywhere. Everywhere I am."

"Do you know where he lives?"

"No."

"Damn. But, at least, you've noticed that he goes literally everywhere you do."

"Yes."

"Well, you have to ask yourself, what are the odds of that? What are the odds that he just happens to share all of the same interests that you do, enjoys going to all the same places, and doing all the same things? That he just 'happens' to be into everything you are?"

"Well, maybe he—"

"Amelia, he's not required to share your tastes, he's just required to lie about it to your sister."

"Maybe he's taking extra initiative—"

"You're starting to sound like an apologist. I mean, I know he's cute, but do you actually like him?"

"Ever since he forced that kiss on me, I really haven't. I feel like ... there's something wrong about him. Did I mention that, on a few occasions, I almost feel as if I've seen his car outside my apartment building?"

"Like when?"

"After we had all that champagne, remember?"

"Regrettably, I do. The worst drinking parties are the ones where you remember everything. But, in this case, I don't remember a car outside your building. Then again, I have no idea what his car looks like, nor was I looking for one."

"I get that. But I really feel like I've seen it there. I've certainly seen it enough to be able to recognize it. And when he saw me at the park, it wasn't enough that I just ran into him. But rather, after I went back to you guys ... He stayed there, watching me. Remember?"

"Yeah ... Yeah, I do."

"He's ... just ... always trying to be there."

"Yeah, imagine if he were outside right now," Wendy said, rolling her eyes.

Amelia took a sip of coffee, then looked up.

Wendy was staring, wide-eyed, out the front window of the café behind Amelia's back. Suddenly, Wendy darted her eyes sideways, as if pretending not to look.

But Amelia could definitely see the color drain from her face.

She didn't dare turn around and look out the window herself. She didn't even want to risk the possibility of meeting his eyes. She was afraid that if that happened, he would assume it was an invitation for him to walk into the café and invite himself to the table.

"Come on," Amelia whispered.

Both women stood up and collected their things. First, Wendy just sort of hung around and wasn't sure where to go until Amelia prompted her to follow her toward the back of the café. There, they found a young barista, whom Amelia approached.

"Is there a back exit to this café?" she said quickly. "There's somebody out front who might be ... well ..."

The look on the barista's face went from professional to sympathetic. She was a woman who understood completely.

"Past the back kitchen," she said hurriedly, "there's a fire escape exit with a warning that if you open it, it'll sound an alarm. It's broken; there's no alarm. Use that and go through the alleyway to the street up ahead and turn right; then there's an exit into a subway."

Amelia smiled at her gratefully, and she and Wendy made their way into the back staff room, through the kitchen, past several staring employees, before they pushed their way out through a fire escape, noiselessly.

They rushed down the alleyway to the street, and to the right, just like the sympathetic barista said, was a stairway leading underground to the subway.

The two women practically dove into it.

They quickly paid and jumped on the first train that was moving. They didn't care where; they could always transfer.

On the train, Amelia sat down next to Wendy and turned to her. "Don't joke with me. Did you really see Damon outside the café?"

Wendy was breathing heavily. She was obviously distraught. "He was just standing there by a car. His car, I guess. And he was staring at us."

Amelia looked down into her lap. She didn't tell anybody other than Wendy that she was going to this café, deep in Brooklyn. She didn't tell anybody that she was taking the subway. She didn't let anybody know where she was going, or how.

If Damon had been waiting outside her apartment building, he would've seen her exit the building and go to the subway. He could've quickly checked which train she'd hopped onto and driven out to any destination along that line.

Perhaps even all the destinations on that line.

Amelia had a hypothesis. She'd tested it. Unfortunately, it had turned out to be true.

Damon was stalking her.

## 20

"Hey, Amelia, me again. So, listen, hope you don't mind me bothering you. I just wanted to let you know that you're an amazing artist, and you're going to be great at that new gala of yours. That's impressive, considering you only just had a gala. Your paintings are so damn beautiful, I wish I could buy every single one. I will always appreciate your amazing work. You're going to be one of those legendary artists of our time. I can see it in you. Well, I'm just calling to say good luck, and I can't wait to see your next gala. Or maybe we'll run into each other again. I'm sure I'll see you soon. Can't wait! Thanks a lot, babe. Talk to you soon."

And that was the most recent message that Damon had left on Amelia's phone. It was the last of many.

His four previous messages were also logged in her voicemail.

There was a time when Amelia would simply erase the messages. Problem with that was, then there would be space for him to leave more. These five, plus five legitimate messages that she needed to hold onto from her agent and her mother, filled up her inbox. And as such, he couldn't leave any further messages.

But even if he couldn't leave messages, that didn't stop Damon from calling.

After a time, it became apparent that he was calling at least once every hour.

After that episode at the café in Brooklyn, Amelia was extremely careful not to step outside her apartment unless she was absolutely certain that she would be able to go about her day without being followed. For the most part, that meant asking Mark for more favors and hoping he would keep bringing her groceries home.

He never asked why; he never criticized; he never complained. He just said he was always glad to help and trusted that she knew what she was doing.

This was the kind of contact she needed now, more than anything. Mark was just the sweetest thing.

Unlike Damon, of course. Who was blatantly stalking her.

It was clear to Amelia now just why stalkers were so intimidating, even if they never actually got close or pushed their way in. Because the ones who were very careful about their stalking, as she was discovering firsthand, found a way to invade somebody's personal life in the most generic of ways. Amelia couldn't prove what was happening with Damon was anything more than a casual acquaintanceship.

So Damon left plenty of messages. So he called a lot. So she had a friend who spotted him outside a café where she happened to be. If she ever brought accusations like that to the police, they would just give her that look of, "So what do you expect us to do about it?"

And she wouldn't blame them. Even Amelia knew that an accusation of stalking wasn't going to hold much weight if he was simply calling often and showing up to places. Regardless of how unnerved she had become. How much she didn't invite phone calls, how she didn't want to see him anymore. How he was always there, even though she wasn't paying him anymore. How he always seemed to interpret situations that invited far more intimacy and closeness than she actually allowed.

She hated how casual and, frankly, devotional he started to sound over the phone. She hated never being certain if the car she was looking at was Damon's or some other similar vehicle. She hated how she couldn't prove anything.

Finally, going stir-crazy and desperately wanting to ensure that she still had control over her own life, Amelia made the bold move to leave the building through the back exit typically reserved for the building super. She simply told him that she was worried that there was somebody out front whom she didn't want to see. He allowed it, though he did ask her if there was any reason for her to be worried, and if perhaps she would like him to call the police.

Amelia felt ashamed that she'd said no.

Altogether, though, it seemed to have worked. She was able to sneak through the basketball courts behind her building, walk down a pedestrian stairway, and come out to a busy street. She headed to an art supply store to pick up a particular pigment she had run out of.

She hated that she wasn't able to simply enjoy the walk. Her spine went cold every time she approached a street corner, wondering if she would run into Damon as she turned it. She kept looking behind her, and felt like she couldn't trust her eyes anymore, always double-checking, triple-checking, to be absolutely sure he wasn't there.

This wasn't fair, she thought, trying not to cry. She didn't do anything wrong, and now she was completely on the defensive.

She was so distraught that by the time she got to the art store, she had to linger there for a minute just to remember which pigment she needed. She had completely forgotten.

The walk home was no better. The sun was out, and it made the snow on the ground glitter. There were happy couples out enjoying the day. There were families with kids and dogs.

Amelia mistrusted all of them. She didn't want to. But she couldn't help herself. All these people were potentially somebody who was going to hurt her.

She didn't want to live like this. She never asked for this.

Almost powerwalking back to the rear exit of her building, she texted her super, telling him she'd be there in a moment, so by the time she approached the emergency exit, she just had to knock on it, and her super was there to open it up for her.

He looked concerned and was obviously expecting some kind of danger, maybe somebody determined to assault Amelia.

Now she had gotten her building super involved. A man she hardly knew. He certainly deserved better than having to deal with her nonsense.

Well, all the same, it had worked. She had managed to step outside her building for the first time in about a week. As she boarded her elevator, she was wondering if this was going to be her life now, measuring her excursions by the length of time it took her to organize and accomplish them.

Wasn't fair, she thought. Wasn't fair.

She stepped off the elevator and rounded the corner to her apartment. And had to stop herself from screaming in fright when she realized that her door was slightly open.

Amelia had never, ever forgotten to lock her own door. But she had to admit, she didn't remember locking it this time either. After all, why would she? It wasn't exactly a major event, and all in all, the building was itself pretty secure.

Maybe it was a stress-induced mistake. Or maybe Damon was inside, going through her underwear and smelling her shoes.

Or maybe that was just too ridiculous, she thought.

Maybe he was waiting behind the door to strangle her when she came in.

Her whole body went cold, and she had to fight a rising surge of nausea.

And then, before she was able to tell herself what a stupid idea it was, she slowly opened the door and peeked inside her apartment.

There was a trail of melting dirty snow leading into her entryway and then stumbling around in a line, through her living room, over to her little art room, where a man lay, pathetic and slumped, against the wall underneath the large windows of her studio apartment. He was in a sharp suit that had clearly been destroyed by snow and God only knew what else. His disheveled appearance matched the sorry state of this human being. Whether he lay against the wall because he was exhausted, intoxicated, or dying, Amelia wasn't sure. It could've been all three.

Staring at him for a while, she also thought that he

wasn't quite tall or broad shouldered enough to be Damon. His hair color was wrong, too.

It wasn't until he looked at her directly, with that slack-jawed drunken stare of his, that Amelia realized she was looking at Sam.

It wasn't Damon, yet somehow, she didn't feel particularly relieved. If anything, she felt infuriated. Which, considering everything else she was going through, was not at all what she needed.

"Oh God," he said weakly as he struggled to get up. "Amelia!"

"Are you—" she managed to spit out before stopping and changing direction. "You can't be fucking serious."

"I love you," he drawled, swaying a bit as he finally got to his feet and extended his arms toward her. "Thank you for saving me."

"Get the hell out of my apartment!"

"This was our place," he said, stumbling toward her. "Yours and mine. We built it together."

"It's a studio apartment in one of the world's most expensive cities. My parents pay for it. Even by familiar connection, this was never your place."

Sam tried to sit on the corner of the coffee table and missed it completely, plopping his butt down on the floor. "What did I do to get you to hate me?" he said. "Well, no, that's stupid. I mean, I know why you hate me. I cheated on you with your sister."

"Fuck you and get out of my apartment."

"But where am I supposed to go? You're the only person who's ever loved me."

"Oh, whatever."

"But there was always something between us. That's why you would've considered getting back with me, right?"

Amelia shook her head in exasperation. "What the hell has happened to you?"

"Cara broke up with me. I was waiting for her to get back because I hadn't seen her in a while. And I started thinking some really horrible thoughts, so I had a glass or two of whisky to soothe my nerves. And then she showed up, and she said, 'Are you still here?' And I got all upset about it, and she told me to get the fuck out because she was only screwing me to hurt you. Like, I can't believe it. She actually said to my face that she was using me."

"You were using her."

"No, I thought I loved her."

"And now you think you love me?"

"Well, don't I?"

"And you thought she loved you, and you think I love you, and you were just slightly off every time?"

"No. I mean, I really did ... I don't know. Please help me."

"How did you get in here?"

"I know the pin code, and I've always had a key, remember?"

"Thanks for admitting that. But I didn't want you to have it, and asked you to give it back, so what you've done might be breaking and entering."

"Well, she did it too."

"What are you talking about?"

"Well, the last time Cara and I talked, she yelled at me to give her your apartment key and the pin code and tell her where you lived. I asked her why, and she said she wanted to see if she could find Damon's phone number."

"Holy shit, mother of God!"

"I know, right? Like, she wasn't even trying to hide it from me that she wanted to go out with Damon. No way that's fair, right?"

Amelia couldn't take any more. She marched over and grabbed Sam from the floor, yanking him up, struggling to shove him toward the door. "Get out!" she yelled.

"No, please," he stammered. "Come on, for all that we used to have, isn't there a little part of you that can forgive me? I feel so bad. I'm sorry. I'm begging you, please, can't you see I'm in pain here?"

Amelia dropped him and took a step back, clutching at her temples. She really had to get through to him. "Here's the thing: at any—*any*—time, you could've told Cara not to call me or to simmer down or whatever. You never did. I don't know if you enjoyed humiliating me, or if it meant nothing to you, but you accepted it. You were presented with the opportunity of hurting me, for sport, and you allowed it.

"And that's how I'm going to remember you. I can't even describe what you used to be like when we were married. It's like remembering an old TV show. All the memories are distant and alien, like they happened to somebody else. The only way I know you now is as this ... monster. That's it."

"But—"

"It's who you are. If Cara were a normal woman, you would've left her eventually too. You only want to entertain yourself, please yourself, and for the first time, it has back-fired, and you got used. And you've pushed me to the point where watching you suffer feels ... right. You deserve it. I'm happy. And I will never, ever forgive you for making me into that kind of person."

Sam stood there, lowering his shoulders and his head,

like a little child being scolded, waiting for his mom to forgive him.

Amelia had just spent the better part of the day and week terrified that she was going to get assaulted by a stalker. She was not in the mood to be some sort of heroic or sympathetic Florence Nightingale figure now. Sam didn't care about what she'd been going through recently, and he was just using her again. She had no more energy left for this.

She grabbed him again and practically flung him out the door.

Sam turned and looked back at her. "I mean, we can still keep in touch, right? And maybe if there's any feelings that develop or—"

Amelia slammed the door and marched back to the couch.

Behind her, she could hear Sam knocking on the door.

"I am calling the police," she called out. "And if you think I'm kidding, fucking try me and see what happens. Do you want to be arrested for this?"

She wasn't sure if she would actually call the police. But Amelia was grateful that at least Sam believed her, because the banging on the door immediately stopped, and it sounded like he had finally left.

She sat on her couch, resting her head in her hands, hoping she wouldn't have to take painkillers to be able to handle this evening. She was hoping that simply drinking a lot of water would suffice.

Finally, in total frustration, she got up from the couch and gazed out her window. She saw a stumbling, drunken man heading off toward the subway. She was really hoping it was Sam going away, out of her life, forever.

Then she caught a glimpse of a bunch of other people

heading to the subway, including what appeared to be a rather large man.

Memories of how she'd needed to sneak out earlier came flooding back, and she wasn't sure of what she saw. It was from a very great height, and it was getting dark outside.

She didn't want to believe it was Damon.

But with everything she'd been through today, she was hoping that maybe, just maybe, it really was him. If for no other reason than to know that he too was going away.

## 21

A melia had not heard from Damon at all. No phone calls. No texts. She thought she had seen his car around, but she wasn't positive.

About a week after Sam had headed off into the night, she received the first text from Damon in all that time.

A very simple and straightforward one.

> So, any more birthday parties?

It wasn't a romantic message. It wasn't an obsessive one. It was terse and, given what she'd hired him for, appropriate subject matter.

She started measuring out the possibilities of the situation. It was true that, for the past week before Sam's untimely arrival, Damon had been calling and texting rather frequently.

He'd behaved almost boyishly. Immaturely.

And then ... nothing. By all accounts, if he was obsessing over her, he would've intensified his demands.

But he didn't. He backed off. It was almost as if he was now treating her professionally again.

Amelia had a moment of inspiration. There was the possibility that Damon had screwed up.

Maybe Damon had a crush on her—she had to stop for a moment and be impressed with herself—and he got a little too pushy. He acted unprofessionally, but people did that all the time without it being some sort of psychosis. Maybe over the past week, he'd realized how badly he'd conducted himself, and now he felt extremely embarrassed by his actions. Embarrassed by the fact that he had an infatuation with a client. Especially considering that his job was to become physically aroused in order to please clients.

Perhaps a genuinely heartfelt infatuation shocked him. And he felt so awkward about it that he backtracked and tried to make things professional again.

Still, she didn't want to forgive him. His conduct had been terrifying and inappropriate. But she had to admit that there could be an explanation for it, as ridiculous as it was.

After thinking it through, Amelia had to consider the possibility that maybe this was just a matter of her thinking highly of a man who'd acted incompetently but was not actually dangerous.

And after dwelling on that notion very carefully, wondering too if she was being naïve, she started thinking that maybe she had interpreted Damon in that way simply because she wanted all of this bullshit to stop.

And that was when she decided that even if that was true, she still wanted it to stop. It had to stop.

Enough was enough.

So Amelia replied to Damon's text with a simple request

that they meet up at a nearby café. An hour later, she was there, watching Damon approach her.

"Hey, stranger," he said with his devilishly charming grin. "Long time no see. What you got there?"

Underneath her arm, she carried a canvas. It displayed one of her earlier paintings from the past few weeks. A simple image of her apartment, looking out the window at a sunny skyline of New York City. It made for a lovely gift now that it was all painted and finished.

A great present for a fond farewell.

"This," she said, holding it up for him to see, "is something I've been working on. I guess it's a little simple, but I was hoping you would enjoy it anyway. Plus, it can be a nice memory between us: I'm really grateful for the meditation techniques that you taught me; I'll be using them to develop a lot of confidence in the future."

She stopped short of admitting the real reason why she chose this painting for Damon. After the work she did for her galas, she knew that this simple painting would never sell anywhere else.

"What do you mean a memory between us?" Damon said, looking perturbed. "I mean, it's not like we'll never see each other again."

Amelia was hoping that it was an innocent remark, nothing more, as she kept a straight face and reached into her purse to pull out a large sum of hard cash.

"I hope that's true," she lied. "I hope that if I ever require your services again, then I'll know exactly where to come. But, that said, I'm afraid the job is done. Just last week, my ex-husband broke into my apartment. He was, well, a pathetic mess. Apparently, my sister dumped him. She failed to accomplish anything, and she screwed herself over by showing she had no more use for him. So they both failed. And now they're both out of my life. Easy peasy, quick and sleazy." She held his gaze before continuing.

"I can't thank you enough, Damon. Without your help, I never would've been able to reach any kind of emotional closure on this or feel like a stronger, bigger, better person. I wish things between us could keep going, I really do. But if they did keep going, well, that would mean my sister was still trying to hurt me, so, in the grand scheme of things, it's probably best that they're not."

Damon simply stood there, very stone-faced.

Amelia was waiting for him to do something, react, anything really. After a while, as it started to appear that he wouldn't, she reached out, grabbed his hand, then slapped the money into it.

"Here's the remainder of your pay," she said, also handing him the painting. "I hope you like it. The painting, I mean, not the money. Obviously, anybody would like the money. As for the painting, well, maybe someday you'll be able to tell people it's an Amelia Gray original, and then you'll be able to sell it for your children's college money or something. Heh!"

Damon continued to stand there, stock-still, holding the painting by the fingers of one hand and looking down at the cash in his other hand.

Amelia wasn't sure what to make of his silence. Frankly, it was unsettling. She was starting to think it would've been easier if he had tried to kiss her or something. At least such behavior would confirm her suspicions.

Finally, he pocketed the money. "Well," he replied, "I guess that's that. Thank you for this amazing painting. It's

wonderful. And, in all honesty, I am glad you found everything you were truly looking for."

Amelia kept her smile on and politely nodded. It was all
she could do to keep from panicking.

"Take care, Amelia," he said. "See you around." And with
that, he gave her an attractive smile and nod before turning
on his heel and heading back the way he'd come.

Amelia wondered about the way she'd just dismissed
Damon. Should she be worried? On the surface, there didn't
seem to be a problem. He accepted payment, took his gift
graciously. He seemed stuck, even uncomfortable, but he
had kept control of himself. And then he just walked away.
As if there was nothing between them.

And yet it unnerved her.

Damon had been so still, so calm about it. As if this was
nothing to him.

# 22

Amelia did everything in her power to live a normal life now that she had something of a normal life restored to her.

Except, if this really was genuinely a *normal* life, then she'd had virtually no experience with it as an adult, she came to realize.

She'd gotten married ten years ago and spent that time being a dutiful wife. She painted but wasn't trusted to contribute to the family finances by means of her painting. It was always very small scale until recently.

Before that, her relationship status was largely defined by how long she could hold onto somebody before her sister ruined it. It was a weird way to live. Yet it was so common for such betrayals to happen to her during those times that they were what counted as "normal" back then.

And now, here she was. Single. Independent. And at least in a minimal way, financially independent. Her sister was out of her life. Her mother had nothing to complain about anymore, which ultimately meant that she rarely contacted

Amelia at all. It was a double-edged sword. On the one hand, at least her mother wasn't beating her down with every sentence. On the other hand, her absence simply reinforced the fact that her mother didn't really want anything to do with her unless it was to criticize her and make herself feel better by doing so.

But, ultimately, it was a decent enough way to live. Few problems, only optimism. This was going to be her new normal. She wanted to live it. She wanted to keep this normal for as long as possible.

Until, somehow, Sam found a way to ruin it.

Sam just couldn't figure out how to let go. His bullshit explanations about him being heartbroken and regretting his mistakes didn't make any difference. The reality was that even if those explanations were true, they wouldn't excuse the fact that he was not wanted and was becoming very abusive and frightening.

Now that she was rid of one stalker—Damon—she had to deal with a new one. Sam.

After that first encounter with him in her apartment, she'd very sensibly asked her building super to change the locks on her door. The only reason he'd got in was because he used to live there and still had a key. She didn't believe he would ever give it back now, and she didn't want to have to talk to him about it.

Then, one day, Amelia was home when she suddenly heard rustling at the door. It sounded as if somebody was desperately trying the lock. And it just went on and on. Somebody was really struggling with that lock. And they just wouldn't let it go.

Amelia determined that it was Sam long before she heard him muttering, "What the fuck is going on here?"

There were more utterances of "Dammit," and "Come on," as increased force was applied to the lock, and a constant, frustrated jiggling of the doorknob could be heard as well.

Clearly, Sam was under the impression that he could use his same old key to enter the apartment again. He obviously hadn't gotten the idea into his thick skull that Amelia could've changed the locks. Or perhaps he had, but was just choosing not to believe it. As if wishing reality away would make the door open.

Finally, there was a vicious kick to the door, followed by the sound of Sam storming off.

She didn't know if that was going to be the end of it. She didn't know if he was coming back with the jaws of life or a hacksaw or something. In any case, she figured he'd probably show up later in the week.

Amelia put his antics out of her mind and was able to focus again on her painting before hearing another, softer knock about fifteen minutes later.

She felt her phone vibrate next to her, revealing a message from her building super.

Hi. Are you home right now?

She had never felt quite so relieved. She didn't realize how much tension she was holding in her body until it faded away. She gingerly tiptoed to the door and, looking through the peephole, saw that it was, indeed, her building super.

She opened the door. "Hey," she said. "What's up?"

"Uh, have you seen anybody come to your door recently?"

"Yes, my ex-husband was here about fifteen minutes ago. He kept trying to get in. Why?"

"Damn, did he hurt you?"

"No, I didn't even open the door or make any noise. Is everything okay?"

"He came to my office in the basement. He demanded to be let into his ... Well, your apartment. I refused, and he got really angry."

"Oh my God."

"I told him I'd call the police. Then, as I started dialing, he ran away."

"I am so sorry."

"No, it's all right. At least he didn't do anything stupid."

"That's debatable."

"I mean, he didn't try to attack you or me, but I see your point. Do you want me to call the police?"

"Look, if you feel it's necessary, I'll cooperate. But I don't really see the point. I don't even know where he lives or how to find him. And best I can tell, they'll probably treat it like a domestic dispute and say there's nothing they can do."

"Yeah. Yeah, I know ... shit. This building is supposed to be secure for our residents. How did he even get into the building?"

It was very much a shit situation, but Amelia felt like there was really nothing they could do, and then she recalled the pin code on the building entrance. "I forgot to tell you when he got in here the other day that he knew the pin code to get in. Can it be changed?"

The super frowned. "I can see to that, but I wish you'd told me that before. I assumed last time he just waited for someone to open the door and got in that way. Damn. That means I'm going to have to provide every resident with a new code. That's going to be such a pain. People hate having to learn new codes."

Amelia wanted to believe that he was a sympathetic man, but she was wondering if he secretly thought that she was responsible for all this hassle.

And on top of that, the hassle just never stopped.

In the weeks that followed, even though Sam could no longer get into the building, that didn't stop him from buzzing at the door at all hours of the day. The super did call the cops, but he was right back at it a few hours later. When he called again, they told him they were too busy dealing with real criminals and to let them know if he managed to get in.

Amelia told herself that she didn't have many reasons to leave her apartment, except on occasion to help Mark with the dogs, so she was usually home and working on a new painting. But all the incessant door buzzing, the calls, and the texts on her phone. Infuriating. She would block him, but then she wouldn't know what he was thinking, and that was a scarier thought. Didn't make it any less annoying though.

She didn't want to give him the satisfaction of basically ruining her private time, her creative time, the time when she would be painting. But, for now, there simply was no other choice.

When she had to leave, she snuck out the same way she did when she was avoiding Damon unless she was with Mark and the dogs. Sam kept his distance then. When she was on her own, she arranged with the super so that she could leave through the back service door, across the basket-ball courts, and head off to the local bakery to pick up some bread.

Then, as she turned onto the street, all of a sudden Sam was there. In all his washed-up glory.

He looked a complete mess, like he hadn't shaved or showered in days. And the dehydrated, blotchy skin on his face suggested the initial signs of alcoholism.

"Hi, Amelia," he started, approaching her.

"Get away from me," she replied, turning sharply and heading back home.

"No, please," he said, reaching out to grab her arm. "Just let me talk to you for five minutes. Please."

"No!"

"Oh, come on. Don't I deserve five minutes? What's wrong with hearing me out?"

"No," she insisted. "I'm done."

"I just want to talk to you," he said, grabbing her arm so forcefully he compelled her to stop. "What's wrong with you?"

"Help!" Amelia screamed at the top of her lungs. "Rape!"

Everybody within earshot—which, considering her volume, meant quite a lot of people—immediately focused on what was going on. They were staring right at them.

Sam let go of Amelia and looked around at the men in the crowd. "She's crazy," he said, backing off, panicked. "She's crazy. I'm just trying to give her the medication. It's okay."

Amelia appreciated everybody's attention stopping him, even if inadvertently, but she was starting to feel like she herself was under a microscope, and it was very off-putting. She turned away and briskly walked back to her apartment.

"Hey, wait!" Sam yelled behind her.

She could hear his footsteps as he ran after her.

By the time she turned to look at him, ready to defend herself against his assault, she saw that some of the men and women who'd heard her yelling had leaped upon Sam and forced him to the ground.

"Help me!" Sam shouted. "Help! Help! I'm being mugged!"

Considering that he was surrounded by about a dozen witnesses who'd seen the entire encounter where he was grabbing Amelia against her will, she wasn't surprised that his cries weren't well received. But she also knew that she didn't want to be a part of this.

She could feel her anxiety coming back to her, her chest tightening. This was too much. This was supposed to be a relaxing day of working on her painting, then going out to the bakery. But now, she'd had to defend herself against a violent assault.

And it was all because of Sam. It was all his choice.

He was making choices for her life again.

He was finding new ways to hurt her.

Some of the other people—probably very good, very decent people, she knew—implored her to stick around, maybe report the offence to the police. But, instead, she did everything she could to block them out as she turned back to her building and ran for home.

The throbbing pain in her chest. The shortness of her breath. She didn't want this. She didn't want any of this.

Back at her apartment, she dropped her bag of baked goods and fresh bread on the floor as soon as she was inside. She didn't even care if they got dirty. It really didn't seem to matter anymore. She just wanted to stop pacing, calm down, keep her hands from shaking.

She wanted to crawl into the darkest corner of her apartment, one that had no connection to Sam whatsoever, until she realized that, since this had been their home, there really weren't any places where she could truly escape him.

He was still there. She could feel it in her bones. She couldn't stop them from shaking.

At last, when she finally started feeling as if she might calm down, there was a violent banging on the door.

"Please!" Sam was yelling. "I don't have anywhere else to go!" he yelled and banged some more, the noise blurring into a cacophony.

Amelia started crying into her hands. The super had changed the pin code to the building, so how had he gotten in? Did some hapless resident just allow Sam to tailgate them in through the door? Or did he simply break and enter?

What if he always showed up? What if he was never going to leave?

"I love you!" he cried. "Don't you love me? Isn't there anything left? Don't you believe in us anymore?" He banged on the door again. Then he started rattling the knob.

She had to trust that he would be incapable of opening the door, but she still started to shake as if she was nauseous.

Suddenly, as the doorknob was held firmly, there was a tremendous bashing against the door, as if he was trying to force it open by throwing his shoulder at it. Over and over again.

And then, almost as suddenly, she heard Sam mutter something and then more banging.

But not at the door.

It was near, though. Almost as if it was just outside the door.

And then she heard Sam's voice again. Only, this time, no discernible words.

He was screaming again.

In fear.

In panic.

And then more violent bashing. Amelia stared wide-eyed at her door. Had Sam lost his mind? Was he now trying to break his own head against the opposite wall?

Not impossible, she thought. But, also, a wild explanation. After all, hitting yourself against the wall really took a lot out of a human body. It would stop him from doing anything else, especially if he was intoxicated.

Sam sounded as if he was screaming. He also sounded as if he was ... Amelia couldn't quite describe it ... Clawing against the floor.

Still feeling nauseous and very afraid, Amelia approached the door and looked through the peephole.

She thought she could discern a desperate, weak arm near the floor. Sam's. But for the most part, all she could see was Damon. Standing tall and aiming down with his fists.

He was beating Sam into the ground.

Terrified, Amelia couldn't stop looking. It was so unbelievable.

He looked like he was beating him to death.

Damon.

Damon was here!

Suddenly, with a final scream of adrenaline, Sam reached up and smacked Damon's face away, temporarily disorienting him as Sam leaped to his feet and made a run down the hall.

Damon shook on his feet, seemingly ready to chase after him, until he stopped himself and simply tried to control his seething rage. Amelia could see him standing there, staring down the hall, his jaw clenched tight and his fists shaking.

His fists looked like there was blood on them.

This was impossible, Amelia thought. This was fictional. This wasn't happening.

Suddenly, Damon turned and looked to her door, and Amelia felt as if she was going to lose consciousness and fall back into the apartment. It took everything she had to stand upright.

"Hey, Amelia?" Damon said, his breath heavy. "Are you in there?"

Amelia didn't dare say anything. Damon had no proof that Sam wasn't crazy and just attacking the door to an empty apartment. Amelia wanted to keep it that way.

There was an extended silence before Damon spoke up again. "Amelia, are you in there?"

Amelia watched with frozen horror as Damon stood there staring at her door. And then, as if he hadn't done anything at all, he closed his eyes and smiled a beautiful innocent smile toward the door.

"If you are in there," he said, with that husky, masculine voice of his, "I'm glad you know I will always help you." He gave a slight nod and walked away as calmly as ever.

Amelia was certain that the last part of him that she saw was his fist. She couldn't be sure, but she didn't see any blood on it.

Maybe, she told herself, she'd just imagined it.

## 23

After the awful altercation between Damon and Sam outside her door, Amelia had spent the better part of the afternoon switching between hiding in her bed and running to the windows to see if there was any sign of either of them out on the streets. She was fully expecting to hear more knocking on her door. Maybe from Damon expecting a reward for "saving her." Maybe Sam, having found a way to sneak back into the building.

And if he did, would Damon have followed him? She wasn't sure.

She wasn't sure of anything anymore.

As it happened, there were no other confrontations at the door. No other visitors. Not even her building super, which indicated that he wasn't aware of what had happened, meaning Sam hadn't broken in. One more reason not to arrest Sam, as far as the police were concerned, Amelia thought.

She needed perspective. She needed answers. At the very least, she needed somebody she could trust.

Obviously, that meant Wendy. She called her friend and asked her to come over.

When the knock came on her door, Amelia was so relieved that Wendy had come by so quickly, she rushed to the entranceway and threw open the door without even considering the possibility that it might be somebody else.

She nearly gave herself a heart attack when it opened.

"Oh!" said Mark, looking equally startled at the sight of Amelia. "Sorry! I just, I thought I saw something on the carpet here that looked like blood, and I—"

Amelia threw her arms around his neck and held onto him for dear life.

It was the first time in days that she had been in contact with another human being, one who wasn't trying to hurt her, take her, use her. And it was this sweet, funny man. This decent man, who had always been very kind to her whenever she turned to him for help during her times of loneliness.

She could feel Mark tensing beneath her arms as she gave him the biggest hug in the world. Probably he was shocked by her sudden friendliness.

She didn't care. She needed this.

She felt pressure on the back of her neck as his arms slid around her body and he returned the hug.

This was the normal that she was looking for.

"Oh!"

Amelia looked up, then hastily released Mark from her grip as she realized that Wendy had just arrived and had caught sight of the two of them hugging in her doorway.

She was sure it looked awkward, considering she was embracing Wendy's ... well, for lack of a better term, boyfriend, though she wasn't sure if Mark knew about

Wendy's willingness to play the field, as it were. All the same, the two of them did seem to be spending more time together, and with everything else happening these days, she didn't want to complicate matters any further.

So she just told Wendy that she'd invited her two best friends to her place so that they could all talk about what had happened recently. Admittedly, she'd never even considered the possibility of talking about this to Mark. But he was here now. And all things considered, since he was her neighbor, it would be hard to imagine that Mark hadn't heard what went on earlier.

Also, considering who he was, and how he always made her feel brighter and filled her with laughter, she felt she could trust him. She didn't want to lose that friendship from her life.

She told them about how Sam had accosted her and then somehow managed to get into the building again. "Then he was screaming and beating on my door, and I was so scared."

"When was this?"

Amelia told him how she'd made arrangements with the super to go out the back entrance to do a little shopping and how it had been on her way home when Sam caught up to her. She told him approximately when it had occurred, and Mark shook his head.

"That's when I was out with the dogs. You know if I'd been here, I'd have stopped him and made sure he left. How did you get him to leave?"

Amelia paused for a minute as she looked at both Wendy and Mark, who sat across from her. She explained about how Sam's screaming changed to terrified, and when she looked through the peephole, she saw him being beaten half to death by a man who should not have been anywhere near her building let alone outside her door.

Amelia trusted that Wendy would have the right thing to say, but watching Mark rest his head into his open palm, she was worried about what this might sound like to somebody who wasn't expecting it. She was worried about how he would react.

"I'd love to know what you're thinking, Mark," Amelia finally said, hoping for a sympathetic or calming word.

"I'm not gonna lie," Mark finally said, rubbing his eyes, "I thought he was your new boyfriend."

"Boyfriend?" Amelia scoffed. "Why boyfriend?"

"I've seen him show up here a lot. There was that one time he was holding a bouquet of roses. And then, I didn't mention it at the time because I didn't want to ... well, I didn't want to sound like I was badmouthing your boyfriend. But there was a time when I was coming into the building from picking up some dog food, and he grabbed the door and slammed it shut, preventing me from coming in. Then he wanted to know if you and I were friends."

"Wait," Wendy interjected. "What did he want to know? If you were just friends?"

"Not like that," replied Mark. "It was very strange. Like, he was trying to sound intimidating. It was more like, 'So, you and Amelia. You two are pretty close, right? Good friends?'"

"He said it like that?" asked Amelia, startled.

"Yeah, just like that. He was trying to get up in my face about it and intimidate me. And I was just answering, yes, yes, of course. Eventually, he loosened his grip on the door, and I went in. Then he stood and stared at me as I headed toward the elevator."

"Why didn't you ever say this before?" asked Wendy, raising her voice.

"I don't know," Mark replied, starting to sound defensive. "I thought it was weird at the time, I didn't think it meant anything more significant. In retrospect, it seemed to make sense that he was a jealous boyfriend or something."

"Lay off him," Amelia told Wendy. "He couldn't have known."

"Known what?" asked Mark.

"That he—" Amelia froze as she realized what she was about to say. She wanted to explain what her actual relationship was to Damon. Which would involve her explaining to her neighbor that she had hired the services of a playboy.

Her stomach twisted at the thought. Of developing an image of herself in Mark's mind that she couldn't control. A rather sultry, sexualized one.

"That he was hired help. He was basically an actor. For hire. Through a service."

Mark looked confused. Wendy rolled her eyes.

Amelia wanted to signal to Wendy that not all women were comfortable with the idea that others might know that they'd hire men to sleep with them, but she decided that a glare was all she could get away with at the moment.

"It's kind of complicated," Amelia continued. "But basically, the reason my marriage failed was because my sister stole my husband from me. Much in the same way that she's stolen all my boyfriends throughout our childhood together. So I figured if she was given the opportunity to try to steal another one, and he was specifically hired to turn her down, then it might ..."

Amelia trailed off. She wasn't exactly sure how to end that sentence. Her sister might learn her lesson? Give up?

Feel really bad? And it wasn't until she tried to say it out loud that she realized how ridiculous the whole plan sounded.

Fortunately, Wendy chimed in and finished her sentence for her: "Mess with the bitch."

"Yes," said Amelia, not necessarily with full conviction.

"Oh," Mark said pensively, looking off into space. "I didn't think there was a service for that. But I guess actors need to make money when they're not working in the theater or whatever."

"His job was simply to create the narrative for my sister and mother," Amelia said. "And that was that. This was never supposed to escalate beyond that. He was never my real boyfriend."

"I see," he said, grinning a little. "But the way he spoke to me, it's starting to sound like he doesn't quite know that."

"Yeah, it really does," Wendy agreed. "In addition to what you heard in the hallway, there was a time when we went all the way up to Brooklyn, to have coffee at a café, and I was sure I saw him there too."

"Brooklyn, Jeez," Mark said, thinking deeply. "So he was able to track you all the way across New York. He's keeping tabs."

"Oh my God," Wendy suddenly said, looking off into the distance with wide eyes.

"What?" asked Amelia.

"How did he know to follow you all the way to Brooklyn when you took the subway?" Wendy asked. "What if he followed me? And, and I guess he saw you in the park a few times, with both of us, and that's how he knew to approach Mark. God, what if he's keeping track of all of us?"

"That would explain how he was able to find your ex-husband once he got in the building," Mark added, making the connections. "If he was keeping an eye on anybody coming in here, he certainly would've recognized him."

"Yeah, I guess," Amelia replied. "And I guess it wouldn't be that hard for him to keep track of Cara, my sister. Since she was the one trying to come after him."

"So he's been stalking you and people connected to you," Mark said. "Do you have any evidence of him doing so?"

"Evidence? Why?"

"If you don't approach the police with something tangible, then the most they'll do is start a file on it. It won't be worth their time to really look into it if they feel there's nothing that they can do to pin an offence on him."

"I'm inclined to agree," Wendy added. "Probably the best approach is to go to the people who can have some kind of effect on him. I mean, he still has to work; maybe you can contact Nicolas."

"Who's Nicolas?" asked Mark.

"Guy who manages the escort service," Wendy said. "For lack of a better term, a pimp who—"

Amelia turned on Wendy sharply, staring at her with the most vicious death eyes, demanding that she shut the hell up at that very moment.

At first, Wendy looked confused; then she let out a little gasp, obviously realizing how much she'd just revealed.

Mark looked between them. "Pimp? What do you mean —" And then, just like that, his eyes went wide, his jaw dropped, and he started blushing rather intensely. While looking right at Amelia.

*Perfect*, Amelia thought. *Just perfect.*

# 24

Amelia felt nervous about contacting Nicolas Wan to try to seek some answers about Damon. Maybe Nicolas would automatically believe the man's word over hers. Or maybe he would believe her, and given the level of secrecy of their underground organization, he would do something horrible to Damon.

Regardless of how she felt about Damon personally, she didn't necessarily want that on her conscience.

So, almost instinctively, she needed to work up her courage to come to a decision.

And with that, she decided to go in a direction that always gave her courage in times of great stress and anxiety.

She whipped out a bottle of wine and quickly poured herself a glass.

She also considered using some of her meditation techniques, until she realized that, whenever she heard that soothing voice in her mind, she always thought of Damon, who'd taught them to her.

The idea made her shake so much, she poured herself another glass.

At which point, she didn't really care that she knew this was exactly what her mother would've done in times of stress.

All that mattered was that her muscles relaxed, and her mind relaxed a little as well.

Which was when, all of a sudden, a thought entered her mind: why go to the trouble of contacting the police, or Nicolas, when she hadn't attempted to deal with Damon, face-to-face, one last time.

After all, when she ended their formal relationship, she'd done it professionally, and he'd handled it very well. And going to him before escalating the situation was, certainly, the professional thing to do.

Yes, she decided. She would attempt to stop all this in the simplest way possible. By dealing with Damon directly.

She was so pleased with her decision, she never stopped to consider that she was going to speak to the man whom she last saw beating her ex-husband to a bloody pulp outside her door. The man who had been showing up randomly in her life and kissing her without her consent.

Fortunately, wine really was the only thing that could justify such a level of human foolishness. A little bit of Italian red helped to keep those thoughts out of mind as well.

And so, after prepping her clothes, prepping her words, and—frankly—prepping her escape route, she picked up the phone and dialed Damon.

It barely had time to ring before he picked up.

"Hey there, sexy," he said. "Long time no hear, stranger. What's going on? New job? More family get-togethers?"

"No, Damon," she said. "We need to talk."

"Yeah, sure. What would you like to talk about?"

"No, I mean in person."

"Well, sure, you know I'm always happy to see you. So, where? Walk through a park, or—"

"Let's meet at that café down the road from my place."

"Cool, cool. Maybe after, we can head over to your place and—"

"Damon, this is serious."

"Is everything all right?"

"Look, just get over here. I mean go to the café. Not here. To the café."

"All right ... See you in a bit."

Amelia was about to hang up the phone, and then she listened and realized that Damon hadn't hung up first. He was still there. Listening. Softly breathing.

This went on for a full minute. What the hell was he doing?

Well, in any case, she wanted to get this over with. So she did hang up. And then she put her phone away as she watched the room tilt a little bit.

She realized that, a moment ago, she'd almost invited Damon over to her apartment by accident. Maybe liquid courage wasn't quite the way to go with this.

That said, she certainly felt the strength to get this over and done with right now. She grabbed up her purse, looked around to see if she could find anything defensive—ultimately, she decided that her keys were about the sharpest and smallest things she had available to her—and headed out the door.

Outside her building, she caught sight of Damon's car.

Parked within sight of her building. She took a closer look; it was definitely Damon's car. Not a lookalike, not the same model. It was his car.

And it was empty.

The amount of time between when she finished her phone call and getting down here couldn't possibly have been more than three minutes, she reasoned. Had he been sitting in the car just now?

Well, the thought was rather terrifying in and of itself. Although it strengthened her insistence that this had to be done. She couldn't have any more of this.

Trying to walk as assertively as she could, she made her way to the café. She could already see Damon from a distance, as he waited at their outdoor patio table. It was a warm winter day, and he appeared to have a beverage ready. And he was smiling that sweet, debonaire smile of his.

Everything about this was wrong, she thought.

"Good to see you again," he said, going in for a hug.

She lifted her palms and stopped him, gently pushing him away.

When he backed off, his face looked sad, like he had been personally hurt. "What's wrong?" he asked weakly. "You sounded worried over the phone. Like, this sounded pretty serious. Is everything okay?"

She hated the fact that he stared at her with such worry, such concern. Like he was personally invested in this. This absolutely had to stop, she couldn't stop herself from thinking again.

"Damon," she finally said, "why did you beat up my ex-husband outside my apartment?"

Damon's eyes went wide, and his shoulders rose and

sank as he breathed deeply in what looked like a sigh of relief. He almost looked like he was about to laugh.

"Oh, is that what this is about?" he said happily. "You were in your apartment. I'm sorry you had to see that. He's been harassing you. I wanted him to stop threatening you."

"I said, why did you beat him?"

"To ... to stop him. I mean, in his state, he wasn't going to stop with a firm talking-to."

"How did you get into the building?"

"He followed in some woman as she was unlocking the doors, and I came in right behind him."

"You followed him in from outside?"

"Yeah."

"Right on his coattails?"

"Yes."

"Why?"

Damon suddenly looked unnerved, as if the question were ridiculous or even rude. "I mean ... because he was, he was trying to get in. It's not like you wanted him there."

"I didn't want you in there either!" she said, raising her voice.

Damon looked startled. "What's going on here? Is everything okay?"

Amelia had to do everything in her power to keep her cool. She could feel her throat getting dry and the potential onset of a headache. She really felt like she was about to lose control. This wasn't working.

But she had to make this work. She had to put a stop to it, once and for all.

"Damon," she said slowly and reasonably, "I hired you for a job, which you fulfilled. I'm grateful for the work you did, but we were always just employer and employee. I appreciate the effort and the dedication you showed, but we were working toward reaching an end goal, and we reached it. Sam is gone. Cara is gone. You're paid. It's done. There's nothing left. Anything you do beyond this is unwanted ... and unwarranted."

He was starting to look shocked, even upset. "What are you talking about?" he asked. "I thought we were having a great time together."

"We were having a great time together doing a job. And that's it. I hired you. I was a client. Do you do this with every woman who hires you?"

"What do you mean, every woman who hires me?"

"Every woman who rents you from the escort agency, Damon."

He shook his head and almost laughed again. "Look, if that's what this is about," he said, "then don't worry. There are no other women. You're the only woman I work for. I swear it. You're the only woman from now on."

"No, Damon. That's ridiculous. I'm not angry. I'm explaining to you what your own job is. You fulfilled a service that I paid you for. You're done. We are done. There's nothing else. Now, if you keep calling me, if you keep texting me, then you're going to start looking like a stalker."

"What do you mean?" he said incredulously. "Wait a minute ... Are you breaking up with me?"

*Oh my God*, Amelia thought. She felt like she was about to cry, and forced herself to desperately hold it in.

"What is wrong with you?" she said, more loudly than she might have intended. "We were never together. Our professional arrangement is over, and you are now acting unprofessionally. If you don't stop, I'm going to report you to your employer. Is that what you want?"

His eyes went wide, and his nostrils flared. "After everything I did for you?" he yelled. "I fixed your life for you. I saved you from every person who was destroying everything you ever wanted. Doesn't that count for anything?"

Damon's voice was so loud that people on the street stared at them. Amelia looked over and saw that the café baristas were talking amongst each other.

This was getting out of control. Her adrenaline shot straight up, and she sobered up really quickly.

This was all going wrong.

"Damon, you're making a scene," she pleaded. "I will have to call the police."

"Over what?" he demanded. "Over you hurting me? What did I do to you except everything you ever wanted?" He pressed his hands down on the table, obviously trying to control his anger.

As far as Amelia was concerned, that did nothing to alleviate the heightened emotions of the scene.

"I did everything for you," Damon said at a more reasonable volume. "We were so good together. We were perfect for each other. I wish you could see it like I do. How wonderful this has all been. I can win your heart. You just have to let me in."

With that, he stood up and gave her a sweet smile. He walked off, away from the scene he had caused.

She watched him leave. She knew she should return to her place, since she wasn't exactly sure where else to go, but she worried at the prospect of him showing up at his car, even though he was obviously going in a different direction.

Where was he going? she wondered. What was his plan? What did he mean by "win her heart"?

Everything was already so bad, and now it had somehow escalated. Amelia couldn't alleviate the sense that she was in danger. She always used to think of herself as an intelligent woman.

Now, she wasn't so sure.

## 25

Amelia was about to call the police station to file a restraining order, when a text showed up on her phone. And she was more than grateful that it was Mark.

It simply read:

Coming.

Amelia put her phone on silent, then hid it underneath her couch cushions. She turned off her TV and sat silently.

A moment later, she heard knocking on the door.

She remained perfectly quiet.

Some more knocking.

She didn't move. She didn't dare.

The knocking continued, only briefly interrupted with breaks. But it kept going.

Until, eventually, it stopped.

She sat there quietly, waiting for the silence to continue

for several more minutes before she dared reach down underneath the cushions and pull her phone back up.

Another message from Mark. Which read:

He's gone.

She exhaled rather loudly, and rather happily.

She'd asked Mark for his help when he wasn't with the dogs, and he'd agreed to it immediately. Since he was self-employed, he was often available to monitor the nanny camera the super had let her put in the lobby, particularly when she wasn't around to do so. Amelia had suggested he only keep an eye on the camera when she had to go out, but he'd said he wasn't comfortable with that. He could easily check the camera feeds while he was out with the dogs, and if he noticed anything, he could hurry back. He said he would have a better chance of seeing if Damon entered the building than she would, because she had to focus on her art, and he could multitask. All he would have to do was keep an eye on the camera feed to the front lobby and let her know when Damon came and went. That way she would know when to shut things off in her apartment and stay quiet and when it was safe to continue with what she was working on.

At first, she was embarrassed that she had to drag poor Mark into this at all. But then she started feeling incredibly grateful at how willing he was to help her, which always left her feeling reassured. His kindness really was one of the few things during all of this that made her feel something akin to happiness.

She also wondered if she should compensate him financially, since she was asking him to do a lot of staring at a screen with nothing happening most of the time.

Or so she originally thought.

As it turned out, Mark had a lot to do. Because Damon was showing up far more frequently than Amelia could've possibly imagined.

She figured Mark would have to warn her about him approaching every once in a while, not even once every day.

Mark had had to warn her eight times today. Seven yesterday.

Thank God for Mark, she kept thinking. Without him, she'd probably have run into Damon on several occasions. Then what would she do? Calling the cops was an option, but what could they really do about him? What was the saying? When you need a cop immediately, they're just fifteen minutes away. He could do anything to her in that amount of time.

Now that she knew Damon was back out on the street—in all likelihood, sitting in his car—she got up from the couch, opened the door and looked into the hallway.

Damon had left her an ornate table decoration. A crystal orb, resting atop a beautiful silvery wreath design.

She now had a small pile of expensive gifts that Damon had been leaving at her front door. She kept all of them just in case she needed them as evidence. Maybe even finger-prints. She wasn't sure if they would amount to anything, but frankly, what else was she supposed to do with them? Enjoy them?

She just felt so horrified by him, and she wanted to burn everything that he was leaving for her, erase it from her memory.

Deciding enough was enough, she called the local police

station to discuss the situation. She explained that a man who was nothing but an acquaintance had been stalking her and was now showing up at her home and leaving gifts, and even though she'd asked him to stop, he continued.

The detective on the phone asked her who the man was, and she told him his name and what she knew about him. He then told her that if she'd like, they could arrest him on a misdemeanor charge for stalking, but that it would be a class four and wouldn't do much unless he was a repeat offender.

Amelia didn't know if he was a repeat offender or not, but she figured if he was doing this to her, he'd probably done it to others. Still, that didn't mean that he'd been arrested for it.

"Ma'am, if he hasn't threatened you and is merely trying to get your attention by leaving you gifts, maybe just continue to tell him you aren't interested, and eventually he'll go away," he suggested.

Amelia sighed. "And what if he doesn't?" she demanded to know.

"Look, if you want to come in and file a formal complaint, that's your prerogative, but I can tell you that your case will be of low priority. Your best bet is to try to work this out with him or maybe file for a protective order. If you want, I can give you that number."

Amelia was quiet and silently fuming about how disinterested he sounded. "Thank you. Yes, I'd like that number," she said.

He rattled off the number and then hung up. Amelia's frustration at the situation was palpable. It had sounded as though he thought she should just tolerate his behavior, which was what she didn't want to do anymore.

Going back to her phone, she dialed the number he'd

given her, which was to the private line of an investigative officer at the central precinct in Manhattan. She was determined to get that protective order since it seemed her only option at the moment.

The only issue was she had to go through an extensive interview just to have them file it. Unfortunately, that meant she had to explain the nature and purpose of her request, how everything started, including any details about what was being done to her, or what she had done thus far.

She knew it was going to be difficult. For starters, she wondered how many people she was going to have to implicate.

Obviously, Damon. But she would have to explain her reasoning for why she thought Damon posed a threat, which would require her to explain how Damon got involved in her life in the first place.

And she knew which part of the conversation she was dreading the most. Yes, she'd hired an escort. From an escort agency.

She wondered, with some trepidation, if she would have to explain that she'd learned about this escort service from her best friend. She really didn't want to get Wendy in trouble.

She also didn't feel comfortable about getting Nicolas Wan in trouble. Obviously, he was the one who'd connected her to a dangerous stalker, and to be blunt: he was a pimp. But, those concerns aside, Nicolas had always been wonderful to her. She hardly knew him, of course, but from what she did know from their few encounters, he was simply a dashing businessman doing a job. And, initially, he did it well: she set out to get revenge against her family, and she did. Thanks to him.

And she was going to be paying back his understanding by getting him involved with the police. Him, a man who ran an operation that, by any measure, probably wasn't very legal.

Good old Amelia, she thought. Always a disappointment to somebody.

She remembered preparing herself for the prospect of a criminal record in which she was listed as a "John."

But this conversation was going to be atrocious for an entirely different reason: it would reinforce what she believed about the police. They were a necessary evil, as it were.

When she told them that she had contacted Damon through Sterling Escorts, the police officer who took that report said something that she had fully expected but had managed to startle her all the same.

"Oh, Sterling!" the officer said over the phone. "Right, right, them, okay. Go on."

And she continued with her report. While trying to process what she had just heard.

That there was a male escort service operating out of New York City wasn't shocking. It was probably to be expected. What did shock her was that the police were familiar with them. In fact, they were so casually familiar with them that the officer she spoke to brushed it off as if mentioning them was nothing. Just another organization on another day on the job.

They weren't shocked. They weren't intrigued. To be honest, they didn't even sound critical of her.

They knew them. Because of course they did. How could Sterling Escorts operate in New York City unless it had its backside covered?

Which typically, as far as Amelia understood it, meant bribes and wetting certain people's beaks. Which meant police officers telling other officers to *leave that one alone* because *it's handled*.

Because such bribes were a reasonable source of income and possibly a great way for them to keep an eye on the underworld's criminal elements.

In reality, though, Amelia had to concede, she might have been reading too much into it. After all, it wasn't like she had any proof or anything. Just a casual conversation with an officer.

Once she'd finally finished explaining everything, the officer asked her to give them an hour and then call back to follow up on it. Amelia spent the next hour fretting over her options. Finally, she picked up her phone again and dialed the same number as earlier.

"Hello, you've reached Officer Travers, city central, how may I help you?"

"Hello, this is Amelia Gray. I'm calling to see about following up on the protection order?"

"Oh yes. Right, right. Thank you for calling back. I'm glad you called; there's been a recent development."

"A development?"

"Yes, we are wondering if you have any information about Mr. Chase's current whereabouts. Did he ever give you an address?"

"No, never. But we talked about this. Shouldn't you get that information from his agency?"

"That was the first place we tried. The address Mr. Wan gave us was inaccurate, it's not a residence, and Mr. Chase is not located there. When we followed up with Mr. Wan, he revealed that it was the only address Mr. Chase had ever given him."

"Couldn't you just wait for him to go back to work?"

The officer paused before saying, "Apparently, Mr. Chase has not been back to his escort service job for almost six weeks now."

## 26

A melia had to explain to multiple officers every detail she knew about Damon Chase. She told them about his inappropriate conduct toward her, his actions outside her apartment door, and his reaction at the café down the road. They didn't really seem concerned by any of it.

She was starting to get concerned when one of the older officers asked her if there was any reason for Damon to not expect a kiss, given the type of agency he worked for and the kind of person she'd chosen to hire. Amelia was not surprised but struggled to keep her disappointment under control. What the older cop implied was a very polite way of saying that, as a woman, she'd brought it upon herself. Unfortunately, she'd been expecting this sort of attitude from certain members of the police force. It was why she never really wanted to get them involved in the first place.

She needed help from her city's municipal protection force, not snickering and judgment.

They had also asked her if there were any witnesses to

the event outside her apartment door. She had to regretfully admit that there weren't any. Which wasn't entirely true but was the most straightforward way of dealing with it. Mark didn't actually see anything, he was out of the building at the time, but he'd seen the blood afterwards, which wouldn't go very far in a report, would it? Unless they tested it, but then it wouldn't lead to Damon, merely Sam. And Sam, well, obviously he was the real witness of that encounter, but Amelia didn't want to crawl back to him for his help. In this case, she could see the bigger picture.

As for Damon's blowup at the café, there were several witnesses. But she'd have to assemble their testimonies, and she didn't even know most of the strangers there. She recognized some of them from the neighborhood, and she supposed she could go back to the café and ask any of the employees if they'd be willing to write something out. But all that would take time, and while that wasn't a big deal, she wanted the protection order now before things got worse.

If only, she thought, the police would simply trust a scared victim.

In the end, the main officer taking her report was a little wishy-washy in his explanation of how much this would achieve. Not denying, but not confirming anything either. The most honest thing he probably said, Amelia figured, was that it might take twenty-four hours to process, but then it could be a while before Damon was served with the order, since they didn't have a known address for him.

By which point, Amelia figured, God only knew what would have happened to her by the time they served it. Or for how long she would have had to stay buried in the quiet corners of her apartment.

Thanks to the police, Damon seemed to have decided

how Amelia was going to keep her schedule, and what she was going to do with her life. It simply wasn't fair.

Still, it was what it was, and for the time being, she was reasonably well set up for hunkering down and waiting. She kept in touch with Wendy by phone, and at least she was able to paint and keep in contact with her agent. She had been through enough emotional turmoil recently to release it effectively on a canvas or two. And on top of all that, she'd been developing a good working relationship with Mark. They were communicating more, and Amelia was grateful that there was somebody close by willing to look out for her. He was always available and kept in touch with her about any sudden appearances by Damon.

Of which there were now very few these days. Something for which she was both very thankful for, but also rather trepidatious.

As such, there was little to do except paint and wait.

She was making the best of the situation by trying to see if there was a way she could capture the sensation of waiting, endlessly waiting, forever, with nothing to do, in the visual medium. What exactly would the essence of waiting look like? What would tedium look like?

She started applying clouds of gray onto a canvas. Just a depth of gray that allowed the eye to sink into it. She didn't know what she was creating, but she knew there was something there. Even though she couldn't quite see it.

*How very apt*, she thought.

She felt inspired to work on this new piece, but it was nonetheless monotonous. Which was why she was grateful when a sudden phone call interrupted this monotony.

She picked up her phone and was surprised to see that

the caller display was Pluto Civil Engineering. Sam's employer.

Very strange, she thought, since, by now, Sam would surely have left a forwarding address and phone number to a location other than her own. Also, it wasn't like his job didn't know his cell phone number. Amelia's best guess: Sam wanted to call her again, begging her to take him back, and he'd decided to use his work phone in the hopes that she, stupidly, wouldn't notice it was him.

*Good*, she thought. He was now using company resources to make personal threatening phone calls. A surefire way of getting fired.

She answered the phone. "Yeah?" she said quickly.

"Hello, is this Amelia Gray?"

She vaguely recognized the voice as some coworker of Sam's. "Yes, that's me," she answered.

"Hi, this is Peter. I work with your husb ... with Sam. I hope you don't think this is a strange question, but is there any way you might know where Sam is right now?"

"Why would I know where he is?"

"Well, honestly, we're scraping the bottom of the barrel at this point. Hoping for any kind of answer. You see, he hasn't been into work for almost six days."

"I see," she replied, and restrained herself from adding, *Did you try looking under any of his whores?*

"Are you certain there isn't anywhere you might know of that he might be," added Peter.

She knew what Peter was implying but was too polite to say. He was fully expecting Sam to have been harassing Amelia for the past week. Which, if not for Damon and his intervention, probably would've been true, she thought.

"Don't you have a follow-up number for any of the people he's currently associated with? Maybe Cara Gray?"

"No, we don't have any other contact info for him. Sigh. Shit. Well, please let me know if you see or hear anything, all right?"

"All right," she replied half-heartedly. If she did learn of his whereabouts, she honestly believed she wouldn't have cared.

They said their goodbyes, and Amelia hung up.

So now, on top of Damon not being around, she thought, still holding her phone, Sam was missing.

And the last time she'd seen the two of them together, one was beating the other.

She didn't want to worry about Sam after everything he'd done to her, but she couldn't deny the suspicions growing in her mind.

With a heavy sigh, she called her parents' home. She knew it was a long shot, but there was always the possibility that Cara might—strong emphasis on might—still know something in regard to Sam.

The phone rang, and then her mother picked up. "Hello?"

"Hey, Mom?"

"Oh, hi there, darling," she said, as chipper as Amelia ever remembered her sounding. "How are you and Damon?"

Amelia stopped in her tracks. She'd almost forgotten her mother was supposed to believe that Damon was actually her boyfriend. This was going to be hard to deal with, she thought. But fortunately, only at a later date. Right now, it was about Sam.

"We're fine," Amelia assured her quickly. "Listen, is Cara there?"

"Yes, she's right here. Hold on, I'll put her on."

Amelia figured that Cara must be at home in New Haven. She'd never held onto a job in her life, and when she wasn't living off her parents, she was living off some man. It was the only life she'd ever known.

Amelia could hear the phone being passed over before hearing Cara's voice burst in bluntly. "What?"

"Do you know where Sam is?" she asked.

"What? Why?"

"His job called me; he's missing."

"Why do you care?"

"I don't, Cara; it's just called basic humanity. Someone's missing. I was wondering if he came crawling back to you after I threw him away. Twice, by the way."

"How would I know where he is?"

"Because you were together until you left him for another guy, oh, wait, that's right, no you didn't."

Amelia smiled and almost smacked her hand against her face. Honestly, she was a bit embarrassed. It was a cheap shot and entirely unnecessary. But after everything Cara had put her through, dammit if it didn't feel the slightest bit like justice. Or at least schadenfreude.

"Bitch, fuck you," Cara replied before hanging up.

Amelia dialed her home again and got Cara to pick up.

"Fuck you!" she yelled before slamming the phone down again.

For whatever reason, Amelia didn't like the idea of Sam being missing. Maybe she just wanted to know where he was instead of stalking her. Or maybe there really was something to this whole "human empathy" thing. But one way or another, she wasn't going to let up. She dialed again.

Thankfully, her mother picked up this time. "Goodness gracious, what was all that about? Hello?"

"Yeah, Mom. It's me again."

"What in the world's happened now? Why was your sister hanging up on you?"

"Ironic way of putting it," Amelia muttered. "Look, Mom, have you seen or heard from Sam recently?"

"Sam? Why?"

"Apparently, he hasn't gone into his job for almost a week now. I figured he may have come crawling back to Cara."

"Darling, with him behind all of us, you really should stop examining the past, and start focusing on what's good and beautiful in life again. You have a very good man, and you really shouldn't—"

Now it was Amelia's turn to hang up. This was getting her nowhere, and frankly, she didn't want to hear her mother's lecture about what's good in this world.

Instead, she called up Sam's childhood home and spoke to his mother. Mrs. Altman revealed that she hadn't heard anything from Sam for over ten months. Evidently, not only had he been missing from his parents for the past week, but also, he had chosen not to reach out to them during his harassment, his infidelity, his divorce, and the tail end of their failing marriage. He just quietly disappeared from his parents' lives.

*What a guy*, she thought.

Despite that, Mrs. Altman expressed a lot of worry and sounded as if she might start to cry. Again, Amelia favored basic human decency: she stayed on the phone and helped walk her through the process of who to call and what to say to fill out a missing persons report.

They talked a little bit more, so Amelia could ensure that her former mother-in-law was doing all right, before they ended the call.

Amelia sat there and stared at her phone for a few more seconds. It was very hard to wrap her head around the idea that somebody like Sam—conniving, selfish, stupid, cruel Sam—could still have somebody in his life who loved him that much and so unconditionally. That incredible familial bond, which surpassed any feelings of hatred for a person who would be willing to hurt others with no remorse.

At least for this woman's sake, Amelia hoped that Sam was all right.

Nothing else for it, she figured. She put the phone down and started experimenting with more gray clouds upon the canvas.

The next morning, she contacted Mark and made arrangements for him to get her groceries. She invited him over for breakfast, as a way of saying thank you for everything he had done for her, to keep her safe, and keep her sanity. She felt it wasn't quite enough.

She wondered, as she poured them both coffee, how much time he was spending with Wendy.

Another day, another day of painting. Then the next, and then the next.

And then, after several more days, she finally received another phone call from the police. She assumed it was about the protection order. But, regrettably, this call was quite different.

"Hello, Miss Gray. We're calling about a missing person's report."

"What?" Amelia started before remembering the whole

thing with Sam. "Wait, why am I on the missing persons report?"

"You were listed as a contact by Samuel Altman's mother."

"Of course I was. Anyway, did you find him?"

The fact that the officer on the other end of the line went silent for so long worried her.

"Miss Gray," he said slowly, "we regret to inform you that Samuel Altman was discovered in a warehouse on Thirty-Second Street in Queens. He had been stabbed several times …"

Amelia didn't really hear any of the rest of it. It was just small, insignificant details about the findings and what they were going to do with the body.

All that mattered was he was dead. Sam, her ex-husband, was dead.

He smiled at her when she cooked him food. He asked her about paints. He showed off, so proudly, his first major ten-story design when he was hired to make the tallest building of his career up to that point. She remembered what he looked like when he was on top of her at night. She could feel him hugging her.

All the things that she didn't want to remember about him, all the things that she had blocked from her memory about him. She couldn't stop seeing them.

He was dead. He had been brutally murdered, and now he was dead.

And his mother, who hadn't spoken to him in almost a year and who missed him, would never see her son again.

If Mrs. Altman ever wanted to know when the last time Amelia had seen him was, she would have to tell her that it was when he was being beaten half to death by a crazy stalker in her hallway.

Over her. He had been beaten because he'd been harassing Amelia.

Somehow, she just knew his death had to be Damon's fault.

## 27

S hortly after the discovery of Sam's body, Amelia was contacted by the police department and told that a detective would like to see her at her earliest convenience in order to determine anything about probable cause, as well as pick up any information that she might be able to provide.

It really grated on her because she'd been told that it would take at least eight weeks for her protection order to be processed. Now that a man was dead, of course, everybody was willing to take action. Never mind the fact that she still felt unsafe to leave her own home.

She subtly hinted at it when she pointed out that coming to the station would be difficult because she was worried for her safety when leaving her own residence. Perhaps they could do something about that, she insinuated.

She wasn't expecting them to promise to expedite the protection order.

Plus, thankfully, her expectations were set so low that

she turned out to be right: they told her that a detective would be sent around to her place to interview her.

At the very least, it was hard to imagine Damon approaching her when there was a police officer on the property.

Particularly now that she couldn't imagine Damon not being Sam's killer.

Her ex-husband was dead.

*What a bastard*, she thought. She wanted to be able to say out loud that she was glad he was dead.

But every time she tried, it hurt her inside. She didn't want to believe that she had any emotional sympathy for this man, who'd had his life stolen from him. It was hard to believe that she would have this much emotional connection simply on the basis of human empathy, since she didn't feel this way about any of the other hundreds of deaths that took place in New York City.

Maybe, she thought, she felt bad about what she was becoming. A dominated, controlled, and very bitter woman. Sam's final gift to her. Right until the end, he found ways to hurt her even more.

Maybe he didn't deserve to die, she thought. But he was a bastard.

Complicated emotions.

These were issues she was going to have to deal with on her own. At the moment, she was making her place nice and tidy so she could have a heartwarming and secure safe space for when she had to meet the police officer.

Funnily enough, that was another of Sam's final gifts to her. Having to put up with this nonsense.

When she opened the door—after receiving a text from Mark that the man coming into the lobby was, in fact, somebody he didn't recognize who looked official—she opened it on a well-dressed man with a badge. He was in a suit and tie, which was certainly the definition of a plainclothes detective, though he wore his badge proudly. He had a strong physique, a powerful handshake, and a warm smile hidden behind a bushy moustache. He seemed like the kind of guy who could get things done.

Amelia hoped that he really was.

"I'm Detective Tom Corbett of the New York Police Department. May I come in?"

"Yes, please." Amelia led him to a chair and sat down on the couch across from him. "So, what can I help you with?"

"As I'm sure you know," Detective Corbett replied, "I'm investigating Sam Altman's death. I'm looking for any information from those who knew him as to how it could've occurred. For example, if he might have made any enemies."

"I'm happy to help, though I'm not sure what kind of help I can offer," replied Amelia. "He divorced me while having an affair with my sister."

"Your sister," said the detective. "Are you certain of this?"

"She sent me a recording of the two of them having sex and crammed her tongue down his throat at my birthday party. I'd say it's a guarantee."

"Sent you a ... Really?"

Amelia sighed. This was going to be a long interview. "My relationship with my sister has been extremely fraught our entire lives. She developed a bitter hatred toward me. She spent much of her time trying to make me feel bad by robbing me of any chance at love. Being able to steal my husband from me and ruin my marriage was a triumph for her."

"I see," the detective said. "You sound like you're still pretty bitter about the experience."

"Well, wouldn't you be?" replied Amelia, until she thought about his words and realized that they could be a subtle way of accusing her of being a suspect in Sam's murder. "That said, I mostly just tried to move on with my life."

"Really?"

"Yes ... Why?"

"I've recently been in contact with other departments I work closely with, and running your name through the system, I discovered you recently put in a request for a protection order against Damon Chase?"

"Yes, I did. So how's that coming along? Any protection heading my way soon? Have they found him to serve him the papers?"

"If my theory works out, sooner than you might think," replied the detective, looking down at his notes.

Now, Amelia couldn't help but stare at the man. He was obviously deep in thought, considering something he hadn't said aloud just yet. And all while discussing Damon Chase. What was he going on about? What exactly did he know?

"Excuse me," Amelia continued. "Are you familiar with Damon Chase?"

There was a moment of silence; then the detective looked up at Amelia. He appeared to be sizing her up. "Familiar, yes," he finally replied. "But I'd like to hear more about how you got to know him. After all, I assume you know what he does for a living."

"Escort service."

"Professionally speaking. An interesting acquaintance to have. And around the time that you became single."

"Are you implying something, Detective?"

"I'm just wondering if we're both thinking the same thing."

"And what would that be, pray tell?"

"That Damon Chase isn't what he seems to be."

Amelia froze for a moment. She was prepared for this police officer to snidely imply that it was dirty or provocative in some way that a grown woman was jumping into bed with a prostitute the moment she got divorced. But she wasn't prepared for this.

"If you don't mind me asking," the detective said, "what involvement did you have with Mr. Chase?"

Amelia was fully aware that the police department already knew this, since she'd filled in as much information about it as she could on her protection request. And that if this detective knew about that request, then he'd already read it. So she wasn't sure what exactly he wanted to hear now.

Maybe he really was accusing her, she thought.

"All right," she said. And then, deciding to throw caution to the wind, she explained her entire plan and how Damon had helped her execute it.

"Were you hoping to get back together with your ex-husband after this?"

"Once I realized that he was knowingly complicit in my sister's actions toward me, I fell out of love with him pretty quickly," Amelia told him truthfully. "I have to admit, I was focused on getting revenge against my sister. Whatever happened to Sam didn't really matter to me anymore."

"So how did you react to the news of his death?"

Amelia paused for a moment, considering. "I felt heart-broken by that. And I felt so angry that I had to be heartbroken by it. I hated him, but I didn't want him to die. He just had to do that ... That one last thing to, to really screw me over."

Another moment of silence, and then the detective spoke up again. "I have to admit, I'm glad to hear you say that."

"Excuse me?"

"I said I'm glad to hear you explain your feelings in that way."

"You're glad ... Why?"

"I was legally obligated to consider you as a suspect in your ex-husband's murder, but now, I'll have to explain to everybody I work with that your involvement is extremely unlikely."

"Oh! ... If, if you don't mind me asking ... Why?"

"One, you already had the police involved long before his death, which would've been an extremely terrible choice, though a good one if you wanted to elaborately cover your tracks. Two, we've been looking into Mr. Chase for some time, and we're aware that your own travels have become somewhat limited of late. Sam's body was found in Queens. We can't confirm that you were or weren't in your apartment at the time of his death, but it would've been a rather distant trip, given your recent activities. Also, there was no definitive forensic evidence.

"But that's what gets supported by a detective's intuition. And you answered honestly about human sympathy and human hatred toward somebody who harmed you. It's been my experience that people who want to hide their emotions blanket over them intensely. All of a sudden, people are adamant about how *completely distraught* they are, complete with wailing and moaning. Either that, or they insist that they aren't moved at all. But hating yourself for hating a dead man? It's such a realistic feeling that, frankly, I'm a little surprised no one ever tries to fake it more often."

"Oh," said Amelia, lowering her guard a little more. She had to admit, all her other feelings about the police aside, this guy seemed to be pretty damn good at what he did. "Wait a minute," she said. "You said you've been looking into Mr. Chase for some time?"

"Yes."

"Because of my protection request?"

"Actually, no," replied the detective. "I was wondering if you could tell me about the last time that you saw Sam Altman. I want to know if you may have had any reason to believe that he may have encountered Damon Chase."

"The last time I saw Sam was with Damon. Through that peephole," Amelia said, pointing to the door. "Sam was harassing me, and, all of a sudden, Damon showed up and beat him nearly half to death. Before throwing him out."

There was a long silence, with the detective sizing Amelia up again. Although this time, he didn't look like he was eyeing a suspect, but rather, something else. Amelia couldn't quite put her finger on it. An ally, perhaps?

"You believe Damon Chase killed Sam Altman, don't you?" said the detective.

"Yes."

"But you don't have any proof, do you?"

"I heard about Sam's death the same way you did. I wasn't there. How can I have proof?"

"Then why do you think he did it?"

"For one, the way he's been acting around me lately. He was supposed to be providing a service, nothing more. Then, all of a sudden, he's kissing me and following me. He's personally invested in his aggression toward Sam and my sister, as if he's taking his own satisfaction in hurting them, rather than doing it for work. And Sam's murder happened not too long after that beating. I mean, wouldn't you be suspicious?"

"I certainly was."

"But you're not now?"

"What? Oh, no! No, no, no. I still am, just—"

"Wait, still?"

For a moment, the detective looked embarrassed. "I specifically requested to be the one to work your case," said Corbett, "after I learned that you were looking for protection from a stalker by the name of Damon Chase. Years ago, I investigated Damon Chase and his potential involvement in the death of his wife."

"Whoa, *his wife?*"

"Yes. Years ago, his wife, Ophelia Chase, passed away under circumstances that seemed ... Well, pretty extreme for a suicide."

"What exactly happened?"

"Ophelia seemed to have committed suicide by drowning herself in a river."

"Wait. Her name was Ophelia ... and she drowned herself?" Amelia thought that sounded hinky.

"I take it you're familiar with the works of Shakespeare."

"Hamlet's love interest, Ophelia. She drowned when she fell from the willow tree into the brook, and some characters in the story suspected she did it purposefully," Amelia said quietly.

"Exactly. And, frankly, it was a bit too on the nose for me."

Amelia nodded; she thought so too.

"I thought it extremely suspect that his wife killed

herself in such a way. Her body held no evidence of her tying herself to any sort of weights that would assist her in drowning herself, which meant that she would've needed to drown herself by willingly keeping herself under the surface of the water. Which is, technically, not impossible, I suppose. But have you ever been swimming and tried to see how long you could hold your breath? After a while, it's an excruciating, terrifying experience. Deliberately drowning yourself isn't easy, and it's certainly an odd choice for a suicide."

She agreed. Why would Ophelia drown herself? If she'd wanted to commit suicide, there were other ways to do it. She could have overdosed on medication and died peacefully in her sleep.

"There wasn't any explicit evidence that he had killed her, but there were other reasons why his insistence ... 'bore weight,' sorry for the pun."

"What do you mean by other reasons?"

"Officially, Damon Chase's statement was that his wife took her own life after suffering a devastating personal experience. You see, not too long before that, she was raped by an assailant who was apparently dating her best friend."

"Oh my God!"

"Yes, there was recorded evidence, from medical practitioners and close friends, that she had suffered an assault and had made comments about being suicidal. As such, his insistence that his wife's death was at her own hand was readily accepted. High-ranking officers in the department decided to drop charges against him despite my beliefs after interviewing him, but since it was assumed that he wasn't guilty and ... well, because he worked with a company that, um ..."

"A company that paid you very well."

Detective Corbett glowered at Amelia. "No, Miss Gray," he said sternly. "Not me personally. Never me."

Amelia couldn't help but take a dig at the police in general, but considering how nice this detective had been up until now, she regretted opening her big mouth. Desperately trying to change the subject, she said, "So the rapist and her friend, they didn't say anything?"

"They probably could have if they were still alive."

"They died too?"

"After the death of Ophelia Chase, we looked into their involvement as prime suspects. We discovered their bodies in the man's apartment not long after. They had both been stabbed to death in what looked to be a drug deal gone bad. As best we can tell, they died shortly before Ophelia did."

"Damn."

"By the time I was able to point out that there were suspicious details around the death of Mrs. Chase, we had already abandoned the pursuit of Mr. Chase, and since then, because we're so understaffed, I've had the misfortune of simply being forced to sit on my theories. Until now, that is."

"You think that Damon killed his wife and Sam?"

"To be honest, yes, and I've always wondered if perhaps he killed his wife's assailant and friend, though as I said, it did look like a bad drug deal, but the perp was never caught, and the case went cold. My theory is reinforced by the fact that your ex-husband was stabbed repeatedly, just like they were. The man you described is becoming extremely possessive and protective of you. A man who wanted something from you and wasn't willing to lose it. He has drawn closer to you, and he caused a scene when you threatened him with the police. This sounds to me like the kind of man who would do anything to protect the person he sees as his woman. Revenge, like he did with that rapist. And, well, you saw him brutally attack your ex-husband."

Amelia couldn't say anything. This was a lot to take in. The fact that all logical evidence was pointing in one single direction didn't make it any easier to swallow.

After a moment of silence, Detective Corbett stood up from his seat and headed toward the door. "I'd like to thank you for inviting me into your home, Miss Gray, and for listening to me. Sometimes, I find that fewer and fewer of my fellow officers really do. But it is important to be able to do the right thing in life. And to know whom you can trust. As such, I must ask you to trust me and to listen to my advice: you must remain in your apartment at all times from now on, at least until we catch this man. Do everything in your power to make no exceptions to this. And for the love of all goodness, do not open your door to Damon Chase if he should ever return. Instead, either call the police or, better yet, call me personally, on my private line. I've been waiting a long time to pin down Mr. Chase."

## 28

Looking up from her bed, Amelia could see across the studio to her easel, where her last work—her experimentation with gray clouds all swirling down into an inner journey of different shades of gray—was still resting, incomplete. Granted, the whole thing was covered over with gray, but, when she looked at it, there was something not quite right about it. Something missing. It was missing a piece of vitality. It was missing the answer to what it was. Or maybe it was missing the mystery of itself.

Amelia hadn't been able to approach her easel for the past twenty-four hours. She knew the painting was going to be sitting there on that easel for a while longer. It was hard to feel like she should engage in anything thoughtful or attempt to have fun at a time like this.

She had engaged with a man who was most likely a murderer.

It seemed likely that he had murdered two people who had betrayed his wife, then killed his wife right after.

Thanks to a convoluted set of circumstances, he'd gotten

away with it, even though the evidence pointed directly to him, at least in her mind. She admitted that she was somewhat biased, given that Damon's behavior had really disturbed her. But all the same, he disturbed her for a reason.

What was his reason for killing his wife after killing her assailant and her friend? Did she learn about what he did, and turned on him out of a sense of morality? Perhaps the story of her assault and rape was false, and he simply killed her and her secret lover, though that didn't explain why her best friend was mixed up in it.

Or, and this was possibly the simplest explanation: he was an insane murderer and just killed them all. That thought certainly crossed her mind more than a few times.

Amelia's phone vibrated. There was a message from Mark.

> Coast is clear.

She gingerly, but quickly, went to her front door.

Opening it, Amelia noticed a plastic bag at her feet, filled with what she'd requested Mark buy for her: shampoo, soap, tampons, toilet paper. Basically, necessities.

She grabbed the bag and immediately closed the door, locking it behind her.

Amelia and Mark had worked out a damn good system. For her peace of mind, he continued to monitor the nanny cam so he could report to her when Damon showed up in the building, though he acknowledged that, for the past week, he hadn't seen Damon at all. Which made a certain amount of sense, Amelia thought, since the police were now actively looking for him and were doing drive-bys on their apartment building. Case in point, whenever she looked out the window, she could no longer see his car but often saw a police officer driving by, much more so than before all of this started.

Otherwise, it was absolutely imperative that she keep her promise to the detective and not leave her apartment. Meaning she'd been stuck in here for the past few days.

It really did feel like she was going stir-crazy, but at least it was preferable to the fear of being jumped from behind at any given moment.

Aside from the weirdness of it, Amelia settled into her new routine. At this point, she was trying to figure out how to show her gratitude to Mark for the incredible effort he'd put into keeping her safe. She was wondering if maybe she should offer him some money, though that might make him feel awkward. She wondered if she could bake him something or paint him something. But she didn't really know what his tastes were, except for dogs. Under any other circumstances, she would ask him out to take the dogs for a walk. Not the time for it, though. She considered maybe inviting him over to her place for ...

She suddenly stopped herself. Amelia wasn't exactly sure where she was going with those thoughts. After all, Mark was Wendy's boyfriend. She was wondering how she was going to explain all this to Wendy after it was over. Particularly since she was taking up a lot of Mark's time. He was always so trustworthy, so caring.

She really wanted somebody that caring in her life. How lucky Wendy was.

Except, obviously, these days. When a murderer-on-the-loose was occupying both her friend and partner.

Alleged murderer, of course, Amelia acknowledged.

Although, the writing was on the wall. Even if she completely ignored the whole story about Damon having a wife who had died, along with some of her friends and associates, there was the matter of Sam. Much like the Damon Chase that Detective Corbett described, the Damon she knew had encountered a man who was harassing someone whom he believed to be *his girl*. And he really took it out on him.

And a week later, Sam turned up dead.

None of which happened much longer after Damon went into a meltdown about the thought of losing Amelia. And insisted that he would prove to her how much he loved her.

Her verbally abusive ex-husband had turned up dead. Just like the people who had hurt Ophelia Chase. Her abuser and the woman who betrayed Ophelia for her abuser ...

... the woman who betrayed Ophelia for her abuser ...

... Amelia's entire body ran cold. She couldn't believe she could be so stupid as to not even realize it.

She knew exactly who the next target was.

She immediately picked up her phone and dialed.

The phone rang and was answered after a brief moment. "Hello?" her mother said.

"Mom, is everything all right over there?" asked Amelia, hurriedly.

"Yes? Why?"

"Is Cara there? Is she okay?"

"Oh God, what did she do now?"

"Just put her on, please?"

"Well, very well then," her mother huffed into the phone. "And don't raise your voice at me."

There was an awkward silence that went on for some time until finally Amelia heard Cara grab the phone. "What?" she asked bluntly.

"Cara, listen to me. Damon murdered Sam."

"Wait, what?"

"Damon! He killed Sam! They found Sam in a warehouse in Queens; didn't the cops come talk to you?"

"Well, yeah, but I didn't know anything, so ..." She didn't sound very bothered by the fact Sam was dead.

"Cara, listen to me. Damon killed him!"

"The fuck are you talking about?" she said skeptically.

"I think that Damon is coming to kill you next!"

There was an awkward pause, and then finally, Cara spoke. "Holy shit, did you break up with Damon?"

"No! Listen to me, Cara. He's a murderer, and he's coming to kill you."

"Holy shit! He dumped you."

"We were never together, okay? It was, I don't know, a stupid thing, the point is, he's obsessive, and he's—"

"Doesn't feel good, does it, bitch?"

*"For the love of God, Cara! The man is coming to murder you! He thinks he loves me and wants to kill you for me!"*

"Oh, this is just beautiful. He dumped you, and now I'm actually going to get to have him."

"No! Cara, you aren't listening to me!"

"Fuck you."

And then she hung up.

Amelia stood there, astounded by how heavy her chest felt. She dialed home again. It rang again. It picked up again.

"Is this you?" said her mother immediately.

"Mom," Amelia said urgently, "Damon is a dangerous stalker with a history of murder. He murdered his previous wife and two of the people around her. He's obsessed with me, and he believes he's going to ingratiate himself toward me by murdering Cara, just like he murdered Sam!"

"Oh, dear God, you require medication."

"No, dammit, Mom!"

"You were so, so close. You actually had the perfect boyfriend for once. And you couldn't even hold onto one, just one decent relationship in your life."

*"Mom! Listen to me!"*

"I tried. I really did. Now I have to spend the rest of my life paying for a totally useless daughter. And I'm never going to get anything out of it. You just ... You just can't do anything!"

"Mom, this is serious—"

Amelia heard a definitive slam on the other end of the line. Her mother had hung up on her.

This was insane, Amelia thought. Her sister was going to die.

Amelia realized that Cara was going to die. She also realized that under no circumstances did she actually want that.

She had spent her entire life hating her sister. Now, the thought of losing her was like having her heart ripped out of her chest.

She dialed her parents' number again. It continued to ring for a very long time until there was a click, and an automated voice told her that the person she was calling had rejected the call.

Amelia hung up and tried again.

A different automated voice told her that she could no longer access this number.

Her parents had actually blocked her.

If she drove out to New Haven now, Amelia thought,

she'd probably not make it in time, if Damon happened to be headed there right now. If she raced, maybe she would get there just in time to meet Damon, at which point he would kill her family anyway and then kill her as well.

Or maybe she would meet him on the road.

Or maybe just outside her door.

Amelia collapsed to the floor in tears. She was powerless. There was nothing she could do.

And her sister was going to be the one who would pay for it.

All. Over. Again.

But then the thought struck her that she should have called the police as soon as she realized that Cara would be on Damon's hit list. So she immediately contacted Detective Corbett and told him what she feared would happen. She told him, too, that she'd done everything in her power to warn her sister, but, due to their prior relationship, she simply couldn't get through to her.

The detective assured her that he would do everything he could to deal with the situation, then urgently hung up.

Amelia was left on the floor of her apartment. Looking up, she found that she had collapsed not too far from her easel. Cold, distant, lifeless, but her art felt like the only friend she had left in the world right now.

---

## 29

It was the next evening. After a day of anxiously awaiting news of her sister being safe, or Damon being caught, Amelia had made plans. Despite her admiration for Detective Corbett, who genuinely seemed like a good man, she decided to make her plans without either his knowledge or consent. She secretly hoped that, if they ever had a chance to meet again, he would forgive her.

She couldn't stay in her apartment any longer. Everywhere she looked, she could only remember how Sam used to be there, and now, he was never going to be there again. Now, on top of that, she couldn't stop thinking about Cara.

And she couldn't stop thinking that this was all her fault.

The detective had recommended that she not leave her apartment, for her own safety, since Damon wouldn't have access to her unless he forced entry to the building. Perhaps reasonable, Amelia thought, but Damon already knew where she lived. In fact, if he eventually figured out that she never left the apartment, then he would have all the time in the world to sneak up and camp somewhere nearby in the building. How did she know he wouldn't kill the building super and maybe live in his room? What about her neighbors?

What if he did something to Mark?

No, not anymore. She wasn't going to put other people at risk just for her own safety.

Added to that, there was another good reason for not telling the detective about her decision: the police had, thus far, failed to track him down.

It had been weeks. And they still couldn't find him.

They knew he was obsessed with her. They knew what his car looked like. They knew where they met, and where Damon would expect to find her. And they still couldn't find him. He had managed to elude the police force every step of the way.

So as far as Amelia was concerned, either the entire NYPD was incompetent—and she hadn't necessarily ruled that out—or, more likely, Damon wasn't the mouse in this scenario. He was the cat. He was the one keeping tabs on the police.

Meaning, if the police force was under the impression that Amelia was trapped inside her apartment, then that was the absolute last place she should be. But if she left them thinking she was still there, well, all the better.

And so Amelia had talked to Wendy. They'd talked about getting Amelia out of her place and somewhere safe, maybe to a hotel or somewhere Damon wouldn't know to look. In the end, Wendy suggested she move into her apartment in Clinton Hill for the duration of the police hunt for Damon. Amelia wasn't sure if it was a smart move or not. Damon was aware of Wendy's existence, but as far as Amelia was aware, he didn't know where she lived. Wendy said he didn't even know her last name and that he would have a difficult time tracking her down now, and therefore he wouldn't be able to find her either. Amelia wasn't so sure, but she decided to give it a go. It was better than sitting around her own place, waiting for him to show up.

Now was the best time to make this move. Since Damon was on the run, Amelia could be reasonably assured that he wasn't actually keeping an eye on her apartment building. He wasn't anywhere nearby, at least, or the cops would have captured him already. He wouldn't notice when she left. By the time he got back—more of a matter of *when* rather than *if*—she'd be long gone, and hopefully, he would never know.

If she did it smoothly enough, it would work.

She packed her bags, contacted Wendy to pick her up, and then asked her building super to help her escape.

But first she had to say goodbye.

As her building super was taking her bags away, she went next door and knocked.

Mark opened the door and stood there, staring at her.

She stared right back.

There really was nothing left to say at this point. The whole situation was out of control, and she just wanted him to understand how grateful she was for his help.

All they could do was silently give each other a hug. And say goodbye.

While hugging, she reached over and gently gave him a little kiss on the side of his neck. She backed off after realizing what she was almost about to do, and hoped that maybe the kiss was so soft that Mark might not have even noticed.

She hoped so. She had no idea what just came over her.

Mark escorted her to the basement tunnel, where he

held her hand briefly for one second more before letting go and waving to her.

She traveled with her building super for a few hundred meters and then exited through a service door into a parking garage she recognized at the opposite end of the neighborhood from her building. Wendy was there, and she grabbed Amelia's bags, loaded them up into her trunk, and let her into the passenger seat as the two of them thanked the building super before driving away toward Wendy's apartment.

Amelia had an appointment to keep. And she didn't want to be late.

It was the other major reason why they were traveling to Wendy's home. Apart from the fact that it was a good place to hide out, they could bring in other people without risking them being seen approaching Amelia's apartment. Without them risking Damon seeing what was going on and figuring out whom to put in his crosshairs next.

Amelia had asked Wendy to make arrangements with the man she was going to meet. She needed answers, and he was going to give them to her. Using Wendy as an intermediary made sense. Largely because she was the reason any of this got off the ground in the first place. So Amelia knew that if Wendy said her contact was going to be there, she could feel confident that he definitely was.

After just twenty minutes, they drove into a parking garage underneath a very old New York building that was filled with all sorts of history, personality, and unfortunately, the occasional rat. But Wendy liked it and called it home, so it was good enough for Amelia. And to be honest, from the outside, at night, it did have that old college rustic charm.

There was something very adventurous and inviting about the place.

Once they were parked, Amelia grabbed some of her things and traveled up the four flights of stairs to the top of the building. There, Wendy let her in.

Where their visitor was already waiting.

"Ladies," he said, getting up from his armchair. "I'm glad to see you returned safely."

"Hello, Nicolas," Amelia said to Mr. Wan. "Long time no see."

"Indeed. But at least you are safe, and that gives me great comfort and pleasure."

"Please sit down."

Amelia could tell from the way he was speaking that he was trying to be charming, much in the same way that he had been almost completely enticing when they first met. But at this point, Amelia couldn't care less. If she told him to sit down and listen, he would. End of story.

Quietly, Wendy grabbed Amelia's things from where she'd placed them and moved them into a side room. She would remain there for the rest of the night, giving Amelia and Nicolas some privacy.

Amelia sat down across from Nicolas. "I learned a lot about your organization in recent times," she began. "As such, I assume you know what's been going on with Damon Chase?"

"In truth, only as much as you know. The police came to me very early on and asked me to provide any information I had on Damon. I did so. A few days later, the police revealed to me that all the information I provided them was inaccurate. Damon Chase never offered any of his real private information, as it turned out. He lied to me. I never knew the man."

"Do you feel you 'know' many of your employees? How do you treat them?"

He nodded. "I've always taken care of the people who earn a living for me. In effect, I want to be more than just an employer, but something other ... a protector. As you can imagine, people in this line of work can feel as if they've lost all hope. I want them to believe that they have a certain amount of safety that I simply never had when I was younger."

"So Damon made you feel like you could protect and care for him. As a result of you giving him every benefit of the doubt, you never doubted him."

"No, I always knew there was a mathematical probability that somebody would take advantage of me. But I thought I was too smart for it. I ..." He paused. "Amelia, I can't even begin to tell you how sorry I am for what happened to you. For what is still happening to you. Nobody should ever have to be terrified to live their own life. Nobody coming to my agency should ever have to feel like they are in danger. You deserve better."

"Nicolas, you made an extremely serious mistake, and people have paid for it with their lives. And, odds are, based on what I know about you and your company, you won't end up liable financially or legally. But I feel I also know you well enough that this is something you're going to be paying for with your heart and your soul. And given recent events, although I understand you deserve that, I also wish you didn't have to feel that kind of pain. I mean that. I really do. And for what it's worth, I'm grateful for your help."

"And you have it, my dear. As I said, I am so very sorry you are going through this."

"It's just, being realistic, you have to understand that you hired a man who was responsible for three murders when you met him, and by all accounts, while he was associated with your agency, he committed at least one, maybe two more. We have a killer on the loose, who has potentially killed five people, and he is specifically targeting people who are associated with me. So, for example, his target could include the man who introduced me to him in the first place."

"Me." Nicolas seemed taken aback at her words. As though he hadn't considered that he might also be a target for Damon.

"You swear to me that you haven't seen him for several weeks now?"

"I haven't lied to the police, and I'm not lying to you now."

"Then do you know where you're going to go?"

"I suspect, much like you, I'll be finding new accommodations. As will all of my employees. And I certainly won't be having any contact with him ever again, except, possibly, to keep him busy somewhere while having him arrested."

"That's good to hear," Amelia finally said, with a smile.

She really didn't want anyone else's blood on her hands.

## 30

It had been five days since Amelia moved into Wendy's apartment.

Damon probably didn't know that she was residing there now, but she decided not to put any more of her friends in danger by risking being spotted.

This was what life must feel like for people in the witness protection program, she thought. All her activities were carefully monitored. All her movements were carefully arranged. Because, for whatever reason, a dangerous individual had become obsessed with her—someone who shouldn't have these sorts of rights over her—her whole life was basically being manipulated by him.

And Damon had the protection of the law.

It wasn't something she felt comfortable saying out loud, since she was very aware that the police would object to that kind of statement. However, it was true. They could've gone after him after he killed his wife. They didn't. They could've gone after him when he was stalking Amelia. They didn't.

They should have hunted him down by now. But they seemed to have lost him.

And every step of the way, by sheer negligence and incompetence, they allowed Damon to live out his life the way he wished to. In her mind, that effectively meant that the police gave him a pass. Maybe not literally, maybe not even intentionally. But they did.

And she was the one who had to pay for it. By being locked in this apartment, which she could not leave without putting herself in danger. Or, more likely, putting Wendy in danger.

This was absolutely intolerable, she thought. But it was also the life she had right now.

Currently, she sat at her easel. She hadn't brought it with her since it was too large to fit in the car, so Mark had met up with Wendy and gotten it to her after Amelia left. She was working on an abstract. It was a series of paintings that she had been recently inspired to work on, focusing on how the white space around various geometric shapes implied the kind of freedom and innocence she longed for, yet also checked on the shape of borders in boxes, which made the viewer feel trapped. The irony did not escape her. She knew exactly why she was feeling this way.

She came to realize a lot about her life while painting. Early on, her family had been abusive toward her. Whether through intimidation or simply by ignoring her. Or, in the case of her sister, actively taking advantage of her trust and innocence. For a while, she felt as if she'd spent her life trying to get away from them. Up until very recently, when she realized she'd spent most of her life trying to gain a sense of normalcy from them, to gain their approval. To gain a real life with her family.

An ordinary, normal, loving life.

But now, in exchange for her efforts, she had this awful sense that Cara was probably dead. And based on the fact that Cara was living with her parents—as per always—there was a very good possibility that they were dead as well.

Calling them would be fruitless, since, to the best of her knowledge, her family was still blocking her phone. And if she did get through, she was entirely confident her family wouldn't believe her about the danger they were all in. But if they did listen, and maybe even believed her, there was also the possibility that the only person left to pick up the phone was Damon himself. Or a police coroner.

She didn't want that kind of pressure on her mind. Perhaps it was selfish, but she did appreciate having the ability, at Wendy's, to try to gain some kind of normal life. Even if it meant just sitting at her easel, painting a few new pieces, and believing that, somewhere, out in the world, her family was still doing its thing.

The alternative was to claw at her face and bang her head against the wall in torment.

Even if she was being a little overdramatic in her thoughts, her response sure felt realistic enough.

She finished applying the last bit of a metallic navy blue to the border of her most recent piece and stepped back to look at it in full. Lots of two-dimensional shapes, mainly squares, but with variations on them that made them look like microchip wiring, very contemporary, very twenty-first century. But all of it was holding in the picture, tightening it, closing it in.

This was the fifth piece she'd made that had this kind of theme, and it still felt very pure, very novel to her. She liked it. She wasn't sure if her agent would agree that it had pop-culture marketability—she wasn't frickin' Piet Mondrian, after all—but she certainly liked it. Which was a good sign.

She picked up her phone.

"Hey, Margo," Amelia said as soon as she heard her agent's familiar greeting.

"Amelia," Margo replied happily. "My God, it's been too long. We can't really make a living if you keep cancelling galas."

After her two successful galas, given the way everything had escalated, Amelia had cancelled all the future ones they'd planned, without even really thinking about it. In fact, she had almost entirely forgotten about it.

"Yes, well, sorry," Amelia replied.

"Are you?"

"Really, I'm very sorry. It's been … It's been pretty bad on my end for a while."

"I'm sorry to hear that," said Margo. "I do like it when my talents are able to live full lives and create something mean-ingful and wonderful. I'll try to ignore the fact that, after you die, your stuff will be worth ten times what it is now."

"Well, at least one of us has something to look forward to." Amelia snickered, knowing Margo was teasing her.

Margo laughed. "Seriously though," she continued, "I do hope you're all right."

Amelia sighed. "I am for now. I assume you heard about Sam on the news?"

"Yes, I was sorry to hear of that. I know you were divorced, but it's still hard to fathom that someone you once loved has been murdered."

"Yes. Well, the police and I think it was my stalker who killed him, so I've got some serious personal things going on right now."

"Are you safe?"

"I think so. I've got people helping me, so I think I'll be able to manage. And I'm working on a new series, if you still want to consider a gala in the near future, once this is over with."

A hopeful offer, Amelia thought. Of course, if they were to hold a gala now, she wouldn't be able to attend.

"Oh, interesting," replied Margo. "Are they anything like your emotional whirls?"

Amelia laughed. "Well, I suppose that's up for interpretation. They're certainly equally as colorful."

"Are they as appealing, though?"

Amelia rolled her eyes. She knew that Margo always focused on the commerciality of her work. "I'm sure every college kid is going to stick these up on the walls. They are abstract, geometric shapes, explorations of colors on white space. It really looks very comfy when studying for exams."

"Well, I suppose it will appeal to everybody who likes that kind of stuff and who is sick and tired of Piet Mondrian."

"Preach."

Margo laughed. "So let's just get these over to my studio, and—"

"Right, Margo, on that subject, I can't really leave my place for the time being. Actually, I'm not even at my place. I apologize for requesting this of you, but I was wondering if you could come to me? I'm staying with a friend. I needed out of my place because of everything going on, and I can't show myself out, well, anywhere. But if you come here, I can give you the paintings; will that work?"

"Sure, that works," Margo responded; then after a pause,

she added, "Oh, I almost forgot. I got a really strange phone call the other day to do with you."

Amelia froze. She didn't remember ever explicitly telling Margo about Damon being her stalker, merely that she had one.

"What are you talking about?" Amelia said quickly.

"Somebody called up here. A man claiming to be your boyfriend, said his name was Damon? Anyway, he said he was trying to get in touch with you. He wanted to know where to find you, because you'd apparently moved from your apartment."

*Oh God*, Amelia thought. She figured Damon would find out that she wasn't in her apartment, but she wasn't expecting it to be so soon. He'd probably found out the same day she left, for all she knew.

"What did you tell him?" Amelia asked.

"Well, obviously, nothing much. One, that if you'd moved, that was the first I'd heard of it. Two, regardless of whether you moved or not, we have a confidentiality agreement. I'm not going to give out your home address to anybody. And three, frankly, he claimed to be your boyfriend, and I don't remember meeting him at the galas or anywhere else. So I certainly wouldn't trust anything like that, particularly since I'm a little amazed that a genuine boyfriend in this day and age wouldn't know how to get in touch with you. Like texting doesn't exist."

"Margo," Amelia started, "that man who's been calling? He's my stalker. His name is Damon, but he doesn't have any kind of relationship connection to me. He's been harassing me, and—"

Amelia choked on her words, not wanting to talk about Sam again. She took a shuddering breath. "He's been following me around and making threats. The police are looking for him, and I've been trying to avoid a steady routine for the time being."

"Oh, honey, I am so sorry to hear this! Is there anything I can do?"

"Well, you're gonna have to hold off on booking me a gala for now, unless I'm not advertised, which sort of defeats the whole point. And I would like you to gain access to my work, but we've got to get the stuff into your hands safely somehow."

"Say no more. You have no idea how many of my female artists have people who are obsessive around them. I have a place I use for secure trade-offs, very clandestine, very out of the way. And that means we won't compromise your current location."

"You have no idea how concerned I am that you have to have a specific location for your talent to be able to sell their work without having to deal with stalkers. Like, you antici-pate this."

"I was going to say 'welcome to the twenty-first century,' Amelia; but let's be honest: when have talented women ever had a break?"

Amelia agreed, but she didn't like hearing it.

Instead, she simply made arrangements with her agent to have the paintings delivered to the warehouse apartment on the outskirts of New York. They said their goodbyes, with Margo expressing concern that Amelia should keep extra safe; then they hung up.

Amelia stopped and put her head into her hands. She needed to have the paintings delivered, but she also knew that she couldn't really leave the place she was stuck in. Meaning that she would probably have to ask Wendy to do it for her or get a courier, which could be expensive but was probably the safest thing to do. The sad thing was, Wendy would jump at the chance to help, even though Amelia knew that she didn't want her to because it was honestly too dangerous. There was no reason to lose her as well, and she really hoped Wendy would see that.

On top of her ex-husband. And, presumably, her sister and the rest of her family.

So much of her life right now was being dictated by Damon. He decided where she would go, what she would do. He decided who would be responsible for taking risks on behalf of Amelia.

He decided who would live and die.

## 31

J anuary was coming to an end. It was cold outside, and snow still covered the New York City streets.

Not that she would know about any of that first-hand. Amelia hadn't stepped out of Wendy's apartment for over a week now. She regretted making Mark go out and buy her personal items, her food. Now, equally she regretted making Wendy do it, but she knew it was necessary.

The snow certainly looked pretty through the windows, and it was clear that it was chilly based on how the frost was sticking to the windowpanes. But it was all a distant matter to her, as if watching it through a TV screen on some movie. She couldn't feel any of it.

Her phone was plugged into the wall, where she was able to keep it filled with charge while it suddenly began to receive a flood of texts from Damon. Every so often, she would look over and catch one she didn't recognize. He had started texting her so frequently that there was never anything on the screen that she saw more than once. Unless it was a repeat.

And curiously enough, he always seemed to have something new to say. Or at least, the same old thing to say in a new way.

When the texts started, she'd begun forwarding them to Detective Corbett, but so far, they hadn't been able to find him using them. All she'd been told was they were coming from various burner phones.

She found that, being locked inside all the time, she mostly occupied her time with painting, exploring her inspiration. But even then, she became exhausted even from doing what she loved. Her wrist felt dead from constant brush stroking.

So she was taking a break today. No painting. Not any kind of research on techniques or things that inspired her. No, she was going to dilly about the apartment. Which was kind of a form of entertainment in itself.

Somewhere behind her, Amelia's phone vibrated. She'd received another text from Damon. She didn't even look at it; she already knew what it was going to be. At this point, what else could it be?

Amelia sighed and circled the apartment. Wendy had a desk in her living room covered with a bunch of books and various papers. Amelia almost thought it resembled the desk of a librarian or some sort of fantasy wizard, given that it looked like layers of dust had accumulated on the books. In the right lighting, she would love to paint a picture of them. Explore this side of her friend.

Elsewhere, there was an armchair and a few other chairs, which looked like they belonged to a dining room table but were moved to this space because they were more useful for putting things on top of them. People in their generation never truly *dined* anymore, she thought. It got in the way of their ability to eat while watching TV.

Around here, she found all the things that made Wendy's life: one or two condoms, unwrapped. The occasional bra. Cards from various restaurants she probably went to with any cute guys. Various things her day job forced her to read, crammed into corners of the room where she obviously tossed them with the intent of forgetting about them.

All the while, across the room, Amelia's phone vibrated.

This was very different from her own home life, Amelia thought. She never got to settle into a lived-in space, she realized. Growing up, there was always a housekeeper working to keep everything in her childhood home tidy despite her best efforts to have the place covered with toys or, later, magazines. When she got older, her living spaces were flooded with canvases and paints.

Then she got married. And her husband complained that everything was covered in canvases and paints. He kept tripping over them, he often yelled.

Of course, he never seemed to pay attention to where they were either, Amelia thought.

By the time she was older and divorced, at first, she didn't paint and barely touched her own apartment except maybe the bed, which she needed for crying. Later on, she painted, but far more neatly. And even that wasn't something she got a chance to experience for very long. Shortly before this whole ... mess of her life started.

By the time she had circled the apartment twice over, she got back to her cell phone and looked at the screen. She had received thirty new text messages. Her voicemail had been flooded long ago, and she just left it that way.

She knew that any sane woman in this situation would simply block the caller. After all, literally every phone service in the world provided the feature. It wasn't exactly a difficult thing to stop somebody from contacting her.

But Amelia never did. She wanted Damon to shoot himself in the foot, metaphorically speaking. Every single phone message she received from him, she passed along to Detective Corbett. Every time she received a collection of texts, she screen-captured them and forwarded them to the detective.

Whenever Damon presented her with long diatribes of how much he loved her, what he wanted to do for her, how he wanted to make her life better by being in it, she captured all of that and moved it on to Detective Corbett.

If she blocked him, all these messages would stop. And then she wouldn't be able to collect massive amounts of evidence of his stalking and forward it to the police officer, whom, frankly, she had grown to trust. The detective was always sympathetic and willing to hear everything she said. He always believed her, and he never talked down to her. The most critical thing she could ever say about him was that he appeared a bit intimidating, and sometimes he seemed to be thinking three steps ahead of her and every-body else in the world. Which, at the very least, she couldn't deny were qualities she wanted to see in a detective.

Hence, why she passed along everything to him. Making sure he developed a large file of behavior that, if and when Damon Chase was finally captured, would put him away for a very, very long time. Fingers crossed.

There was also the possibility that, maybe—fingers crossed again—Damon might reveal information in his messages that indicated where he was, or what he was planning to do. Stuff that might lead the police to finding him.

There was another good reason to allow the messages to keep coming. Namely, if Damon continued to text, then that indicated to Amelia that he was still under the impression that he was able to communicate with her through this method quite comfortably and easily. And, therefore, he would continue to do it. If she ever blocked him, perhaps he would go into a rage, much like the one outside the café when she last saw him. He would become despondent, bitter, vengeful ...

And then he would put extra effort into tracking her down.

What if he went after Mark? she thought. What if he tortured him until, desperate for release, he revealed exactly where she was?

The thought crossed her mind that Mark, of all people, would probably hold onto that information no matter what the cost. He really did seem like the kind of guy who would keep her protected.

She hated how that made her feel a little warm inside.

All the same, it wasn't a risk she was willing to accept. She needed her friends. She needed them to be safe. And so, if that meant having to deal with about a thousand texts a day from some guy who didn't seem to understand that not being replied to typically meant being ghosted, then that was what she was going to do.

Evidence in and of itself, Amelia thought as she picked up her phone. If he really did text her this often and continued to do so without any evidence to support him that she was actually listening, then he really was living in his own little world.

Opening up her phone, she saw the long string of texts. There was a time when she used to read each one, to ensure that she didn't miss the slightest detail, hoping to gather some important clue.

There never was one. And after a while, all the texts just sort of blurred together.

They were all terrifying, all nerve-racking. At this point, Amelia could simply internalize the panic, the terror. It was all she could do to keep from screaming.

She put the phone down, let it rest, and allowed it to collect more evidence. She started wandering around Wendy's apartment again. Maybe she would plop down on the couch and watch some TV. Pretend the world wasn't moving on, forget that it felt as if nobody cared about her.

Wondering if this was what it felt like to be dead inside.

## 32

A new problem. One that Amelia realized she had effectively brought upon herself.

No matter what her intentions.

Ten days after she had spoken with her agent—in which time, their plan of using a third-party studio apartment as a trading-off location for her work was going reasonably well; there hadn't been any complications, and Wendy had thankfully agreed with the courier idea even though it was an added expense—Amelia finally did receive a real call on her phone. She was expecting that it would be Damon again.

However, when she looked at her screen, she picked it up eagerly. She desperately wanted to hear good news. "Yes, hello?" she said, every bit of excitement clear in her voice.

"Yes, Miss Gray," replied Detective Corbett. "Are you doing all right?"

"Yes, yes, quite all right! And, and how are you?"

"Well, frankly, concerned."

"Are there any new developments in tracking down Damon?"

"I was hoping you could tell me. Have you seen or heard any suspicious activity in or around your apartment recently?"

Amelia's spine went cold, and her chest felt heavy. She had to smack her hand up onto her cheek in great surprise.

In all the time that she had been stuck in Wendy's apartment, painting away, she somehow forgot the detail that her arrangement to live in another woman's apartment was hers and hers alone. She'd never informed the police. She'd done it in secret, and she'd kept it that way.

They still thought she lived at her old apartment.

"Um, no, why?" she said, trying to sound calm and collected. But she already knew she'd left a rather long pause after the detective's question.

"There were a few sightings of Chase in the neighborhood. We thought that maybe you would've seen something. Maybe you would've seen him enter the building? Or somebody else may have? We were hoping you could help by saying if there was anything you would've noticed."

"Um, no. No, I haven't seen anything." Amelia took a breath, debating on whether to tell him where she was or not.

"You're certain of that?"

"I am ... I am a little surprised, Detective. If someone reported to the police that they've seen something suspicious, why weren't they able to go in and arrest the guy?"

"I assure you that we're doing everything we can."

"But until then, I just have to be holed up here?"

"Where?" he asked, sounding suspicious.

"At ... um ..." Amelia moved her mouth away from her phone and let out a deep sigh. All things considered, there was a possibility that the detective knew exactly where she was and what she was really doing. How uncomfortable of him to be so polite about it. "I'm safe, Detective. I might not be exactly where you want me to be, but I am safe."

He didn't say anything for a full minute. "Very well. Please let me know if you see anything suspicious wherever you are, and hopefully, we can get there in time," the detective replied. "We're all in this together. Nothing is accomplished by any one of us taking it easy during these hard times."

"Of course," replied Amelia.

"Thank you, Miss Gray. Have a nice day." And with that, the detective hung up.

Somewhere else in the apartment, Amelia heard the shower turn off. Wendy had finished her time in the bathroom. Which was good because she needed a car.

Wendy came out with a towel around her. She used another towel to rub the water out of her hair. "Hey, who was that? Damon?"

"Worse. It was Detective Corbett."

"Oh shit. He knows you left the apartment?"

"Well, he didn't, I don't think, but he does now, though not where I am exactly. The point was, he called up and wanted to know if there was any suspicious activity around my apartment. The place where I am supposed to be."

"But if there was any suspicious activity there, wouldn't you be in a worse state than you are now?"

"Exactly. Pretty sure that was how he knew I wasn't there."

"Shit ... well, I mean, I hope he could see that you being here is much safer."

"Wendy," Amelia interrupted, "can you get dressed? I need you to drive me back to my place."

"Wait, *what*?"

"I need to check on the apartment."

"That's so stupid. That's the worst thing you can do right now."

Amelia simply leaped up and started assembling outdoor clothes and stuffing things into her purse.

"One," Wendy continued, not letting up, "Damon will be looking for you there. Two, the police are probably stalking the place, so they'll see you showing up. Three ... you know what, that's all I have, and it's already pretty bad."

"Can you please get dressed? I need to go; we'll be in and out fast."

"But ... But why?"

"I'm just going to check on the place, see if there's anything wrong, maybe grab some stuff, and, and maybe Detective Corbett will be there seeing to things. I mean, he did know I was missing. Either way, it would be better him being there than Damon, anyway."

"And if Damon's there?"

"Then the police detective and I will really have something to talk about, because seriously, if Damon is there and they haven't grabbed him, then what the fuck are they doing for their paychecks?"

"Seriously, Amelia, what if Damon is there when you show up?"

"Let's just be in and out fast, okay? It'll be alright ... It'll be alright." Amelia knew that Wendy would never actually say that, so she was the one saying it, over and over again. She needed to hear it.

Wendy hopped into black sweats and a black hoodie—evidently, she was under the impression it was time to be a ninja, Amelia thought—and they went down to the parking lot to meet in front of the building to hop into Wendy's car and head back to Amelia's apartment.

Along the way, Amelia texted her building super and asked him if he would meet them at the entrance to the old tunnels. He warned her that she could be risking people's lives, including her own, by coming back, but Amelia was determined. Eventually, he agreed to keep watch, and if he saw any sign of Damon, he would text her. Amelia had agreed to text him when they arrived, and if the coast was clear, then they would hurry to the entrance, and he would let them in. It was the best, if not the only, way to get in and be assured that Damon wasn't around when she did so.

Parking the car in the same parking garage they'd left almost two weeks ago, Amelia looked around. There was no sign of Damon's car or the man himself. She wondered if there was any possibility that maybe he was watching her from the trees or the bushes just out of view. She thought how absurd it was to be so paranoid, jumping at the possibility of every shaking bush or gust of wind being her stalker. She texted the super to see if he'd seen any signs of Damon, but he gave them the thumbs-up.

With the coast seemingly clear, the two women got out of the car and approached the emergency door quickly. When they reached the metal door, Amelia didn't even have to knock; it was opened almost immediately by her building super, who waved them in.

Everybody believed her coming back to her apartment, even for a moment, was a bad idea.

Frankly, so did Amelia. But she had to know. She had to alleviate her concerns.

She wasn't going to let Damon force her to live her life in hiding.

Going back into the building through the basement, Amelia and Wendy climbed into the elevator and headed up to her apartment floor. The elevator doors opened, and the hallway was clear. *So far, so good*, Amelia thought. Turning right out of the elevator, they made their way to the end of the hall where Amelia's apartment was.

When they passed by Mark's apartment, Amelia pointed to it and turned to Wendy. "Maybe you can stop in, if you like."

Wendy looked a little taken aback. "Why?"

"I don't know," Amelia replied, shrugging. "I just thought you might like to—"

"Holy shit." Wendy froze.

Amelia looked behind her and understood why. Her door was closed, certainly. But there was damage to the wooden frame next to the doorknob. It was picked out, splintered, and forced. The paint job was scratched and scraped off. There was evidence that tools had been used. Probably a crowbar.

Somebody had broken in. They weren't even in the apartment, they didn't even try the door yet, and the assault on the doorway was so heavy and obvious, there was no way anybody could think somebody wasn't trying to break in. This work was shoddy.

Damon had been here.

"I'm calling that detective of yours," Wendy said, pulling out her phone.

Amelia didn't turn the knob; she just pushed against the door. She had to know what he'd done to her place. It opened easily. The doorknob was evidently damaged and now completely unusable.

As the door swung open, Amelia was too scared to turn

on the lights, so she simply squinted in the low light of the setting sun. Still though, the evidence of breaking and entering was obvious. There were muddy shoe prints all throughout the hall, suggesting that somebody had entered from the snow without trying to cover their tracks. Heading into the room, Amelia and Wendy carefully listened and observed, trying to sense if anybody else was in there as well.

*So far, so good*, Amelia thought, feeling the ice-cold air filling her chest.

"I explained to the detective we were here; he's on his way; he told us to stay out though—" Wendy started.

Amelia ignored her. She needed to see what he'd done. As she stepped into the apartment, she noticed her things had been ruffled around. The cushions of her couch were thrown to the floor, and her bedsheets looked like they'd been roughly handled. She wondered if somebody had been sleeping there.

"Amelia, look!"

She turned to Wendy and saw what she was referencing. Her intercom, the one that allowed her to buzz people in, had been violently ripped off the wall; it was now dangling from a few wires, the rest of them cut. Amelia knew why: this intercom system also doubled as a basic building security system. It would have gone off if there was any kind of forced entry. The fact that the wires were cut was the only reason it wasn't blaring right now.

The two women looked around the apartment for a little while longer, to see if there was any evidence of what Damon might have been doing. The bathroom had been used and not cleaned up after. There was a water glass in the sink. Her closet had some sweaters removed, which were tossed onto the bed. Shoe prints were everywhere. But all in all, it didn't look as if anything was taken or destroyed apart from the door and the intercom. By all accounts, Damon had entered the apartment, searched the place, and left.

If she had been there, Amelia thought, Damon would've found her. This was why her instincts were right for her to leave this place. She hoped Detective Corbett would understand that when he saw this mess.

She walked past her closet again to see if any of her jewelry might have been stolen and stopped when she noticed a little red light.

She looked closer and saw that the light was emanating from a tiny electronic device.

A spy camera!

Amelia couldn't believe it but couldn't stop staring at it as well.

It was an actual spy camera. Damon had broken into her place—extremely blatantly—and still had the nerve to hide a spy camera.

She ran the possibilities through her mind. Would he come back to pick up the recorded footage? Perhaps he really was that stupid, but there was a more obvious answer.

He wouldn't have to pick it up if it wasn't recording. If it was transmitting.

Because an obsessive psychotic like him would be watching through a camera like this all the time.

Which meant he was watching now.

He knew she was there.

## 33

"Wendy, come take a look at this."

Amelia was looking at the camera hidden in her closet. Damon Chase had broken into her apartment while she wasn't there, and installed a camera to alert him when she returned.

Wendy came across the apartment and asked, "What is it?"

Amelia pointed at the red light.

Wendy looked down. And then she stared. And then she stared some more. And then she just dropped her jaw and let it hang there, slack. "Is that a camera?"

Amelia barely registered her voice. It was like it was coming from far away through a thin length of tube. Somewhere miles away. Somewhere that didn't really exist. It might as well have been imaginary.

Amelia's world was stretching out. She felt dizzy. All she could see was that little red light coming from the camera. It stretched out until—

*"Hey! Amelia!"*

Amelia felt someone shaking her shoulders. It brought her back to reality. Wendy was witnessing Amelia descend into a state of shock, and needed to snap her out of it.

Amelia could take the camera right now and smash it. Better yet, they could drive down to the police station, hand it over as evidence, where it would be a means of tracking the signal to figure out where he was.

But Damon knew there was no point in leaving behind a camera that he wouldn't be able to follow, just so he could be found out and turned over to the police.

No, he was too smart for that. And far, far too obsessive.

The camera would be transmitting a live feed, which meant Damon had to be watching right now. In fact, he was probably hiding somewhere, watching, and waiting for his moment to strike. And the camera was small, with no external antenna. So its reach couldn't possibly be that great.

Which meant he was close.

Amelia looked over at Wendy. There was a look of terror on her face, just like that day outside the café in Brooklyn.

"We have to go," Amelia said. "We need to get out of here right now!"

"All right, let's go," replied Wendy.

Amelia started to run for the door, when Wendy called out behind her. "Should I take the thing?" she said, pointing back to the camera.

Amelia genuinely didn't know what the best option was. The camera was evidence; it was tech that the police could use to find Damon. If they left it, he might be able to pick it up later and use it on them again or maybe just get another if the cops confiscated it. Maybe he'd put it somewhere else, somewhere where they wouldn't find it, wouldn't suspect it.

The danger in Amelia's life felt really intense right now, and she wasn't thinking too clearly.

Except, she reasoned, if she grabbed the camera now, whatever feed Damon was watching would still be active. He'd see where they were and where they were going. Hell, maybe it had a GPS unit in it. Amelia couldn't promise that she would be able to turn it off. Maybe it would follow her all the way to the police station. Then, effectively, it would become a race to see whether Amelia or Damon could get to the station first. There was an obvious threat by taking the camera with them.

Amelia snapped to her senses. Damon was close. And he'd already had plenty of time to see the two of them on the camera. There was no point in worrying that she was putting the two of them in greater danger.

They already were in terrible danger no matter what they did. So they might as well do something that might help them in the process.

"All right, grab it," said Amelia, waving Wendy over. "Just go!"

Wendy grabbed the camera and quickly pocketed it.

The two friends ran for the door and were out in the hallway. They hopped into the elevator and hit the lobby button. They rode it down to the fifth floor, where it suddenly stopped.

The elevator doors opened.

Damon was standing there.

He looked surprised and happy to see Amelia.

She wasn't.

"Oh my God," he said, extending his arms for a passionate hug. "I thought I'd lost you."

He was about to say more, when Wendy reached out and

gave him a straight punch to the gut. Damon was walking full force at Amelia, and he hadn't been focused on anybody other than her, as if nothing in the world existed. He didn't even register there was another woman in the elevator, so he basically walked straight into the punch.

Keeling over, he grabbed his stomach in pain and grimaced, like he was about to be sick.

Before he could react, Wendy pulled her fist back, laying into him again. Then she clenched her fist and swung it upward sharply, straight into Damon's chin, sending him hurling backwards, into the wall of the elevator.

Amelia narrowly managed to miss him, stepping out of the way in the nick of time.

"Go!" Wendy yelled, grabbing Amelia's arm.

Whatever shock Amelia experienced evaporated. At that point, she certainly didn't need to be told twice.

The two of them stepped over Damon's legs, hopped onto the fifth floor, and bolted for the emergency stairway. Somewhere behind them, they could hear Damon scrambling to get back up and run after them.

They flung their weight against the metal emergency door, moving its massive weight out of the way so that they could make a break for the concrete stairway that would lead them down to the emergency exit.

Behind them, Damon yelled, "Amelia! Wait! Please! I'm sorry!"

They only got down about one and a half floors before they heard a huge crash, telling them that the door that gave them trouble was no problem for Damon. He simply rammed that door and blasted past it.

They weren't far enough ahead. And they weren't fast enough.

They did everything they could to run, all the same.

Leaping down entire stairwells, Wendy and Amelia kept a hand on the railing at all times, hoping that all their momentum would cause them to swing around and go down the stairs a few flights at a time. An irresponsible and dangerous way to tackle stairs, they knew, but, at this point, a twisted ankle would hardly matter, so long as they managed to escape this man.

When they got down to the second floor, Amelia glanced upward and could see Damon running, quickly and powerfully, just around the bend, a flight of stairs above them. He was being more reckless with the way he plummeted down the stairs. He was much faster than they were.

Amelia realized that Damon would surely catch up. And her body felt like it was going to go numb.

She didn't want him touching her. She didn't want to know what he felt like. She could taste him on her lips. She felt nauseous.

The numbness she was experiencing in all her extremities made it virtually impossible to know what the ground felt like underneath her feet as she ran. But she ran anyway. She charged so forcefully and so violently, she didn't care if she went crashing into anything sharp or dangerous.

For a moment, Amelia wondered if she was actually in a nightmare. It certainly felt like one. But she knew what would happen if Damon caught her. She couldn't picture having that much imagination when she was asleep.

She knew this was real. And she hated it.

She got to the emergency escape door just a moment before Wendy did, and she used all her momentum to throw her shoulder against the handle, forcing the door open with a violent strength she never imagined herself having. Practically stumbling as she exited the door, she caught her footing and only slowed down to look behind her to see if Wendy was still there.

Fortunately, the door was thrown wide open, so Wendy charged on through, top speed. She was still there.

Unfortunately, so was Damon.

Amelia turned. In front of her was a rampway that led down into a small parking area next to all the basketball courts. If she ran down that way, she could go around the basketball courts and make a break directly for the parking garage where Wendy's car was located. It was the only option she had left.

She raced down, with Wendy hot on her heels. She could hear Damon's weight hitting the ground behind her.

As she was about to come up on the basketball courts, Amelia's body froze again when she realized what a horrible idea this was. They were running farther away from the main street, where all the cars and local traffic were speeding by. Here, nobody would see some guy was chasing her. There were no streetlights here; it was hard to make anything out. If she called out for help, nobody would ever hear her.

She could see the parking garage. She ran for it. It was all she had left.

Somewhere behind her, she heard commotion and had just enough time to register it before she felt an impressively large arm reach around her waist and apply pressure, slowing her down. She was flipped around and forced against the chain-link fence that separated her from the basketball court.

Damon was pressing her up against the fence. He was struggling to grab one of her arms, as she realized what he was trying to do and started flailing her other arm, hitting him against his shoulder, his head, trying to push him away. For the most part, trying to keep him from grabbing her other arm.

She didn't want Damon to lock her wrists together and hold her up against the fence by force. With his strength, she knew that he could use just one hand to hold her wrists down and effectively put her arms out of use.

"Oh God," he said, struggling with her arms, forcing his face into the crook of her neck. When he wasn't talking, she could feel his tongue gliding up and around her ear. It felt thick, like Vaseline. It melted. It felt like it was staining her. "Oh God, I thought I'd lost you," he said.

He almost had her in his grasp when Wendy flung herself over and started bashing him on the back of the head. It obviously affected him, but not severely enough. Still powerful, he flipped around and punched her in the chest, sending her heaving to the ground.

Then he was back on Amelia. But her arms were loose now, and at least she could punch him with her fists as much as she could. Damon would have to start over now if he wanted to hold her down.

In a second, he grabbed her left wrist and shoved it up against the chain-link fence again. She knew that he wouldn't have to wait very long.

Her whole body shook. This didn't feel like a nightmare anymore.

Nightmares ended. This wouldn't.

Amelia felt Damon apply his lips to her throat and heard him moaning in a hideous ecstasy. The whole situation was so awful, she didn't register that she heard barking as well for a moment.

The barking got closer and became a snarl as Damon turned around and just barely got his own arms in front of his face before a poodle leaped out of nowhere and nearly bit it off.

Amelia dove out of the way, watching in a kind of terrified amusement as Damon wrestled with the vicious poodle. His brute strength was just about to get the dog off him, when a small gang of Labradors, Great Danes, and various other eager dogs leaped out from the darkness and hurtled straight at the man. Mark's dogs, Amelia thought.

Now, Damon was the one howling in fright.

She ran over to Wendy, who had a murderous look on her face, like she was infuriated that she wouldn't be able to get her hands on Damon again. Too many dogs, and a hell of a good opportunity to get out of there. They both knew it.

She looked around for Mark, but didn't see him anywhere. He had to be close by, but she didn't have time to find him. She and Wendy needed to get away and call Detective Corbett again. Amelia wondered where the heck he was; had he gotten to the apartment yet? Was he wondering where they were? Would he look for them?

They bolted, not stopping for anything, not even to glance back and see if Damon was being torn apart. The fact that they couldn't hear him running behind them was good enough.

First thing, they made their way to the parking garage where Wendy's car was parked. They hopped in, powered up the engine, and started to reverse with full force.

Wendy put the car into drive and was just turning for the exit when they both caught a glimpse of Damon limping after them with several dogs chasing after him.

Wendy floored it, pumping gas into the engine and driving straight for the exit.

Amelia looked back and saw Damon shaking off the dogs and then hopping into a car and slamming the door. She looked on in horror, praying the dogs got out of the way. The worst part was he'd parked almost right next to them. They never even knew it.

The biggest thing she noticed, though, was that he wasn't driving his usual car. It was an old clunker and a hideous pink. Obviously, Damon was rolling around in a new vehicle.

He had deliberately gotten himself a new vehicle so he could escape surveillance by the police in order to keep going after Amelia. Hell, maybe he even stole it. And somehow, in the back of her mind, Amelia knew that the crazy bastard still didn't think he was doing anything wrong.

When Wendy was out on the street, she didn't let up on the gas and likely violated several traffic laws by running various red lights and making extremely sharp turns throughout the streets of Manhattan. By the time she finally slowed down, Amelia couldn't see the pink car anywhere behind her.

"Thank God," Amelia said, finally breathing a sigh of relief. "But the camera. What if it has GPS or something?"

"Central precinct is not too far away; call Detective Corbett and tell him we're headed there," Wendy said, driving far more sensibly now, but still trying to control her breathing and her anger. "Even if he was tracking the camera, it'll be in the hands of the cops by then."

"That sounds good," Amelia said, whipping out her phone.

She made the call and briefly spoke to the detective and then quickly texted Mark, planning to thank him.

> Where were you? How did you get those dogs out there?

After a moment he texted back.

> I just let them loose. Now I gotta go find them all. Worth it?

Amelia smiled. She texted him a winky face, followed by:

> Totally! Thank you so much!

Mark had saved their lives. She wished he were here. She wanted to hold him. She wanted to know what it felt like to be held by somebody who felt ...

... Who made her feel good again.

And, of course, just as the thought entered her mind, another text came up on her phone.

> Get back here. You're mine.

## 34

A melia and Wendy sat in the police station, at the desk of Detective Corbett, who'd said he was turning around and would be right behind them. When he arrived, they handed over the camera, which he slid into a plastic evidence bag.

Amelia realized something she thought was important. She told the detective that surely the reason why Damon stopped the elevator on the fifth floor of her building was because he was *staying* there.

Detective Corbett promised to investigate. He then took a very deep breath, exhaled, and asked, "So are you ready to tell me where you are living now?"

After giving Wendy a quick glance, she confessed that she'd moved over to Wendy's place and basically kept herself locked down there. She provided the detective with an address and contact info.

Corbett gave off the feeling of a man who was calm and rational about everything. Like a teacher. Or maybe a protective father.

It was a little strange, but Amelia thought how she wished she felt this more often in her life.

She also sent the detective the latest round of texts from Damon and asked if he'd seen her apartment yet.

"Not yet, I was nearly there when I got your second call. You shouldn't have gone in there; however, from what you've told me, it wouldn't have mattered, since you ran into him on the elevator." He frowned. "We'll get some officers over there to secure the apartment. I'm glad you weren't there, just for the record. I know I told you to stay hunkered down, but considering what happened, getting out of there when you did was a wise decision."

Amelia felt a little better about her deception after that.

"My only complaint would be you keeping me out of the loop. Had he gotten to you, I wouldn't know where to start looking. Don't do it again," he said sternly.

"Yes, sir." Amelia nodded.

She went on to tell him what she could about the car Damon was currently driving. Mainly that it was pink and would hopefully be easy to find, considering the color. How many pink cars could there be? The detective then gave them permission to head on out and get some rest. Now, it was time to go home.

Along the way, Wendy couldn't help but point out that, rather obviously, a police car was tailing them.

"You know," Wendy finally blurted out, "somehow, I imagined that if the police were following me, it would be because some guy was making out with me while I was driving. Not for something like this."

"At least this way you won't get a ticket," Amelia responded. "Glass half full."

Soon they arrived at Wendy's apartment. She pulled into

her underground parking lot, and the police car, mercifully, didn't follow. Both women knew, however, that the car would probably be circling the neighborhood or parked nearby.

Wendy's block was now their new stakeout location.

The two of them called it a day. They both went to bed, but struggled to sleep. Fortunately, Amelia didn't have anywhere to go the next morning, and Wendy decided to tell her job to either fire her or give her a day off the next morning. Effectively, the two of them could sleep into the afternoon all they wanted. They felt they'd earned it.

Once Amelia finally did wake up, she found Wendy making them pancakes with strawberries. She gratefully accepted a plate while checking her phone. There were, of course, the hundred or so texts from Damon. New ones that she hadn't gotten a chance to show to the detective.

The detective had also left a message. The camera found in her apartment was transmitting to a fifth-floor apartment, where Damon was staying. Even though that apartment, she knew, was rented by a retired and wealthy nice elderly couple. Apparently, according to Corbett, nobody had heard from them in a while. He said they would stake out her old home and regularly check on the apartment where Damon was squatting.

And there were several phone calls from her mother, from first thing this morning.

Amelia called her parents immediately.

"Hello?" her mother yelled into the phone the moment she picked it up. "Cara?"

"No, Mom, it's me," Amelia said. "Why were you calling me? What's going on with Cara?"

The moment Amelia said her sister's name out loud, her body froze. She remembered what all of this was about.

She already knew.

"God, Amelia," her mother cried. "Have you heard from Cara? She hasn't called; she hasn't accessed her father's bank account in three days. Is she with you? Do you know where she is?"

"Mom," Amelia said, her heart breaking, "I tried telling you, almost a week ago, remember? Damon killed Sam. I tried to—"

"What does any of this have to do with where Cara is now?"

Amelia shook her head, letting it sink into her open palm. "I think Damon may have killed Cara."

"Oh, what the hell is wrong with you?" her mother snapped. "We don't have time for your mental illness, Amelia."

"What?"

"Do you know where Cara is or not?"

"Mom, I tried to tell you what was going to happen to her. You cut me off. She cut me off. Didn't the police come by and talk to you? To her?"

"Amelia, I couldn't believe you dragged the cops into your delusions! I told them it was ridiculous."

Amelia wanted to shake her.

"I can't believe you think Damon has actually hurt your sister. That is what you're saying, isn't it?" she demanded.

"That's what I think happened. I tried to warn you it would happen. You brushed me off. That's what the police believe too. He's gotten to her, I'm sure of it."

"I can't believe that handsome man has anything to do with this; it's unrelated."

"That's ridiculous, Mom."

"*Ridiculous!* You think I am being ridiculous? No. It's you who are being ridiculous!"

"Yes, you are! You weren't listening to me then, and ... and I can't imagine you're listening to me now. I mean, you're going to find out about the same time I am, I guess. And that's all there is to it." There was no reaching her mom.

"I can't believe this, you selfish little—"

Amelia didn't quite hear the rest of her words, as by then, her mother had hung up.

Didn't matter. They both got what they needed, Amelia realized. Her mother confirmed that Amelia didn't know anything about Cara's whereabouts. And Amelia now knew that her sister hadn't been seen anywhere for three days, three days during which she hadn't accessed her parents' funds. Which, knowing her, was quite impossible.

Wendy looked over when Amelia put down the phone and asked her what had happened. Amelia told her everything.

And then she couldn't understand why she was crying. Her sister was a horrid little monster. She had destroyed everything she was ever given. She had hurt Amelia so much.

And Amelia felt now like her sister had died all over again. Even after when she first knew Damon was after Cara, and she knew somehow that her death was inevitable.

Now it was done. And the world felt hollow for it.

Wendy held her, and they swayed together. Amelia didn't know why she felt so torn apart. But she needed her friend.

After that, she sat down and finished her pancakes. They didn't taste like anything, and they didn't feel real. Then she slumped on the couch and let the world pass her by for another day.

The next day, Wendy revealed that Detective Corbett had called her, trying to reach Amelia, as she wasn't picking up her phone. Somewhere in the background, Amelia vaguely heard Wendy telling her that they had found Cara's body in an upscale hotel suite. Wendy was crying for her friend and for her dead sister.

Amelia wasn't certain if she was crying or accepting the news emotionlessly. It all felt the same at this point.

Then the day just kind of existed. She knew Wendy was being very kind to her, very gentle. Feeding her, walking her into the shower. Amelia was aware of it happening, just not feeling connected at all.

Then the next day, Amelia was vaguely aware of Wendy answering the door and bringing back Detective Corbett. The police hadn't completed a full investigation of the crime scene or even a full autopsy investigation yet, but he asked Amelia to come down to the coroner's office. They needed a family member to legally identify the body of Cara Gray.

Amelia asked him why she was the one called to do it and not her parents. He explained that they had asked her parents to identify Cara, but they were angry, blaming the police for allowing their daughter to die and refusing to go to the coroner's office.

So Amelia and Wendy found themselves in the backseat of a police car.

And then Amelia found herself in the coroner's lab. Some official in a white lab coat was reporting to Amelia about what they'd found in her sister's body. A puncture wound in her neck, plus lethal amounts of heroin. They asked Amelia if Cara had a history of drug use.

Amelia knew that Cara wasn't, by any means, prudish. But

at the same time, she wasn't necessarily throwing herself toward drugs either. Her sister was more into sex than anything else, really. It was entirely possible that she had gone her entire life without ever experiencing recreational drugs unless it got her laid somehow. Or negatively affected Amelia.

Also, Amelia knew that vain, vapid Cara would never use her neck as an injection site, since it would be far too visible and ruin her perfect appearance. In her mind, this was the strongest evidence that she didn't use drugs: they just got in the way of seducing men.

Amelia shook her head, and Wendy, amazingly, pretty much repeated to the coroner exactly what Amelia was thinking, almost as if she could read her mind. She explained to him that there was no way that Cara's death could be a suicide or an overdose. That, given recent events in Amelia's life, Cara was more than likely the target of her sister's stalker.

Amelia smiled for the first time in days. She knew she had her best friend in the world standing next to her.

After the questions, the lab staff finally wheeled out a gurney, on which lay a body covered by a blanket. They then asked Amelia to identify her as they removed the covering from the body, revealing the upper torso and face of the corpse underneath.

Amelia had never seen a dead body in real life before. And she'd certainly never thought that it would be somebody in her family under such circumstances.

But now, any stupor, any fucked-up-beyond-the-universe state she was floating in, immediately erased itself as the adrenaline forced itself into her blood at the sight of her sister's dead body.

Cara was pale. Everything on her torso was sagging and horrendous.

And the look on her face. Not serenity, not horror, not terror. Just a sad acceptance that this was happening. This was happening, and there was no stopping it.

Because, in Amelia's mind, there was no stopping Damon.

Damon chose to do this.

*No*, Amelia said to herself with conviction. *No, not again. Never again.*

She would put a stop to it. There was no hope for her stalker, her sister's killer now.

By the time they got back into the detective's car, Amelia still hadn't said a word. There was nothing to say, and those around her simply accepted it as Amelia being overwhelmed with shock and sadness, so they gave her all the time and space she needed.

Amelia didn't feel overwhelmed with shock and sadness. If anything, she felt like she could punch through a wall.

Once the two women were dropped off at Wendy's apartment with an armed guard outside the building to be sure they stayed safe, Amelia whipped out her phone and dialed Damon Chase.

It hadn't rung long when he picked up.

"Hey, babe," he said casually.

"My sister is dead. You killed her."

Damon half-heartedly laughed on the other end, as if feigning awkward surprise. "Excuse me?" he said.

"You murdered my sister. You murdered my ex-husband. You murdered your wife. You murdered her best friend, and you murdered her partner. You killed my sister. *Fuck you,* you killed my sister!"

"Amelia, you need to calm down. I think you're going a little overboard here."

"I'm going to get you caught, and you're going to go in a hole, and if there is some way to make sure you are executed, I will be there to watch it happen to you. I will end you."

"Okay, Amelia, I think you need to call me some other time. You're hysterical, and you're not making any sense. I mean, seriously, think about it: even if I did kill her, which, again, you're being completely crazy right now, I mean ... she wasn't a good person to you. I would think you'd be happy that you were finally free from her."

"You are going to die."

"Yeah, well, not before everybody who has hurt you."

"What?"

"Trust me, Amelia. Just hold on a little while longer."

"Wait, what are you—"

Damon hung up.

Amelia wasn't confused or even the slightest bit unsure. There were only two people left in her life who'd hurt her, who were still alive.

## 35

After Amelia had identified her sister's body, Detective Corbett scheduled a visit with her parents so he could tell them about Cara's death in person. Amelia went with him, especially considering she suspected Damon was going after them. She had extremely low expectations about the visit, but she still had to try. She hoped the detective would help make them understand what had really happened to their youngest daughter, and realize the danger they were in.

"Apparently," said Detective Corbett, "the hotel cleaning staff ignored the room at first because the door handle had one of those 'do not disturb signs' on it. However, when the lobby clerk checked if the room had been cleaned for the next guest, the cleaning staff informed them of the sign, so the clerk double-checked their files. The client had only rented the room for a single evening, so it was assumed the sign was put up in error. That's when they entered and found young Miss Gray on the bed. Dead."

Amelia nodded. She looked over to her right and saw her

mother and her father in the room, sitting and standing respectively, listening. She wanted to see if there was any reaction from either of them about Cara's death.

There was none from her mother. Her eyes were dark and red from crying, and she was evidently spending the afternoon struggling to look composed. She stared off somewhere into the distance, trying to fathom the idea of her daughter being dead. Her favorite daughter. Gone forever.

The look on her face, Amelia thought, spoke volumes: she was obviously under the impression that this death was unfair. A slight against her and her family. It was wrong. She wanted somebody to blame. But first and foremost, she wanted the nightmare to end. She wanted her baby girl back.

As for her father, Amelia couldn't see his face at all: he was turned away. Standing up against the wall, leaning toward a bookshelf, one hand in his pocket, the other hand holding a small glass of whisky sour. It looked like he was desperately trying not to be seen.

Amelia presumed that the detective was allowing this because he assumed that her father—a real man's man—didn't want a stranger to see him crying. Amelia knew better.

"As you can imagine," the detective continued, "the hotel notified the police immediately. At first, I wasn't involved, until they identified your daughter's car in the hotel parking lot. The license plate was traced back to, well, you, Mr. and Mrs. Gray."

Amelia could tell why the detective was stammering on the subject of the car. Given that this was a tragic experience for the two parents in front of him, he was trying not to be rude and accusatory, but Amelia picked up on the small detail: if the reason they couldn't fully identify Cara was because she had no ID on her, then how the hell could she drive a car without a driver's license?

Amelia already knew the answer: her parents pretty much let Cara do whatever she wanted. Amelia wondered if Cara had ever even bothered to get a driver's license. Her mom and dad would just let her have the car and call it a night. Actually, if they knew she was going to use the car to go round up Damon, they'd probably have encouraged it.

Amelia was sure that her mother had been thinking, *Cara? In trouble? With Damon? Perish the thought.*

Detective Corbett set out photos of the crime scene on the table. Amelia had insisted that he bring photographic evidence of Cara's dead body. Anything less, and her parents wouldn't believe it.

"As you can see from the photographs," the detective continued, pointing to the evidence, "there's a clear puncture on the right side of the neck, which is the entry point of the syringe used to inject lethal amounts of heroin into the bloodstream. Overdose would've been severe, but, mercifully, it would've been relatively quick."

The detective had trouble making eye contact with Amelia's mom and dad. He sounded as if he was about to stammer. As far as she could tell, Corbett was having difficulty communicating with her parents because he was presenting them with photographs of Cara's naked corpse and detailing the manner in which she perished. He was waiting for some sort of reaction.

The more Amelia looked at her parents, the more she knew the detective wouldn't get a reaction from them. But he didn't know them as well as she did.

"As you can see here," he said, pointing with a shaky finger toward one photograph of Cara's head, "there's some bruising around the neck and a lot of pressure upon the jugular. Although, it wasn't strong enough to damage the trachea or even prevent breathing. This would typically be the type of indentations found on a person who was being held by the neck rather than strangled. It's currently assumed that the perpetrator was simply trying to hold Cara down, and applying strength to keep her from struggling as he ... used the syringe." Detective Corbett took a deep breath.

Amelia saw her mother's gaze gravitate toward the photos of Cara. She started shaking a little, and her jaw dropped the slightest amount. Evidently, she was wondering if this was all she would ever see of her daughter again, just these naked, dead photos. She was trying to reason it out, fathom its meaning.

She was trying to comprehend that this was all she was ever going to have of her daughter from now on.

"Forgive me, if this is upsetting," said the detective, "but I should let you know that in the interest of following up on details from another related investigation, we checked Cara's body for evidence of assault of a ... sexual nature. And what I can tell you, if it will ease your mind, is that there wasn't any. In fact, there appears to have been no sexual activity, at least not for several days before. The bruising on her wrists probably came from—"

"What?"

Amelia and the detective looked up at her mother, who had finally spoken up. She wouldn't stop shaking though.

"I'm sorry?" asked Corbett.

"What do you mean? She was in a relationship. With a man. At the time."

Amelia desperately wanted to speak up but remembered

her last phone conversation with her mother. And, frankly, all the ones before that. This was not the time to get into a fight. Maybe the detective would have more luck. Though she wasn't counting on it.

"Can you elaborate?" asked Detective Corbett.

"She was going to that hotel to meet with her boyfriend. Damon, a young man whom ... Amelia knew."

"Damon Chase?"

"Yes, that's his name. He's such a charming man. Have you been able to find him?"

"We're still working on it. But we've been held back by a lack of—"

"He has to find out what's happened to his girlfriend. I don't want him to think that we were keeping it from him." Her mother started wiping her eyes, pushing tears away.

Detective Corbett, however, looked even more confused. "His ... girlfriend?"

"Yes. At first, I thought you were going to tell me that he was found there, as well. Maybe whoever attacked her went after both of them. But if he's still alive ..."

The detective turned to stare at Amelia.

Amelia shook her head and closed her eyes. She couldn't begin to imagine how to explain to the detective that her parents were completely unaware of the truth of who Damon was.

"Mrs. Gray, as I've explained before," the detective said slowly, "Damon Chase is the suspect here. When I called before and warned you about Mr. Chase stalking Amelia, you said you understood. Now we have evidence that your daughter Cara had been using her cell phone to contact him and, in fact, called him several times the night of her death. We have hotel security camera footage of the two of them going up to the room, but only Mr. Chase leaving. We've also accumulated significant evidence about Mr. Chase's obsessions with your daughter Amelia. As I mentioned before, he's been stalking her, threatening her and people associated with her. We also know that he has a history with women he knows being found dead."

The detective didn't receive any response from her mother, which obviously shocked him even further.

She knew her mother wouldn't say anything because she liked being the queen of her household and did not want to appear to be hysterical or embarrass herself in front of a stranger invited into her home.

But Amelia was not surprised when her mother gave her a look. A silent glower, a disdainful, stabbing glance.

That stare of accusatory disappointment. With which she wanted to make it clear to Amelia that her accusations were simply not allowed.

In that angry look, her mother told Amelia that she was being selfish for destroying Damon's image. What a pathetic waste of a daughter.

And how dare she—with her very presence—have the nerve to make it clear to her mother that she was all that was left of her family.

With the exception, of course, of Amelia's father.

Amelia took one last look at him still leaning up against the wall. He was trying to keep his expression hidden, but, from her standpoint, she could make out the expression on his face.

He was angry and disappointed, yes. But he also looked like he was finally released.

## 36

D etective Corbett strongly urged her parents to move to a friend's house or to a hotel because Damon had made a threat toward them as well.

But they flat out refused. They did not believe they were in danger. They simply believed that their only remaining daughter was being selfish for focusing on herself. They believed she was grateful that Cara was dead.

In truth, Amelia wasn't grateful that Cara was dead. She wasn't happy that anybody ever died. She just knew that Cara's death was unnecessary and cruel. It was painful and sad, the conclusion to a painful and sad life.

With nothing left to say to her parents, Detective Corbett drove Amelia all the way from Connecticut back to New York. He was in a plain car, though, Amelia noted, he did have a black strip on the windshield and all the equipment for flashing lights and a siren, in case they were needed.

Looking forward, she couldn't help but notice that there were a few other cars heading back along the same freeway on the same route toward New York for a very long time.

And they all had these black strips on their windshield as well.

The detective had arranged a police escort. And it wasn't hard to figure out why.

If Damon couldn't find out where Amelia was hiding, now that he knew for certain that she wasn't in her regular home, he would surely start going after all the locations associated with her and see if she would show up there.

And from there, follow her home.

It was something that she only realized when the detective came to pick her up to take her to New Haven in the first place. Damon had been to her parents' home on several occasions. They would've been an obvious target for him to track her down. Perhaps that was the only reason they were still alive. If they were all dead, then Amelia would have no reason to ever return to this place. And, therefore, he would've lost the only opportunity to catch her coming here.

Despite the fact that Damon knew she hated her parents. Amelia never wished to be anywhere near her mother again.

Which, Amelia had to concede, was probably a conclusion that Damon would arrive at eventually. It was only a matter of time before his sick, twisted mind decided that maybe the reason Amelia didn't want to be with him was because she was still too depressed, thanks to all these mean people in their lives.

And he would, probably, take care of them as well. He'd said as much.

But Damon was also smart enough to know that her parents were the last people she wanted to be near. After Cara's murder, the police would be swarming all over her family.

If anything, Damon would be out looking for her other

contacts. Wendy was the obvious one. He had seen her on several occasions, usually on their dog walks. Once in Brooklyn. And certainly on the night he assaulted her, when she was doing her damnedest to beat him to a pulp. There was a possibility that if he'd started stalking Amelia early enough, then maybe he would've already known the address of her best friend. The fact that there wasn't any indication that he'd ever gone near her place was a good sign, but Amelia knew it was only a matter of time.

Another person she hadn't considered was her agent. Damon had already contacted Margo, pretending to be Amelia's boyfriend, wanting to get more information from her. She would be a very logical choice to go after.

Amelia knew her agent was not to be trifled with. After all, Margo was practiced at dealing with lots of clients, many of whom were dealing with strange scenarios, including unwanted attention from obsessive individuals. However, that didn't change the fact that Damon wouldn't think twice about torturing the information out of her. And since she wouldn't knowingly have anything to give to him, then he might well torture her until she died.

And that would be another death that would hang upon Amelia's shoulders.

Margo was the woman who gave Amelia her livelihood and her confidence. She didn't want to repay her in such an awful way.

Amelia was so lost in thought that she hardly noticed that Detective Corbett was getting closer to Wendy's apartment building. She was only minutes away from her new temporary home.

She kept looking around, and saw the various police cars breaking off, though a few remained. They were probably going to go back to whatever it was they had been doing before driving up to Connecticut. She imagined most of them were simply heading home.

*Home*, Amelia thought.

She wondered if Damon would put two and two together and realize that it wasn't sensible for him to get assaulted by so many dogs in a single evening. And then make the connection to her little dog-walking ventures, which he'd obviously spied upon.

Maybe he would track down Mark.

What if he went back to hurt him?

She'd held Mark so close that she could still feel the way his face glided past her neck when she closed her eyes. She didn't want that body scratched. She didn't want to think that any harm that might come to him would be her fault.

She also didn't know how to warn him. After all, how do you warn somebody that they have to hide because somebody might be coming to kill them?

That was not how she wanted to be remembered by Mark.

She didn't want Damon to define her life. She didn't want Damon to win.

Finally, Detective Corbett's car was the only one left, and he pulled up to Wendy's building, confidently and without looking around, though Amelia saw the unmarked police car parked on the street with the officer in it. Despite her previous opinions about their incompetence, the other officers had probably confirmed that Damon was nowhere to be found. A double-edged sword, really.

He escorted her to Wendy's door and said goodbye once she was safely inside.

Wendy gave Amelia a big hug. She didn't even know

what had happened today, but she knew well enough to understand that her best friend would probably need one.

Amelia had no idea how to repay Wendy's kindness. She had no way to express to Wendy just how grateful she was that Wendy was helping to save her life. And risking hers in the process.

Amelia realized that pretty much everyone she knew was now in danger. Mark. Her agent. Her best friend. Her parents.

Cara's death was the continuation of a problem that her mother refused to acknowledge, but Amelia knew was ongoing.

Damon was still out there. And he was going to find ways to make her life much, much harder.

## 37

Amelia handed off her most recent series of paintings to the courier. Then that courier headed off to the secret location to deliver them to her agent or to one of the selected few people whom Margo trusted to represent her.

Wendy had gone off to do some shopping and hadn't been there when the courier arrived. She'd said she'd be back later in the afternoon, and that Amelia should try to relax and stay safely inside. She had assured Wendy that she intended to lock herself up in the apartment. First though, she briefly took a moment to text Mark and be absolutely certain that he was okay. He insisted that he was and, to help alleviate some of her concerns, even sent her some photos of himself holding some of his happy dogs.

It felt weird to be laughing and enjoying herself, but those goofy pictures, of all things, could actually pull it off.

Otherwise, it had been a pretty silent time. Ever since she'd learned that the police had been staking out her old home, visiting the fifth-floor apartment where Damon had been squatting—the old couple, the Perrys, who lived there had still not been located—she expected that Damon would be extra careful about his actions. To a certain extent, she was right. She had not seen or heard from Damon ever since the assault.

Ever since his final messages.

Which was a very worrying thought. Because it surely meant that he was planning something.

Hence, why she'd spent the last several days painting. Channeling her inner violence, her inner screams. Attacking the canvas in new ways. She suspected that this burst of creativity would probably come to nothing, and this would likely be her worst series of paintings out of everything she'd created recently.

But that didn't really matter to her. The important thing was that she remained active. That she constantly have some work to do so that she would never find herself bored or contemplative.

She knew that if she weren't screaming on the inside while jabbing paint at her canvases, she would likely be screaming on the outside, ripping out her hair and bashing her fists against the wall.

If this was to be the rest of her life, she wondered if she should even try to keep going.

That thought gave her pause. Granted, she shook her head, cast the thoughts aside, and realized that it was only frustration speaking. But she didn't like the idea that she would even entertain it.

She never asked for her life to be like this. Or for it to include this hardship.

At this point, all she could do was simply paint through

it. Pick up a brush, a palette, and start seeing where the slashes and jabs took her.

Now, resting in the dark—she had painted for several days straight and desperately needed a break; all the while, there was nothing on the TV or the radio that she cared for —she simply stared up, trying to see if the streetlights of New York would be bright enough to make all the little dots in the ceiling look like something different. Some sort of film noir environment? An imaginary array of mountains and forests? Or simply some plaster? It could be anything; it could be everything.

All she knew was that it was scarcely a distraction. She was obviously very restless and very aware of the danger her friends and family were in. She just knew that occupying her time with counting the dots kept her from thinking that she was helpless to stop any of it.

Detective Corbett insisted that there were some promising signs. That by tracking the signal from the camera she'd provided, they were able to identify the IP code of the computer Damon must've been using to view the images from the camera. It was obviously a computer with Wi-Fi capabilities if it was picking up the signal from the camera, so it wasn't offline. Now, if he ever used that computer, connected it to a network, they would have a chance to find out when and where that activity was happening.

Assuming they worked fast enough. And that the network provider was compliant with police tracking.

So, ultimately, it came down to luck.

She was upset by this and tried to think about it as little as possible. But she was also trying not to be too upset by it. As she'd gotten to know Detective Corbett, she could tell that he was genuinely concerned. That he was really trying to help her by finding Damon.

That it was bothering him that the man wasn't already caught.

As long as Detective Corbett was on the case, Amelia could feel confident that no matter how frustrated she felt, there was somebody out there who understood. For whatever that was worth.

In time, Wendy returned to the apartment and began putting away the shopping she'd done. That afternoon there was a ping on her phone, alerting her to the transfer of funds into Amelia's bank account, exactly as she'd anticipated in exchange for the paintings. *Good*, Amelia thought. More money she couldn't spend as she might want, possibly for the rest of her life.

Then she looked at Wendy's positive face and reminded herself to try to be less cynical. After all, her friend was doing everything she could to help her.

At about the same time that Wendy went off to her room to get changed, Amelia saw her phone vibrating on the table. And then vibrate again.

So unless it was a series of texts—which, she wouldn't put past Damon, though he had stopped recently—then it was a phone call. Also, something she hadn't experienced in quite some time.

She looked over at her phone, with trepidation.

She saw that the number belonged to her mother. This, though obviously much safer than the Damon option, also gave Amelia pause. Her mother could've been calling for any number of reasons. To cry about Cara. To blame Amelia for Cara's death. Since Amelia wanted to know where her mother's mind was going, she decided to answer.

"Hey, Mom," she said.

"Hey, beautiful."

The whole world caved in. She felt like she was about to vomit up her own stomach. Everything she'd done to try to relax had just come to a sudden stop and been replaced with all the intensity of any anxiety she had ever felt. She felt completely helpless.

"Hey," Damon continued, "you still there?"

"What are you doing in my parents' house?"

"Oh, good, you're still there. I was worried we'd been cut off. You know, I remember using landlines as a kid, but I don't have any recollection of them being shoddy, so it's not like I was expecting something else—"

"Why are you there?"

"God, I've missed your voice. I love you."

"What is this? What is going on? Are my parents dead?"

"Hey, your wish is my command."

"*No!* God, what are you doing?"

"I'm just finishing what I promised. We were supposed to make sure that all the people who have hurt you would never hurt you again. That was the brief, yes? I've taken care of Sam and Cara; now they're the last ones. I've got them here."

Everything in Amelia's chest felt like lead. She'd known this was coming, but she'd been desperately hoping it never would. That maybe she was wrong.

Despite knowing it was just a matter of time.

"Don't worry," Damon continued. "They're alive for the moment. Both of them tried to jump me, or jump as much as senior citizens can, I guess. So I gave them a shot of heroin. I wish I'd done more to them. I know they've been horrible to you, but I didn't want to risk you missing out. I know you would've loved this."

Amelia didn't want to bungle up her words, so she tried to keep it straight in her head. This was going to require a lot of improvisation and quick thinking. "Fuck no, you, um, you've done enough to them. I'm all good now. I love you."

It was really all she had left. If she made Damon feel as if his job was over, as if he'd finally won her love, then his *mission* was over. No more killing.

Her parents would still be alive.

There was a long silence. Amelia could hear whimpering from her mother on the other end.

Finally, Damon spoke up, sounding like he was about to cry. "What?" he asked.

"I-I said I love you," Amelia said as convincingly as she could. "I want you. I want you in my life. I need you. Please let me come over there; then we can run off together and leave all this behind us."

And hopefully, she thought, leave her parents safely behind.

She heard the sound of furniture moving on the other end, as if Damon was so elated that he just started knocking over chairs and tables. He let out an incredible scream of pure elation. As though everything he'd ever wanted was coming true.

Amelia realized that she was hearing Damon at his most honest. At his happiest.

At his most deluded.

"Please come over to your parents' house," he cried out, almost sounding like he was about to cry. "I'll keep them here until we're ready to get rid of them." And then he hung up.

Amelia did not like the sound of that. She didn't want to think that he was holding them as some sort of congratulatory reward for when she arrived.

Most likely, he was lying to himself about how he had just taken a house full of hostages.

She called out, "Wendy!"

"What happened?" Wendy said, running into the living room.

"It's Damon. He's holding my parents hostage." Amelia ran around the room hysterically, grabbing her phone, her purse, hopping into her shoes.

"Whoa, no!" Wendy yelled. "You can't go. He'll kill you. Or he'll kill them."

"He'll kill them anyway. I have to go."

"Well, call the police, then."

"He'll murder them the moment he hears the sirens. I can't let that happen, Wendy, I can't. I may not like my parents very much, but I can't let him kill them." Amelia fretted.

"Call Detective Corbett; he'll have a plan on how to get to him without going in sirens blazing."

"He'll hold me at gunpoint if he knows I'm going, and he'll stop me." Amelia stopped and turned to Wendy. "Can you call him after I'm already on my way?"

"Amelia—"

"He already knows Damon is going after everyone I know who he thinks has hurt me. Corbett has to know I have to go and try to stop him, convince him that I've made up with my parents. I have to try, Wendy."

"Fine. I'll wait ten minutes. Maybe he'll meet you on the road."

"Thank you," she said as she picked up Wendy's keys.

Amelia violated every traffic law on the freeways between New York and Connecticut. She got to her parents' house in record time. She was terrified the entire way that maybe Damon would get bored or angry or change his mind on a whim. And start shooting.

She had to put a stop to this.

Pulling into the driveway and leaping out of the car as it came to a stop, she dove through the front door of her childhood home ...

... And saw two bodies.

## 38

A melia gasped. The bodies belonged to two of the cleaning staff. One of them was a new girl she didn't know. The other one was an older woman. Maria. Amelia remembered telling her jokes and playing around with her when she was about eight or nine. She used to love making her laugh.

And now she lay in a bloody heap. A bullet to the neck.

Amelia stepped around the bodies—she hated it, but it was all that she could do—and marched over to the dining room, where Damon had apparently executed another staff member, whom Amelia recognized but didn't personally know. She also found her parents there, bruised and bleeding and clearly terrified, but otherwise alive.

And, of course, Damon. He appeared frustrated that her arrival on this scene of devastation was taking so long.

But now, looking up, all the frustration fell away from his face, replaced with tears of joy. He jumped up, grabbed Amelia, and dragged her out the door and across the driveway. Damon flipped her around and pushed her down on the hood of his car. He then lifted one of her legs with his arm, pressed into her crotch, and started to forcefully kiss her.

She lay there and struggled to restrain her gag reflex. But she had to allow it. She couldn't afford to have an argument with Damon as to why she didn't want to French-kiss him. She was worried that if he found her conduct to be less than ideal, then he would question her dedication to the "relationship" and put up a fuss.

The last time he put up a fuss, he caused a scene in front of a coffee shop and threatened to be with her for the rest of her life. This time, she knew for sure he had a gun.

So the moment had to be perfect. Everything had to be exactly the way Damon wanted it.

He briefly let go of the kiss, to lick her jawline all the way over to her ear, and whispered, "God, I've missed you."

"I've missed you too," she lied, trying not to recoil as he slobbered like a dog across her face. She was paying careful attention to the way she pronounced her phrases. She wanted them to sound at least a little realistic.

"Come on," Damon said. "Get in the car. We're getting out of here."

She complied and hopped into the passenger seat of his tiny pink car. She noted that it didn't have any high-tech radio capability, only a cassette player and an old lighter, with a little cigarette symbol still on it, fading away after many, many years. Damon had evidently bought the oldest clunker he could find. Probably the cheapest.

God only knew how he'd been living for the past weeks, she thought, but it was obviously rough.

"Where are we going?" she asked once they were back out on the road.

"Now that we're together, my love," he replied, still grinning like an idiot, "we can go anywhere. The world, the future, is ours. Ours and ours alone."

"That's beautiful," she lied, through a fake smile. "But I mean, literally, where are we going?"

"Oh! Well, first off, I think I'm going to have to end my formal relationship with my employer. And I need to make a withdrawal."

"You mean Nicolas Wan?"

"Yep. If we're gonna be starting our lives together, then appealing to dried-up old broads and pig-ugly whores isn't going to be much of a viable career direction now, is it? But the thing is, I'm fully aware of what he has tucked away and where. We can get money, guns. Maybe even drugs, as he has a side gig in selling amphetamines. I know some people who would be willing to buy those, in case we need a steady income."

"Oh ... And then?"

"Hard to say. I mean, we can't stay in New York. Not after ... well, they wouldn't understand. I was thinking Canada. Wouldn't that be great, to build ourselves a little cabin, up in the woods somewhere? Living out our lives, skinning bears and selling pelts? Keeping warm by cozying up next to each other by the fire? I could think of worse ways to live our life. But I can't think of a better way than doing it with the one you love."

"Huh ... Okay ..."

"You know, there are so many people who can't find love in this world. People who just drift and never get to live out their lives with any meaning."

"Hm."

"I've done things in my life. I've made some choices.

Largely with people who didn't understand me. Who didn't treat me like a person. Always believed they knew me without ever talking to me or asking me anything. They never loved me. They never respected me ... Not like you. You believe in me. You love me. You make me feel like I matter."

Amelia glanced forward. She saw a car, with hidden stripes on it, which she now knew were police lights. Behind them, another car with officers in the front seats. To the right of that car, another undercover cop car.

She wouldn't be surprised if they weren't currently surrounded by police cars. But Amelia was worried that if she turned her head any more, then Damon would notice and get suspicious.

Amelia cautiously, casually looked out her window at the car next to them.

Detective Corbett was looking right back at her. He smiled and nodded.

She nodded back. She hoped he understood. The time was now.

"Hey, sleepyhead," Damon said with a laugh. "Are you even here? What, are you a thousand miles away? Come on, what the hell is going on with you?"

It took everything she had not to jump in fright. She should've been paying more attention, because now he was suspicious. And he was probably prepared to stop at nothing.

It was go time.

She watched out of the corner of her eye as Detective Corbett did a sharp left turn and immediately aimed for the back wheel of Damon's car, attempting to execute a PIT maneuver. She heard Damon gasp, catching it too quickly and swerving harshly to the left to avoid getting hit.

Amelia looked to the left. She recognized the people in the car next to them as more officers. They were preparing to collide safely with Damon's car.

He saw them as well. He knew full well that something was going on. He pressed his foot on the gas and blasted down the freeway.

Suddenly, the car in front of them flashed their lights. Amelia glanced over at Detective Corbett's car, whose lights were now flashing as well.

The car to their left turned its lights on. The car behind them also. Then several more cars Amelia hadn't noticed.

The small pink car was surrounded by flashing red and blue lights.

Damon was quiet for a moment before looking at Amelia. "You set me up," he said.

"You tried to kill my parents," she said harshly. It felt good to drop the veneer.

"They've been horrible to you," he yelled. "They mean nothing to you."

"You murdered your first wife after she found out what kind of a person you really were, didn't you?"

Every sign of certainty from Damon's face drained away as he realized she knew everything. He looked horrified to be revealed for who he really was.

"You don't know me," Amelia said as he navigated away from another cop car. "You don't know anything about emotions. You just want to feel good. But me? I sure learned a lot about you recently."

He actually appeared terrified for a moment.

Amelia felt happy about that. She reveled in it.

But that brief moment was over when Damon realized that the police cars were closing him in and slowing him down, at which point he floored the gas again and desperately tried to squeeze out between two police cars. They tightened their positions, trusting that he wouldn't be stupid enough to try to force his way through.

Amelia watched Damon prove just how stupid he could really be.

He tried to press his car through. The two police cars tightened. He floored the gas, scratching and grinding up his car in between the two police cars.

The force of the impact bent the axles of the old pink car out of shape, and the vehicle began to spin out of control. Several of the police cars backed off and gave him a wider berth, as it was clear that he could no longer keep the car moving in a straight line.

His car was heading toward the metal crash barrier in the median. Amelia watched in slow motion as they were about to collide.

She realized that, after they crashed, he would still have his gun. And a hostage. Trusting that he would be unconscious from the collision wasn't good enough.

She wanted this over. She wanted this done. And she was going to make it happen.

In one swift movement, she unbuckled Damon's seatbelt and tossed it toward the door. As she did so, she announced, "Don't you ever touch me again, asshole."

Like a flash of lightning, the car careened into the median, started to spin, and then the front end of it caught one of the oncoming posts. It collided in a way that caused the entire engine block to cave in, bringing the car from full speed to near zero in less than a second.

Amelia's body was thrown forward with such intensity that her seatbelt nearly choked her. She felt as if her neck was going to rip out of her spine, and several of her internal organs were going to follow close behind. But then the horror faded away, and she fell back in her seat. Alive and in one piece.

Damon seemed still too shocked from watching her undo his seatbelt, so Amelia only just caught a glimpse of his wide, terrified eyes before his entire body flew up over the steering wheel, his head crashed through the glass of the windshield, and he was hurled half out of the car.

Exhausted and in deep shock, Amelia lay back, her mind registering nothing but the massive flashing red and blue lights. Somewhere next to her, she felt some gentle tapping on her cheek.

She briefly thought of Mark.

Turning her neck slowly, she saw that it was Detective Corbett trying to coax her back into full consciousness.

"Please don't take this the wrong way," he said with a smile, "because I am very, very happy that you're alive and well. Now, that said ... I caught the bastard."

"Is he dead?" Amelia said, also struggling to smile.

"No such luck," said Corbett. "He's unconscious and badly injured, but he's still breathing. God only knows what his brain will be like when he finally wakes up."

The smile faded from Amelia's face. She didn't care what state he would be in when he finally woke up.

He was alive. It wasn't over.

## 39

Amelia was aware that trials didn't happen in the real world the same way they happened in movies or on television. Those media were for entertainment purposes, so they had to keep things snappy. In the real world, trials were lengthy, rigid procedures. The courts prided themselves on being purportedly immune from all systems of bias; their methods were based around careful examination of the evidence and, of course, the truth. As such, they never left anything to chance.

*Good*, Amelia thought while sitting next to the prosecutor. She wanted to ensure that this was going to be flawless. That this was going to work.

When she entered the courtroom, Amelia looked over at Damon. She couldn't help it, given his new appearance. Portions of his face were cut up and healed; she guessed from all the glass from when he went flying through the windshield. A portion of his beautiful, wavy hair was now missing, revealing a scar over a patch of his skull. Presumably, he'd needed some brain surgery done after the crash.

At the very least, Amelia wanted to know if Damon was still himself. Or if the accident had left him without proper brain function.

As she looked at him, he stared right back at her. With that same obsessive grin. Maybe now, happier and prouder than ever.

If he had suffered any mental impairments, Amelia decided that they certainly didn't show. He was as evil as ever.

The trial proceeded just as well as it could. Damon was being charged with multiple counts of murder, attempted murder, kidnapping, stalking, and a handful of other things. He'd managed to get a decent lawyer though, who was known to be a bit of a shark. He was going to try to get everything dismissed, but Amanda wouldn't let that happen. She was determined to have her say, and the prosecutor had agreed.

Amelia took the witness stand and gave her account of everything that had happened. From beginning to end. Truthfully speaking, it was hard to describe it as such a series of events. Once she was able to see the entirety of her actions, the whole affair seemed pretty insane, out of control. It certainly made her feel foolish.

The prosecutor had coached her on how to handle herself during examination and cross-examination. He taught her that the best thing she could do was simply tell the truth. Always answer every question. Don't give away more than what was asked. And don't contribute anything of your own volition.

The prosecutor had a strong idea of the manner in which Damon's lawyer would defend him. Since Amelia was making the claim that she was being stalked by an extremely dangerous man who went on to murder her sister, ex-husband, her parents' staff, and then took her parents hostage with the intention of killing them, the defense would likely focus on the fact that she was the one who put herself into this dangerous situation in the first place, thus causing all of these killings by approaching a male escort. He would try to paint her as irresponsible, incompetent. Worst-case scenario, he might even try to convince the judge that she was in on it.

From every law show she'd ever seen, that was what these defense lawyers did. They didn't care about the fact that their client killed a bunch of people. They just tried to get them off the hook for their crimes and pin it on someone else. In this case, her.

But Amelia stuck to her guns. She told the truth and refused to concede anything that she knew wasn't true. She also kept her fists held firm and digging into her thighs as she was seated on the witness stand. This was excruciatingly hurtful.

Then it was over, and she got to sit down by the prosecutor again. She was aware that the entire time she was on the witness stand, and even now when she was back next to the prosecutor, Damon was eyeing her.

The prosecutor told her that his attention on her helped their case, by making it abundantly clear to anyone in the room that Damon was quite the obsessive stalker. She accepted that, but it didn't make it any prettier.

The defense lawyer struggled to find any evidence that Damon was the real victim here when the man was a known serial killer, but he managed to get all of Mark's testimony dismissed, given that he never actually saw anything directly when he released the dogs, and only heard information about Damon secondhand through Amelia.

Nicolas Wan, Wendy, Margo, and her parents were all questioned and cross-examined. Her mother, who was very complimentary about Damon, wasn't very helpful and made the case more difficult. Her father pleaded the fifth.

Amelia couldn't believe her parents were so delusional after Damon had murdered their daughter, their staff and nearly murdered them. She had to think that the trauma of everything that happened had them blocking all of it out. It was the only reasonable excuse she could think of for their statements.

Things were starting to look a little complex, if not outright bad, until the prosecutor called Lori Norris, the mother of Ophelia Chase, to the stand. She was the perfect witness. She looked distraught, like she'd been hiding in fear for years. And her testimony explained why. Shortly before her daughter's death, Ophelia had visited her mother. She had called her on numerous occasions, explaining that she was terrified that her husband, Damon, had become somebody very dangerous. Damon had told Ophelia that he was going to solve all of her problems for her. He kept saying he was going to take care of all the people who had hurt her.

As part of her testimony, Lori played phone messages of her daughter telling her that Damon had killed her best friend and her best friend's boyfriend, the man who had raped her. Damon had insisted that Ophelia should understand. According to her daughter, Damon insisted that he would make her understand.

At this point, nobody believed Ophelia's death was a suicide. But even if it miraculously was, it was easy to interpret it as actions resulting from fear of those threats. Everybody was turned against Damon now.

Amelia, for the first time in ages, felt relieved. She felt like somebody genuinely cared about her.

She knew Damon was staring at her the entire time, grinning. It just didn't seem to matter anymore.

After a short recess, everybody returned to the room.

The judge entered last and pulled out his reading glasses with a summary decision held in front of him. "Order in the court," he said calmly. "After careful investigation of the available evidence, as well as witness testimonies and police reports, we have been able to determine with a reasonable amount of certainty that Mr. Damon Chase has been associated with numerous crimes of which he was accused. Even putting aside the fact that direct DNA evidence does not place him at the scene of the crime of the murders of Mr. and Mrs. Perry, Miss Gray or Mr. Altman, other associated evidence such as video logs and witness testimonies connect him to those matters. Then there are the deaths of the various members employed by the Gray household, which, although the defense put up an adequate argument that those actions were instigated in self-defense, could not adequately be supported by the testimony of Mrs. Gray, who was a victim as well, as shown by the bloodwork provided by the prosecution.

"But even aside from the murders themselves, we have direct evidence of Mr. Chase's possession of an illegal firearm, use of said firearm in a hostage situation, the taking of hostages, grand theft auto, making public threats, disturbance of the peace, breaking and entering, illegal possession of a private residence, assault, and any number of violations of harassment and intimidation laws. I would like to personally thank the New York City police department and its detective force for assembling an amount of evidence that shows that the defendant has knowingly perpetrated those actions for several months now.

"It is therefore the opinion of this court that—"

"Your Honor, I need to make a final statement!" Damon yelled across the room as he leaped up from his seat.

His defense lawyer grasped at his suit jacket, encouraging him to sit back down.

"Order!" called the judge. "Mr. Chase, this is not the time for—"

"Please, Your Honor, I know you have a job to do, but what you're doing is wrong."

"Mr. Chase, I invite you to consider that your legal representation has never called you as a witness, and perhaps he has done that for a very good reason."

"I would like to represent myself."

"Mr. Chase, you will sit down, or I will have you removed from this court."

"We are meant to be together," yelled Damon, stepping out from behind his desk. "I love her more than anything. She was in pain; I was protecting her. That's what a real man does. He believes in himself. Calling it toxic masculinity is bullshit. Amelia, please, I forgive you for—" He stepped forward as if to approach Amelia, but a hefty man in uniform tackled him to the ground before he ever got near her.

Another detail they never showed on court TV dramas: people weren't allowed to wander around in the big space between the lawyers and the judge, like they always seemed to do in movies. If anybody ever entered the pit without the judge's permission, they would be taken out immediately.

*Too bad they didn't show that more often*, Amelia thought while watching the bailiff put handcuffs on Damon as he lay prone on the floor. Because that was rather entertaining. As she watched and listened, a memory started to stir in the back of Amelia's head, something about all of this was bringing up images of her father, but they were fuzzy, as though not quite fully formed, and the more she tried to bring them forward, the more they drifted back to the recesses of her mind. She decided to let them be for the moment and hoped they came more fully into her mind later.

"Mr. Chase," the judge said, "I was about to say that I am finding you guilty on all counts and sentencing you to one hundred and ninety-nine years on Rikers Island. Based on this disruption, I would be inclined to add an additional two weeks, though I suppose that's a superficial punishment at this point."

"I'm in love," yelled Damon as he was being manhandled by the bailiff and forced out of the room. "I deserve to feel happy. Everybody deserves to feel in love. Why can't I just feel love? Why does it have to hurt so much?"

And then he was gone. He was finally gone.

**40**

———————

I t was a restrained and quiet little funeral service.

Amelia watched as an exquisite wooden coffin, carrying the body of her sister, Cara, was lowered into a hole. It was hard to associate that coffin with Cara. It seemed neutral, detached. It wasn't very fitting for all the emotions that Cara had created within her, Amelia thought.

But her parents had paid for an expensive coffin in a luxuriant area of a private cemetery in Connecticut, so here they were.

The funeral attendees included the priest, the surviving family members, and all the people who worked in the Gray household. Amelia wondered how many of them were here because they were worried that they would be fired if they didn't come. From what she heard, her mother invited Cara's old boyfriends, though not a single one showed up. She was also going to invite her friends, before they discovered that she really didn't have any.

Which made sense, Amelia thought. After the life she lived. The life handed to her.

During the eulogy, the priest spoke very generically about how Christ takes all souls with him into heaven and yada, yada, yada. Nothing specifically about Cara, since he didn't know her.

Her parents didn't speak on her behalf. Neither did Amelia.

Amelia watched as the coffin reached the bottom of the hole. Cara Gray. She was a vindictive, evil bitch, who devoted her entire life to proving how much better she was than Amelia by constantly wreaking pain and emotional turmoil on Amelia.

But she was still her sister. And Amelia was not so narcissistic or deluded to believe that Cara's motivation had materialized out of nowhere. She knew it had a reason. She knew where and when it started; those memories that had been triggered during the trial were now fully formed in her mind.

Despite the fact that after a lifetime of being hurt by her, Amelia really didn't owe Cara anything, she decided the right thing to do was to pay back her sister, just once. One last time.

She left the grave and went over to her father, who had wandered off and was leaned up against a tree.

Thankfully, he was alone. Her mother was wandering around, trying to find any comfort she could from anybody who would listen, which ultimately amounted to the priest.

"Hey, Dad," said Amelia, coming closer.

"Oh," he said, startled by Amelia's presence. "Hi. How are you doing?"

"Me? I'm fine. I mean, as fine as any of us, really. And you?"

"I ... I just never imagined ... I would be burying my ... I suppose someday it'll hit me that she's really gone. I don't know what to feel, really ..."

"Do you feel relieved?"

"What?"

"You know what I'm talking about."

"This is ... I don't know ..."

"I'm not an idiot, Dad."

"This is not the time ..."

"I remember you rubbing my shoulders, Dad."

Suddenly, the old man had nothing to say.

"I'm not sure why you thought I would forget. I mean, it's not exactly something that's forgettable. When your dad asks you to come with him into a private room, and he just starts rubbing you."

"I think you're confused."

Amelia stared at him and stated boldly, "I heard you and Cara together."

The truth was, Amelia hadn't heard her father and Cara "together." But she had vivid memories of being very young, and her father talking to Amelia differently, the way he would talk to a grown woman. And how he threatened her before she ran off. After that she always learned to act loudly, brashly, rebelliously, if for no other reason than to make herself into more of a nuisance than an obedient little daughter. To basically keep her father off of her.

She remembered, early on, a point in her life when her father stopped talking to her like that ...

... as he commenced talking that way to Cara. Patting her on the head. Treating her nicely.

And Cara becoming very quiet. And very sad.

And then, not too long after, Cara going from sad to angry and tearing up all of Amelia's clothes and dolls.

And later, taking all her boyfriends. And everything else.

Amelia suspected it. Accusing him of it was a calculated risk. Looking at him now, seeing the way he turned white as a sheet, Amelia knew she was right.

"Cara was the one who got hurt," Amelia continued, knowing her father wouldn't interrupt. "She was the one who was used and then, suddenly, became a plaything. Meanwhile, she had this older sister who could've easily been the plaything that she didn't want to be. She was young, and she didn't understand why she had to be hurt and her sister wasn't. So she was jealous. And she wanted me to know that she wanted my life, that she wanted to be free. That she wanted our roles reversed, that she wanted to be happy and me be miserable. The only way she knew how to express that was the way Mom taught her: by being the best a woman had to offer. Finding a man, getting a man, so on and so forth. Hell, Mom gave her approval, so she probably felt like she was doing something right. I mean, I didn't enjoy it, but at least I understood.

"What I hated was that I understood you as well. I didn't want to understand you. I never approved, but I wanted to be able to live a life where I'd be like, 'Why did he do that? Why would he do that?' It would've been easier to just write you off as a monster instead of knowing that a person could do that. Unfortunately, I guess I was just too damn clever. So I blocked it out. It made life easier.

"Then this whole thing with Damon. And it all came surging forward, right back into memory, being able to compare the two of you. That phrase he used in the courtroom. 'Toxic masculinity.' Men raised to think they're automatically going to be the heroes of their stories, that they're going to get the girl and live happily ever after. When that doesn't happen, they think something's wrong. And they're taught not to blame themselves, so they blame every other possible circumstance around them. Whatever it is, they're allowed to destroy it and, at the same time, fix everything that way. Typical obsessive stalker, really.

"But it explains you too, doesn't it? Parents yelling at you for earning money, like not earning it is some sort of failure. Marrying into money. And Mom, who was raised to believe that feminine independence is not an option, became so selfish and shrewish, that must've been fun for you, being married to that. Divorce was an embarrassment, so Mom would never allow it. You always wanted sons, you never got them, so that made you feel like there was something wrong with you. Side note: thanks for making me feel like that's my fault, by the way. And you, you're surrounded by greed and awful people. And you're taught that love is wrong.

"All of a sudden, you realize you've got this sweet little girl, who was becoming a woman ... And she probably can't say no ... And every love you've ever been denied could come true. Except I did say no. So you moved on to the girl who didn't."

Her father shivered.

Amelia paused. Then she sighed. "Yet another man taught that, by virtue of his masculinity and his awesomeness in simply being born, he's owed a happy life. Or that he's owed anything. When things don't work out, and life is hard, you take something, someone to feel better. And all it costs you is every love that actually mattered ... Right?" She turned and looked at her father.

He turned away, not granting her the same courtesy.

"I could report you," Amelia said, "but what good would that do? I don't have any proof. You probably have the money to stop me. Nobody would believe me because of who you are. I'm guessing, the way she drinks herself stupid, Mom knows too. She just decided long ago that maintaining an image of a successful marriage was more important than confronting a horrible husband and making sure he goes to prison. That would be just too shameful for her, wouldn't it? Dammit, I hate whenever someone says I take after her.

"No, I'm not going to tell on you. Your lawyer would just claim I was bitter and delusional and misremembering things. There's no proof. But that's not the point I'm making here and now. The point is the way you were talking to me a second ago, you didn't know that I knew. Now you do. Maybe you didn't know that Mom knew. Now, in all likelihood, you know she probably does. So consider this: how many of your household staff knew before they died? Are you sure Cara didn't tell any of the guys she slept with what you did to her? Did you ever get drunk with a buddy and tell him that you slept with her? Would you remember? Hell, it's your lawyer's job to protect you; how do you know you didn't tell him one drunken night? Other family members, observant ones, are you sure they don't know what you did and are keeping quiet about it for now? How long will you have before somebody decides to ruin your life over this? Will you spend your last deathbed minutes worried that, somehow, this will get out?

"And that ... Dad ... will be for the rest of your life. You'll always be wondering when, not if someone is going to talk."

He was turned away from her, but Amelia was certain he was starting to cry.

Good.

With that, Amelia walked away. She paused to look at Cara's grave one last time. She could go to Detective Corbett and tell him what she suspected, but she doubted she'd get any justice, so she did this one thing she thought might give her sister some peace, as a good older sister should for her little sister. It was something she should have done long ago, if only she hadn't blocked the memory for so many years.

And now, she could say goodbye. Now it was all behind her.

---

*Springtime*

AMELIA WAS IN A LOVELY DRESS, carrying a little glass of champagne that she wasn't really drinking out of, mostly holding just for show. She was standing next to Wendy, looking equally as lovely, at the art gallery where Wendy normally worked at the front desk.

It was all part of a gala celebrating a new exhibit that featured prominent new artistic presences in the New York scene. They'd invited one of Amelia's works to hang there, one of her gray cloud images.

It started to sound like all the guests at the gala recognized the name attached to the painting more than the painting itself. She overheard, on more than one occasion, people saying, "Oh, Amelia Gray. My daughter has some of her stuff on her dorm wall," or something to that effect. Amelia found the whole thing rather charming.

Thankfully, she still had legal ownership over all her prints, so that kind of free advertising certainly helped her bank account, making her financially independent. Which was always a good thing, especially while living in New York.

In fact, there was only one painting of hers that she didn't have the legal ownership of, and she'd been struggling to get it back. Regrettably, she couldn't convince the municipal government to release it from the evidence locker at Rikers Island. An early painting of the New York skyline outside a studio window.

Maybe that was for the best, she told herself silently.

Meanwhile, thanks to this kind of gala promoting her work, her paintings were becoming somewhat iconic on the New York scene. Margo, of course, was drinking tonight in in absolute bliss, dreaming of the potential of spreading this fame out to increase her client's marketability in Los Angeles or even Paris. Amelia shook her head and smiled. Let her have her dreams.

Amelia wanted to have a relaxing evening, enjoying a gala with at least one of her works in it. She hadn't gotten to experience this in ages now. It was really nice.

And she wanted to make sure that Wendy felt appreciated as well, which was why she had invited her as her guest. Considering everything she'd been through, she didn't want her new roommate to feel as if Amelia was simply still using her.

Formalizing their living arrangements made sense, Amelia knew. Wendy could use the extra income to pay for rent, and Amelia suspected she got off on the idea of telling people she lived with a famous artist. For Amelia's part, she couldn't think of anywhere else she wanted to be. She wasn't even going to keep her old place, not even as a work studio or anything. Too many memories. Dark ones.

Nonetheless, she was going to miss Mark. Now that she was able to live out her life for the last few months comfortably and easily, she was trying to think of something good in her life to focus on and realized that her friends were the only things over the past year that really gave her any kind of comfort. Wendy, certainly. But also Mark. The man who got her groceries. The man who let her play with his dogs. The man who, when she felt the pressure of his arms around her back, made her want to float there.

She would never dream of hurting Wendy, but just the memory of it ... It was nice.

Which was why she almost choked when she looked over at the entranceway to the gallery and happened to see Mark standing there in a smartly cut suit.

"Holy shit," she said to Wendy, smacking her on the shoulder to get her attention. "You invited your boyfriend?"

"What?" Wendy said, rubbing her shoulder. She looked over and then turned back to Amelia. "Mark's not my boyfriend."

"What?"

"I mean, I invited him here, sure. But he's not my boyfriend."

"You broke up?"

"No, idjit, we were never together."

"Yes, you were." Amelia was baffled. Of course Wendy and Mark had been together; it was obvious, wasn't it?

"No, we weren't. He always said he—" Wendy suddenly stopped and stared at Amelia. Before smiling a wide grin. "Aaaaahh," she said, then winked at Amelia and wandered off.

Amelia wanted to follow up on that, but before she had a chance, she was tapped on the shoulder from behind. She turned to realize Mark had approached her.

"Hey," he said.

"Oh," Amelia said, blushing a little. "Hi, Mark. Good to see you. Thanks for coming."

"Wouldn't miss it. You actually got into a major art gallery. This is absolutely amazing."

"Thank you. Sometimes I can't believe it. I feel like I'm here for someone else; then everyone keeps reminding me how much they love my stuff. It's kind of weird."

"I can't imagine."

Amelia smiled, then motioned to the floor around Mark. "I see you didn't bring your dates."

"Huh? Oh! Yeah, I figured the gallery wouldn't approve of a gang of four-legged guests, so it's just me tonight."

"Hm."

"Still, being alone isn't all that fun in the world. I was thinking of going to a café after this. I mean, I'm sure you are super busy, but if you'd like, you don't have to—"

"What?" Amelia smiled at him.

"Well, in all honesty, I'd love it if you joined me ... I think that would be absolutely lovely."

Amelia's chest exploded when she realized that Mark was asking her out on a date. It never seemed very realistic before, although now, knowing that he and Wendy were never a thing, it seemed extremely desirable. She just never expected it to happen right then and there.

Exactly like she wanted.

Her life, opening up for her. Giving her a chance.

Amelia Gray had finally gotten to a point where she felt she could stop crying and smile.

# THANK YOU FOR READING

Did you enjoy reading *The Scorned Wife*? Please consider leaving a review on Amazon. Your review will help other readers to discover the novel.

# ABOUT THE AUTHOR

Theo Baxter has followed in the footsteps of his brother, best-selling suspense author Cole Baxter. He enjoys the twists and turns that readers encounter in his stories.

# ALSO BY THEO BAXTER

Titles by Theo Baxter:

The Widow's Secret

The Stepfather

Vanished

It's Your Turn Now

The Scorned Wife

Made in United States
North Haven, CT
28 April 2024

51872128R00183